Dark Reflections

— Books by Samuel R. Delany —

Fiction

The Jewels of Aptor
The Fall of the Towers:
   Out of the Dead City
   The Towers of Toron
   City of a Thousand Suns
The Ballad of Beta-2
Babel-17
Empire Stars
The Einstein Intersection
Nova
Driftglass (stories)
Dhalgren
Equinox
Hogg
Trouble on Triton
Stars in My Pocket Like Grains of Sand
Distant Stars (stories)
Return to Nevèrÿon:
   Tales of Nevèrÿon
   Neveryóna
   Flight from Nevèrÿon
   Return to Nevèrÿon
They Fly at Çiron
Atlantis: Three Tales
The Mad Man
Aye, and Gomorrah, and Other Stories
Phallos
Dark Reflections

Nonfiction

The Jewel-Hinged Jaw
The American Shore
Heavenly Breakfast
Starboard Wine
The Motion of Light in Water
Wagner / Artaud
The Straights of Messina
Silent Interviews
Longer Views
Times Square Red / Times Square Blue
Shorter Views
1984: Selected Letters
About Writing

Graphic Novels

Empire (with artist Howard Chaykin)
Bread & Wine (with artist Mia Wolff)

Dark Reflections

Samuel R. Delany

CARROLL & GRAF PUBLISHERS
NEW YORK

DARK REFLECTIONS

Carroll & Graf Publishers
An Imprint of Avalon Publishing Group Inc.
245 West 17th Street, 11th Floor
New York, NY 10011

AVALON
publishing group incorporated

Copyright © 2007 by Samuel R. Delany

First Carroll & Graf edition 2007

ISBN-13: 978-0-78671-947-1
ISBN-10: 0-7867-1947-8

9 8 7 6 5 4 3 2 1

Printed in the United States of America
Interior design by Susan Canavan
Distributed by Publishers Group West

It's a pleasure to have such fine reasons to dedicate *this* book, also, to Marilyn Hacker. As well, it's for Vince Czyz (whose story "The Argument" inspired "The Prize"); and Elayne L. Tobin; and Dennis Rickett (without whom . . . well, probably there'd be not much); and Mia Wolff; and Robert Morales. For priceless critical aid, my thanks go to Ron Drummond and Kenneth James; and to a new friend, Robert Loss, for some germane Cleveland lore; and to a great friend, Erin McGraw, for asking him on my behalf; and to my oldest of friends, Priscilla Meyer of Wesleyan University, for invaluable help with the Russian.

Contents

part i

THE PRIZE

for Carl Freedman

In 1987's rainy October, when squirrels stopped, stared, then sprinted along the bench-backs away from the kids with the earrings, combat boots, and dog collars, who for more than fifteen years now had been hanging out in Tompkins Square Park, Arnold's sixth books of poems, *Beleaguered Fields*, won the Alfred Proctor Prize—an award given once every three years that concerned a small circle of New York poets and men and women of letters.

In the late afternoon of the day he'd received the news, as he walked home through the park, a wind gusted among the wet leaves, for moments making a rising roar, like the cheer of thousands. Because so few folks were out that day, Arnold smiled—and dropped his head to the left, then to the right, acknowledging playfully the world's recognition. Leaves quieted . . . and fifty-one-year-old Arnold Hawley left the park at Avenue B.

It was the year after he had stopped working for the City Employment Administration and had taken the teaching job out at Staten Island State University—with its three-thousand-dollar-a-year drop in salary and its hour and three quarters travel time, including the trip back and forth on the ferry, for that extra Monday in which to do his own work.

The prize had been a blessing.

Inconsequential as the Alfred Proctor Prize was in the greater scheme, the award carried a three-thousand-six-hundred-dollar stipend, paid out annually over three years.

It would be nice to get twelve-hundred-dollars a year—for three years.

No, it wouldn't support Arnold, the first African American poet to win, over any significant period, not even living on East Ninth Street in '87. But, from '87 to '89, it would mean for a couple or three weeks not having to buy day-old bread; it would mean walking into St. Mark's Bookshop and actually purchasing that paperback he'd wanted to read; it would mean going to a movie the evening the idea struck him, or seeing a play within the brick-and-glass walls of the Theater for the New City even if he didn't know one of the actors who could get him a comp to this or that performance space inside the converted market building. The Proctor Prize would mean—at least now and then—paying his $396.83 a month rent on time for his third-floor rear apartment, one of three rent-stabilized apartments left in the building.

(The 15 percent raise every two years—the legal limit—more than doubled his rent each decade.)

Its annual certainty?

Its perfect gratuity?

Materially they fortified Arnold.

Spiritually they liberated him.

For a month or two out of the year—out of *three* years,

actually—Arnold could believe he was a little better off than he'd been, and, what's more, the reason was poetry.

Arnold pushed through the glass doors of his building, opened the mailbox briefly—just some flyers and a blue envelope of coupons that he could throw out tomorrow—and started upstairs. A bit later, in his kitchen, he heated up last night's leftover lentil soup. Sitting at the table, covered with books and papers, typewriter pushed to the side and steaming soup plate before him, Arnold thought: What a pleasant ending to a pleasant day. (I should have brought a celebratory bottle of white wine . . . well, next time.) Spooning lentils, celery, and carrots carefully away from himself, he pondered: *Next* time, I must put in some sausage. No matter what Aunt Bea says about what Mrs. Polk says (Aunt Bea had sent the recipe), really, I'm not a vegetarian at heart. And neither is Bea.

—•—

Edena Proctor had lived and died on the south side of Gramercy Park, looking out on the black metal gate around its central garden, to which residents had keys—a square a half an hour's stroll to the north, and of a different size, feel, history, and economy from Tompkins. She'd divided her millions between the Poetry Society of America and Yaddo, where, in 1947, she'd spent a pleasant April trying to finish a novel. It had never appeared. In 1975, the year of her death, she had set up an eight-hundred-thousand-dollar trust to sponsor the Alfred Proctor Prize for Poetry, named after her father, who'd encouraged his only daughter's love of opera, Spain, and the arts.

What other educational projects the Proctor Trust engaged in, if there were any, Arnold was never clear on.

They threw some very nice parties.

•—•

Even without the Proctor, *Beleaguered Fields* had been Arnold's first book to appear in both hardcover and trade paperback: for both he'd received a nine-hundred-dollar advance. It was his second from what he considered a real publisher: Lark & Dove Books, owned by Sid Lark, with an office in TriBeCa and six editors.

In the converted industrial building's ground-floor space— the whole back seemed to be glass and black girders—Lark & Dove had been one of the scrappier businesses to surface among the early '80s catastrophic publishing mergers.

Leaving her job in publicity at Random House for a downtown editorship, twenty-six-year-old Vikki LaSalle, Arnold's editor, had done three things, one, as far as Arnold was concerned, brilliant, and the other two so wackily idiotic that, really, they were, well . . . wonderful!

The brilliant one was to send a set of bound galleys for *Beleaguered Fields* to the Proctor competition. (At a Proctor event she'd met someone connected with the Trust.) A week after the book won, Vikki had these circular gold stickers done up— because the cover had already been printed—which said in raised letters around the rim: "Winner of the Proctor Prize for Poetry," with an embossed seven-pointed star in the center.

Perhaps once a year someone called it the Alfred Proctor Prize.

That Tuesday, with her carroty braids curled on the sides of her head, Vikki—with Arnold—had taken the Short Line Bus and the taped-up carton of gilded peel-offs south along the drizzly turnpike to Lark & Dove's second-floor Jersey warehouse space.

Years later Arnold decided the intensity of her belief in him *must* have had something sexual to it—people just didn't carry on the way Vikki did about books of poetry, any book of poetry.

At Vikki's insistence they wasted forty minutes finding someplace where they could buy six containers of coffee and a dozen donuts. "For the warehouse workers," Vikki explained. "Just like Jackie Suzanne. Really, it *does* help." At the coffee stand they wouldn't take Vikki's credit card and she only had a five in her pocketbook. So Arnold paid the nine dollars and eighty-six cents out of his wallet. "Oh, it isn't fair!" Vikki insisted. "Believe me, I'll see you get that back."

"Don't worry." Arnold chuckled. "It is my book, after all."

Then, over three hours, toward the back of the unpainted loft, frigid with air-conditioning, they peeled loose bright circles and hand pasted them to 852 books—what remained to be distributed of the thousand-copy first printing—piled on the slatted skid.

Downstairs, on the counter in front of a guard-booth window in an orange wall with two asbestos pipes across it and lots of ribbed electric cable looping from the ceiling, they left the carrier carton of coffees and the donuts with the single Russian loader in jeans and denim shirt who'd let them in.

As she handed him the donut bag, Vikki said, "This is Arnold Hawley, one of the truly important African American poets, who cares about language, cares about literature, and cares about the truth!"

The Russian had not shaved that day. "*Ty mnogo zarabaty-vaesh' stishkami?*" He frowned into the brown paper, translucent in spots with grease.

Arnold's three terms of Russian were the only courses he'd gotten A's in at Brown. "*Niskol'ko.*" Arnold had on the dark blue suit and the dark green tie he wore for his students on Staten Island.

The loader nodded. "*V shtatakh chego eshcho ozhidat'.*"

"*Nu da . . .*" Arnold said to end what was beginning to feel uncomfortable, and turned away.

Vikki called, "Thank you again!" as they walked out to begin the twenty-minute hike to the bus stop, now and then glancing at Arnold in monolingual awe. As once more it began to sprinkle, Vikki asked: "What was that about?"

"He wanted to know if poets made a lot of money in America."

That evening Arnold realized he didn't have quite enough left in his wallet for house-special egg foo young at Wo Hop's, six blocks south on Second Avenue. Though they knew him there and would surely trust him for the final dollar seventy and the tip, he made himself scrambled eggs for supper. Eating them from a bread-and-butter plate beside the typewriter on the kitchen table, Arnold reflected again: A three-thousand-dollar-a-year drop in salary actually *meant* something about how you lived your life. He had to relegate even cheap Chinese and *comidas criollas* to luxuries, and start cooking in more regularly—

a fact which, while he'd known it more than a year, the Proctor had allowed him, for a few weeks, to forget.

And the wacky and wonderful ones?

Shortly, Vikki had convinced cigarillo-gnawing Sid Lark to write out a check for three hundred dollars to finance *Beleaguered Fields*' entrance for the coming year's Drew-Phalen Award, a prize presented annually in fiction, drama, nonfiction, and poetry, which had been around since the '20s, so that most literate folk knew of it. Usually its February announcement made page two of the daily *Times* and, for the last fifteen years, page one of the Sunday *Arts & Leisure* section—on the lower half, with a picture of the dramatist: Fierstein, MacNally, Sondheim. . . .

Then, four months later, when 178 hardcovers still remained in Jersey, Vikki had ordered another printing of three *thousand* hardcover copies, with a new jacket, identical to the old, except that, in white letters, along a green band slanting across the bottom third, it read: "WINNER OF THE PROCTOR PRIZE FOR POETRY" and, in gold letters below that: "Nominated for the DREW-PHALEN AWARD in poetry."

That Thursday she phoned Arnold to come in and see the new cover proof.

Craning around the corner of Vikki's desk, Arnold asked, "Shouldn't that be 'winner of the *Alfred* Proctor Prize'?"

Vikki flattened both her hands on the blue blotter. "Oh, dear!" Sucking her teeth, she grimaced. "I forgot again." With her coiled bright braids, Vikki's head appeared wide and heavy with the knowledge of the young. On her office wall hung a large abstract . . . thing, all aluminum and clear plastic dowels. Only on his third visit to the office had Arnold realized it was a barometer, not a clock.

That Friday, Sid fired Vikki.

When a confusing Monday morning phone call finally netted from the receptionist—the third time Arnold had been transferred back to her—that Ms. LaSalle no longer worked at Lark & Dove—indeed, she'd left before the weekend—Arnold decided quietly, as for the second time he was switched over to James Farthwell's assistant (only now did Arnold understand that Farthwell had taken over Vikki's writers), he might as well forget the photo his Aunt Bea had taken of him on her last trip to New York, seven years before, as he'd stood at Avenue B by Tompkins Square's broad brick newel. (Bea had come once almost every ten years, to take in an opera or two at Lincoln Center—and always one at the Amatto—to visit museums, to go to a play, staying a week in Arnold's back room and stoically not complaining about the clutter.) When Vikki had asked him for an author's picture for the book's back, he'd found it in the kitchen drawer and sent it in.

Then, without comment, they hadn't used it.

Arnold had gone through paranoid kippages about their not wanting to put a black man's image on the cover. ("Who let the coon in?"—Wallace Stevens' inquiry at the 1950 Drew-Phalen Awards banquet, when that year's recipient, Gwendolyn Brooks, had entered the hall—replayed regularly up from the kerygma of black literary history, a-broil in memory and imagination, even after forty years.) The picture *was* seven years old.

Perhaps it had looked ridiculously young for a poet now over fifty.

Vikki had said it was a slipup. But she'd said it quickly. Nor had she apologized—

Interrupting Arnold's thoughts, the assistant said, "Oh! Mr. Farthwell just got back to his desk, from Mr. Lark's. Hold on a moment. I'll transfer you."

Then Mr. Farthwell said he would ask in production if anyone had seen the photo; and phoned Arnold a week later to invite him to lunch. "I guess it's a gesture of compensation for the fact that—really, it's embarrassing—we seem to have lost your picture. Basically, though, since you're one of *my* authors now, I'd like to take you out and say hello."

"I'd love to go to lunch!" Wasn't the reason Arnold had worked so hard to get the teaching job at Staten Island State (with its free Mondays), so that when such invitations came up, he could accept them?

The photo had gone with Vikki.

Sexual, yes. But had the object of her desire been the poet, or—as Arnold suspected—poetry?

The second Arnold understood—and shared.

❦

James turned out to be a callow twenty-eight-year-old (white), with wildly bitten nails, who had inherited Vikki's job, Vikki's office, and Vikki's fifty-one-year-old black poet, Arnold Hawley. Going out with Farthwell was fun.

Apparently the barometer had been Vikki's, too. On one taupe wall of James's office—on the floor of which five times the number of manuscripts leaned by the baseboard as had ever stood there during Vikki's tenure—its outline remained near the window, like the line inside a cardboard coffee container, after you'd poured its second-day contents into the sink.

There was no way, when someone was taking him to a seventy- or eighty-dollar lunch, Arnold could ask for a $9.86 reimbursement. Twice, though, he came close.

Some months later, during a third lunch with James, as they sat in a restaurant with a girdered web under the ceiling beside the black columns before some dim tapestry, James leaned forward and smiled: "You know, I'm not supposed to tell you this, Arnold. But the second printing of *Beleaguered Fields* has already half sold out. Borders has just given it front-of-the-store display. And B&N actually called up to find out if Sid wanted to fork over the cash to have it put on the Local Authors table at the Union Square and Astor Place outlets. For twice that, they'll triple their order and put it in the front of all their A-stores associated with universities. Sid's thinking of doing it."

Arnold laughed. "I guess you're not supposed to tell me because they don't want all this attention going to my already very big head—right?" So far his book had gotten all of five reviews, one of which was a pale purple hectographed (!) throwaway from an extracurricular reading club at a Minneapolis community college, surely written by an undergraduate: *The poems in this book are really very interesting.* . . . At the bottom of what school supply closet, today, could you *find* a squishy, hectograph gelatin tray?

James looked uncomfortable. "I'm not supposed to tell you because you're what got my predecessor canned."

"I did?" Arnold frowned. Till then it had never occurred to Arnold that Vikki's dismissal had had anything to do with him. "But what did I—?"

"The reason you see so few books advertised as 'nominated for the Drew-Phalen' is because, Arnold, nomination is just a matter of paying three hundred dollars and sending in six copies. That's all. All publishers nominate their own books. Sure, it's a gamble. But it's a gamble based on a belief in the book's quality. The publisher just has to think what he's entering has a shot. Vikki convinced Sid that yours did. But the nomination fee hasn't gone up in fifty years. The Drew-Phalen Award is an institution drenched—even drowned—in tradition. Fifty years ago, three hundred dollars was more like three thousand. Hell, today three hundred is a fancy lunch for the publisher, editor, and any writer on the bestseller list in town for the afternoon."

Since neither of them had ordered an appetizer, the waiter set before Arnold a broad pink plate on which a square of salmon the size of a new plastic floppy disk had been placed on some plantains, in turn piled on some lentils, atop which, edges reddened with turmeric and red pepper, three shrimp curved around a mint sprig and flaked crabmeat—a low-leaning tower, drizzled about with scallions and cilantro puréed in heavy cream. "He fired her," Arnold said, "even *before* the Drew-Phalen was announced?"

James was having the hamburger. "Sid has a strong sense of . . . tradition—and, as much of a go-getter as everybody tells me Vikki was, Sid felt she wasn't showing the proper—I don't know—respect. Whatever." (That February, the Drew-Phalen in poetry had gone to Richard Howard, a poet whose command of intellectual history and literary minutiae, years before, had delighted Arnold. He'd been ecstatic at the selection, even though he was sure it had really been awarded for Howard's electric fifth and sixth volumes—knockouts both—and not last year's *No Traveler* named. *That* had been merely wonderful.) "Anyway, that's why advertising a Drew-Phalen nomination isn't done. It looks bad to the rest of the book community. That's why Sid sacked Ms. LaSalle—though the rumor is they had some sort of wager that if your book *didn't* win, she'd resign."

"Wow." Then Arnold added, "*Mmm*. And he didn't even wait to see if it *had*."

"Sid said—or at least someone *told* me he said—he was losing patience with her. She had some sort of plan to prove to him you *could* be successful publishing a book of poems."

Arnold grinned. "But even though it *didn't* win, my book has taken off like hotcakes—right?"

"I wouldn't call it 'hotcakes.' But you've sold twenty-five hundred hardcover copies of a book Sid expected to do about one tenth of that."

"Two-*hundred*-fifty? Even *with* the Proctor—and the possibility of the Drew-Phalen?"

"Even with the Proctor." James nodded somberly. Then, from the old-fashioned fluted sundae glass, he pulled up a tongue of Melba toast. "And you didn't *get* the Drew-Phalen." Frowning at it, he pushed it back. "It's not like it's the Pulitzer." Toast crackled among the other tongues. By the flowers, crumbs fell to the cloth.

"Oh . . .!" Arnold said.

A memory flickered from the '60s: checking that year's Drew-Phalen had practically been a Groundhog Day tradition with Arnold and his friend Bobby Horner. Both had always arrived the same week—twice when it had been snowing. They'd bring the Sunday *Times* and have brunch at that Second Street bar—the only bar back then that *had* a brunch. God, he hadn't seen Bobby in years. Things had changed so. . . .

At their fifth lunch on James Farthwell's Lark & Dove expense account, it struck Arnold that this plodding youngster *liked* him—or liked going to lunch with a "successful" poet. Even by someone as stolid and slow as James, Arnold liked being liked.

•◆•

One Tuesday (this term, flouting their earlier promise, Tuesday—rather than Monday or Friday—was his nonteaching day), in the Graduate Center high above Forty-second Street, where he had gone to talk to a CUNY graduate poetry work-shop, Arnold was waiting in the cafeteria for the young woman who was supposed to meet and guide him through the gray and green halls to the seminar room. Sitting at one of the broad cafe-teria tables, he picked up and opened a copy of *Grants, Awards, and Prizes* left there aslant on the tabletop. Absently he began paging through.

Under "Alfred Proctor Prize," the index directed him to a

West Walton Street address in Chicago as the place to send all entries. . . . Arnold frowned.

Sixty West Walton Street, Chicago, Illinois, sounded *awfully* familiar.

Then it hit. It was the address of *Poetry*'s Chicago offices: he'd submitted enough poems to them fifteen or twenty years back. When, in '73, they'd accepted two and Arnold had been doing a three-day residency at the University of Illinois, he'd stopped in to visit and discovered that the place was (one) much smaller than he'd assumed and (two) they were not particularly happy to have poets dropping by unannounced, even when that venerable magazine *had* published you.

Rain chittered on the eighteenth-floor window, obscuring the sumptuous city view, and Arnold wondered: What was *Poetry*'s address doing under the Proctor Prize?

The Alfred Proctor Prize was *so* New York.

◆

The next morning, back on Ninth Street, Arnold keyed open his scratched-up mailbox. Inside, an invitation from the Proctor Trust for one of their seasonal to-do's leaned on the tarnished wall.

That afternoon Arnold called James and asked him if, next Thursday, he'd like to go to a Proctor wine-and-cheese party at Writers' House, up on West Twenty-sixth. "You've been so generous with all these lunches, I thought it might be nice to, well . . . return a little of the favor. I mean, if you wouldn't mind my company."

"Why—that would be great, Arnold!" James was free that evening. "Sure."

They'd gone.

Arnold recognized—perhaps—half the people milling beneath the ceiling's stamped green tin. Most he'd met at the awards ceremony, largely a memory of gladiolas in a crystal vase, half-obscuring a microphone. At a subsequent reception he'd been reintroduced. But, by now, the only one whose name he actually recalled was Jesse Kolodney—certainly because something about her reminded him of Judy Haindel (Arnold's wife, however briefly, fourteen years ago). Arnold had started a conversation with Jesse, a tall woman (unlike Judy) with a short platinum brush (Judy's hair had been tangled and a dark auburn), a black minidress, black combat boots, and an early piercing through her lower lip. Her second-from-the-top desk drawer at her job at Museum of Modern Art Publications was, Arnold knew—with all these people it seemed a running joke—the closest thing the Proctor Trust had to an office: "Hi, Jesse. I've got a question—it's something you should know the answer to. Is the Proctor connected with *Poetry* (Chicago)?" Once Arnold had wondered how to pronounce parentheses. Years ago he'd given up and now said them as if the first were a hyphen and the second not there.

Jesse swallowed a lot from her plastic cup and stepped back, shaking a hand now sloshed with grape-dark spots. "Oh, my God! *Poetry!* They were supposed to correct that two *years* ago! *Three* years, at least. Oh, my God! It was a perfectly *stupid* slip-up. Believe me, it wasn't *my* fault! Really. They told me they'd fix it in the next edition. My God! That's *terrible!* I called them about *that* one myself—*Grants, Awards, and Prizes*, right? Oh, my God—maybe you were looking at an *old* issue . . .?" (It was something in her speech. . . .) Jesse stepped forward again, hopeful. "I *know* I called them about that . . . *four* years—!"

"I saw it the other afternoon," Arnold explained, "up at SUNY. I'm sure it was the current edition. In fact I checked the date on the masthead just to make sure." He had, too. It had been dated '88.

"My *God* . . .!"

Just then, in tweed jacket and open-necked shirt, James strode forward, grinning widely, a coral glow in each ear, his eyes alcoholically sheened. "Arnold, this is just . . . *great!* This is great, man! I feel like a *real* editor—for the first *time!* All these literary people. *This* is what I came to New York for . . . to be an *editor* for. To meet people like *this*. Thank you. Thank you *so* much! This is just wonderful. I mean—" He turned to explain himself to Jesse—"I've already met three people here whose articles I've actually *read*. And Nathan Corner—he's over there—is wonderfully sharp. I mean, I'm kind of a literary type. That's why I went into editing in the *first* place!"

"You're an *editor?*" Lifting her plastic cup beneath her chin, Jesse smiled her smile for nice kids who'd drunk too much. (Was it the smile . . .?) "So am *I!*"

Arnold did not say, *Well, it didn't take a* lot, *did it?* He enjoyed James's enthusiasm, even if it was only from a plastic glass or two of plonk out of the crystal decanter over at the green-covered table on the room's second level, up the carpeted steps. Arnold looked around. It was amazing what free wine, a little Brie, some Ritz crackers, and grapes could bring out in people. Who *was* here tonight, anyway?

•◆•

Beleaguered Fields's third printing sold out six weeks later and, after another eighteen months—and a fourth—went into trade paperback.

In '90, Lark & Dove rejected Arnold's seventh book of poems—*Dashes*. Three and a half months later—after a three-year, ten-month tenure—James Farthwell resigned.

Attenuated by tape hiss: "Hi, Arnold. I'm calling to let you know I am no longer on the staff at Lark and Dove. . . ."

From his shared office, out at Staten Island State, where he'd gotten the blunt message on his voice mail, Arnold phoned James, then rushed back across the sound. Beneath scumbled clouds, Arnold gripped the black wooden rail looking over gray water. Ferries didn't really *rush* anywhere. . . . He got to Union Square on time, only to wait twenty minutes on a cold bench as the winter evening darkened and myriad shoppers passed down to and hurried up from Fourteenth Street. Meeting James, taking him to another Proctor Trust to-do (which happened to be that night), was basically to make the kid feel better.

"Well," James told him, when they were finally on their way, "it could be worse."

"James, I'm *really*—"

"Oh, no! We're celebrating, Arnold," James declaimed with

stolid earnestness. "You've made *two* editors lose their jobs at Lark and Dove, now—"

"James! Really—Really, I didn't *mean* to do any—"

"No."

For all his protestations of sympathy, Arnold felt pretty good. Rejection aside, the day before he'd received a $685 royalty check from Lark & Dove. (It was his only book *ever* to earn royalties!) Earlier the same day, out at school, in the voice mail before James's, he'd learned that Copper Canyon Press had accepted *Dashes*, and while they weren't Lark & Dove, they had a lot more presence in the poetry world. He'd submitted it only seven weeks ago, just enough time to let it drop out of mind.

Both James and Arnold were bundled against January, cold enough to make Arnold's shoulders, at any rate, feel chilly under the black cashmere overcoat Aunt Bea had brought him after his cousin Harold died in Appleton. James wore a bulky parka with the hood thrown back. Leaving Union Square, Arnold followed James into the narrow lobby of the converted loft building, to wait for the elevator that would take them up to the fourteenth floor, where Poets & Writers had their long, bright, blond wood offices.

"No," James repeated. "I wasn't the editor for Sid. And Sid *certainly* wasn't the publisher for me! He's too inconsistent, Arnold. You noticed he *kept* the bits about both the Proctor *and* the Drew-Phalen on the cover for your trade paperback? Then, when I presented your new book at our Wednesday editorial, he had the gall to say he didn't feel we could go on supporting a poet whose work had been sold under false pretenses. Now I *remember* the meeting where Sid approved that cover—for the *Beleaguered Fields* trade paperback, I mean. There's nothing 'false' about the Proctor. And the Drew-Phalen thing, he could have had it taken off then. If he'd had any *real* objections, it's a little late to voice them now. It's not *your* fault. You're a fine poet, Arnold. A *very* fine poet. *I* think so. Everybody involved with the Proctor thinks so. With anybody I meet who reads poetry seriously, I can have a pretty good discussion of your work. Frankly, I don't think Sid's read a line of it, since they accepted your first book." (My sixth, Arnold thought, automatically.) "My father always says the reason you can't work with hypocrites is not because they think they're fooling you, but because they're always trying to fool themselves: *That's* why Sid's so untrustworthy.

"When we were leaving that meeting, Arnold, three months ago, I told Sid, '*You* don't want to have anything to do with publishing poetry at *all*, do you?' Well, he looked at me. Then he said, 'What sane publisher would?' I knew I was going to do this. I've spent ten weeks trying to get the three cookbook writers I'm actually fond of settled so that nothing awful happens to their books once I'm gone—imagine, giving poetry and cookbooks to the *same* editor!—and this morning I went in and told him I was resigning. He did his usual, 'Then have your office vacated by two o'clock.' Bastard! But I *don't* want to work for a publisher who doesn't do *any* poetry—and that's what Sid's become. You're the only poet on his list! You were a *success*, too! And because he's afraid he won't be able to do it again, Sid wouldn't let me take *The Dashes*." He sighed. (Drink always made James slip "the" into the title, Arnold had noted.) The gray elevator door pulled loudly back. "Between three hardcover printings and a trade paperback, eight and a half thousand copies is nothing to sneeze at, even for a novel—much less a book of poems. Arnold, I feel more like a real editor, a real member of a literary community, when I'm hanging out with you, or the people in your circle, the people I've met through you, than I do when I'm in sales meetings or marketing conferences. And *that's* why I . . . well, quit." They stepped forward and turned as, clashing and coughing, the industrial elevator door closed them in.

James pressed a button.

Arnold had always thought his "circle" distressingly narrow—if he had one. But when, on fourteen, they left the gray, gray elevator car and walked down the gray, gray hall to push through the gray, gray fire doors into the . . . yellow wood, polyurethaned, aluminum, and glass opulence of Poets & Writers' not-for-profit offices, Arnold realized he knew the names of perhaps three people there and the faces of another five. While he was trying to decide how to tell James that such idealism, however admirable, was not wise, James strode forward with a hello here and a handshake there. By now, stolid, slightly drunken James (he'd stopped at a bar between leaving Lark & Dove and joining Arnold) knew *every one* of the thirty-five people in that chain of three blond wood rooms!

• ◆ •

About a third of '89's Proctor stipend (Arnold's last, which he had put away for ten months now, for the purpose) went into the first airplane flight Arnold ever paid for himself (rather than some university flying him in for a reading), out to Cleveland for five days with Aunt Bea over the Christmas holiday—because if he didn't do it this year, he might never be able to do it at all.

He'd taken her to Coventry for a steak dinner at the Hyde Park Grill, where they sat like two happy blackbirds amidst a covey of (basically) sedate doves. Bea was the one who'd taught him to be comfortable in such places. "Oh, Arnold, this is *so* good. But if I ever told Mrs. Polk, she'd never let me hear the end of it!" They left through a glow of red neon to attend a Cleveland Orchestra concert in Severance Hall: the Berg Violin Concerto (fingers perched primly on her black pocketbook, beside him in her orchestra seat, Bea muttered: "Imagine—dead of a bee sting, the day before Christmas, at fifty." She'd said it, years before, when they'd gone to hear *Wozzeck* in Lenox. Back then, of course, fifty had been thirty or more years ahead of Arnold; not three years behind) and a David Diamond symphony. While her mind was wonderfully clear, Bea moved around more slowly than he'd remembered.

As the rain stopped and the plane settled into LaGuardia, in the December sun, ribbons of water over the tarmac were gunmetal or scarlet. As Arnold looked out the little window, for moments the plane appeared to tear through webs of crimson and black. He sagged forward, as they slowed to a bumping roll. A minute later, three of Arnold's students he hadn't realized were on the plane crowded past his seat, lugging backpacks. "Oh, gosh! *Hi*, Professor Hawley! Were you in Cleveland, too? . . . See you in class Wednesday!" so that Arnold returned home on the

narrow-aisled bus in a haze of holiday belonging, with the realization—for the first time, actually—that what the Proctor's
three years of moneys, now done with, had meant was that he
could settle more easily into true poverty.

•◆•

Years and years ago, in 1968, between the April his book *Air
Tangle* had been accepted and the October it had appeared,
something had happened that explained why Arnold never
moved from East Ninth Street. A lanky actor, Noel, and another
plump fellow, the singer and actor Lamar Alford (where *had* he
first met them? At this point, Arnold really didn't remember),
used to hang out with Arnold, now at the Annex, now at
Stanley's, sometimes at the Stonewall over in the Village—
Arnold's favorite because there were the most Negroes—
sometimes at the Ninth Circle, or even up at Max's. One day
both of them, with their third, Bobby—all were black; all were
gay—dropped in on Arnold's third-floor-rear apartment one Saturday morning, when nobody had quite enough to go for one of
Speedie's breakfasts (they weren't even *calling* them brunches,
yet) at the Old Reliable—*that* had been the name of the place!—
on Second Street. "What we're gonna *do*," Noel explained, "on
Monday night, is a whole bunch of us—after closing—we're
going to hide, in fourteen different branches of the public library,
all over New York. Me and Lamar will take the Tompkins Square
branch. Bobby here is with some other people up at—"

Sitting on the other end of the gold couch (arrived from

Pittsfield that week), Bobby said, "Hey, man—you're not supposed to *tell* anybody who isn't part of it, now!"

"Oh, Arnold's okay," Noel said from the recliner. "We're going to hide in over a dozen branch libraries, and after they close up we're going to take the signs off the shelves that say 'Negro literature' and put up signs that say 'black literature'— like Dr. Du Bois wanted it called, more than fifty years ago. I mean, what's with this 'Negro' crap, like a race is a *real* thing and you got to put a capital letter on it? Don't nobody ever put a capital letter on 'white'!"

"The day they do," Lamar said, standing by the couch's end, "I'm *leavin'* this country!" For a heavy man, Lamar had so much energy. He rarely sat.

"It's a social fact, yes," Noel said. "A cultural reality—but it's not some biological thing."

"Yeah," Bobby said from the couch, "but there are days you look pretty biological to *me!*" They all laughed, as it sometimes seemed they'd done so much, back then.

The fact was, Arnold wasn't paying lots of attention. But, a week later, first in the *East Village Other* that, outside Gem's Spa, he'd reached in among some clustering tourists to pick up from the paper stand's outside counter, then in a *Village Voice* someone had left on a bench in Tompkins Square, he'd read an article about the "vandalism" in libraries the past weekend throughout all five boroughs. At the same time, the Panthers were pushing the slogan "black is beautiful." Three months later, over the shoulder of a woman sitting beside him on the subway, in the letters column of the *New York Times*, he read his first printed reference to "black people" and "blacks," where, only weeks before, certainly they would have written "Negro." It gave him an astonishing sense of . . . what? Pride, privilege, power? While it hadn't been planned *in* Arnold's living room, those plans had run *through* his living room.

Who, he wondered, had masterminded it?

Bea phoned him that night. "We had such an argument over it—my ladies in the Reading Club. Arnold, you wouldn't have believed it. When I was a lot younger than you, I fought real hard for 'colored' and campaigned against 'Negro' for all I was worth—that capital 'N' sticks in my craw to this day. It's supposed to have something to do with respect? Well, it never meant respect for *me!* It meant white men could call us with another fancy-sounding word that put another mark of scientific alienation against us, this time—like a species of animal in a zoo."

"Oh, Bea," Arnold said, "you *have* to call it—"

"Now don't 'Oh, Bea!' me, honey!"

"—to call it 'black literature'—I mean, because . . ." Though most of the reason was because of what had happened there in Arnold's apartment.

And people all over the country were *talking* about it!

Somewhere in Cleveland, Bea said, "Well, our librarian, Mrs. Polk, she said it was some schoolchildren in New York, who broke into a library—"

"They *weren't* children!" Arnold said. "I . . . *know* some of them. They were highly thinking men . . . and women." The only ones Arnold knew for sure were the three black gay fellows, though he couldn't imagine that—somewhere—there weren't women and even . . . well, *probably* straight black men involved. "And it was *fourteen* libraries! You make sure you tell your group *that!*"

"Mrs. Polk said, as far as she was concerned, they could call it whatever they wanted, as long as it made the young people come in and read it."

"*There!*" Arnold said. "You see?"

Somehow, he saw Noel only a few times after that, but Lamar went on and got a part in a Broadway musical called *Godspell*—and years later Arnold heard he was teaching in Atlanta.

By the bookshelf, in the dark, netted in the myriad physical unpleasantnesses that were his pudgy, fifty-four-year-old body, Arnold stood, a long-nailed forefinger poised on the back of a book. He pulled it free from the shelf, and turned to open it. Before him, he could just see a white field on which he could make out no single word. Is this death, Arnold thought, standing in a dark hall, holding a book you could barely see, opened to a page you could not read?

It was just after three in the morning.

Arnold smiled in the dark—then went to the bathroom. And turned on the light—and looked at the sudden and surprisingly familiar cover of *Air Tangle*. Whenever he'd dedicated a book to Bea (as were all but one of his six books—*Dark Reflections*, which bore no dedication at all), how much she'd enjoyed it! He'd get five phone calls over the next month, telling him what this one and that one had said when she'd showed it off.

Six weeks after *Beleagered Fields* received its Proctor, the Black Women's Reading Group of Cleveland (a hundred years ago the Colored Women's Reading Group) had sent him a long, gleaming box, in which much green tissue rustled about a dozen long-stemmed white roses. In with them was a congratulatory card:

"A token of our Great Pleasure at
your having won a much deserved prize!"

Though, from Mrs. Polk on, all the members had crowded their signatures onto the back, the handwriting on the front was Bea's—indeed, it was all Bea's doing, at once wonderfully sweet, even as it verged on the annoying.

Arnold returned to his sweat-dampened bed, edging toward the far side of the mattress, slipping toward sleep, despite New York's July night heat, an arm wrapping his pillow.

•◆•

Six months after James Farthwell left Lark & Dove, Arnold got a phone call: James was starting his own small publishing company. "I'm calling it Phoenix Press, Arnold—do you like it?"

"You are?" Arnold asked. "How are you doing that?"

"I have a little money," James said, "from my father."

"Oh . . .!" Arnold thought: Had there been any mention of a father before? Is that what it took to be a cockeyed idealist, these days—money from your father?

Then, with the concern of someone who really cared, James asked again: "Do you *like* the name Phoenix Press?"

"Oh," Arnold said. "Yes. It's . . . *very* nice!" He wanted to sound sincere. Probably he sounded snide. James had always been a *little* slow. But Arnold had not realized James was a complete fool. What were you supposed to say, though, when, purely because of inflation, only that year you'd become a fifty-five-year-old man who'd gone from never following scrambled eggs with scrambled eggs or oatmeal with oatmeal for supper, to never following scrambled eggs with scrambled eggs or oatmeal with oatmeal more than three nights in a row?

Of course James was also an *idealistic* fool, Arnold was thinking half an hour later, as he stood at the sink washing dishes, below the doorless cabinets. Of such fools poets should make heroes. Phoenix Press? If James did half of what he wanted, he'd have the entire American art scene bursting up, reborn, from its ashes. And he *was* a nice kid—though he'd only broken thirty a year or so back.

• ◆ •

Copper Canyon, who had almost a two-year lead time, released *Dashes* at the beginning of '92—a week before Arnold's March 15 birthday. So he was still fifty-five. The critical reaction (its three intelligent reviews) produced five invitations to read and two inquiries from magazine editors. In turn, that gave Arnold another encounter with *Grants, Awards, and Prizes*—this one in Nathan Corner's maroon-carpeted office. Corner was a lawyer, who, retired at fifty, now edited and published the journal *Spectacle*. (Fifty seemed rather young to retire. Hell, fifty—to Arnold—seemed pretty young, period.) *Spectacle*'s offices had once been Nathan's law firm's library. Shelves were still full of multivolume book sets in tan and scarlet, gold-leaf letters on their matched spines.

Their acquaintanceship went back to the Proctor Prize days.

Grants, Awards, and Prizes lay on the dark desk. It was the current '92 issue. A flip through the oversized paperback, and Arnold saw that the Alfred Proctor Prize *still* had the incorrect West Walton Street address in Chicago. Shaking his head, Arnold put the fat volume back on the desk's edge.

"What . . . ?" Nathan looked from the shelf where he'd been taking down an art book to show Arnold some collages of which they were planning to do a color portfolio in the next issue. "I thought you said something."

"Nothing," Arnold said. "It's nothing."

But while he looked at the artist's bits of string, mirror, and wood, lovingly glued to the impasto pigments, photographed, and reprinted in what must have been at least a twelve-color plate, Arnold was imagining someone at Chicago's Walton Street, taking mailbags full of misaddressed entries out into the back alley to toss them, with their gray canvas sacks, into some dented Dumpster. How would those folks have even *heard* of the Alfred Proctor Prize?

Probably, from the cover of his own *Beleaguered Fields!*

Whereupon they'd all rushed out to look it up in . . .

Under "Alfred Proctor Prize" alone was no address at all.

•◆•

October light fell through the arched institutional windows by the crowded bookshelves, through the wrought-iron inner balcony rail, down on the broad wood table. I wonder (Arnold glanced up and thought as he always did when he came here) if *that's* where they hid?

As he sat, two chairs away someone rose, leaving a book closed, and, with something of a grunt, moved to the checkout desk, leaning on her cane.

The book's yellow cover framed a photo of the backs of small children, as if in a sports huddle. Smiling, Arnold pulled the volume over to see the title: *Boys Like Us*.

It was the subtitle, though, that raised Arnold's eyebrows: *Gay Writers Tell Their Coming-Out Stories*. Automatically, Arnold moved his hand back to the table edge. Equally mechanically, he sat back in his own chair. He glanced about. Nobody was looking. But why should they?

Not quite smiling, Arnold thought about how many times in his childhood, now in one library, now in another, he had looked up this volume or that because he'd heard it had some reference to homosexuality. But it had always been a secretive search, with glances over his shoulder, or sitting in a seat to read it far from everyone else: somehow pre-Stonewall fear of discovery had been replaced by a post-Stonewall sense of vulgarity in all this public discussion of what, after all, surely should be private. Which one, Arnold wondered, was finally more effective in keeping people off—though, just as he would have done as a teenager, Arnold had already opened the cover and started reading the editor's introduction (somebody named Merla) so that—at least—no one would recognize the cover.

He didn't read it very closely. But it ended with a memorial roster of writers who had died of AIDS. Arnold ran his eyes down the column.

David Frechette . . . was that the heavyset young journalist Arnold had talked to a few times after one or another St. Mark's reading a few years back? Oh, dear . . .

Lamar Alford.

Arnold stopped.

He looked up from the book.

But Lamar had been an actor, not a writer. . . .

Though, of course, he'd been a teacher, too. Perhaps, like Frechette, he had written some articles.

The advent of AIDS in the '80s had been among the factors bringing Arnold's own tentative sexual experiments to an end. Arnold slid his chair back and stood, picked up his briefcase crammed with student papers, and, leaving the book on the table, walked out of the library and down its steps, onto Second Avenue, along the half block to the corner of St. Mark's Place, thick with kids, before, across from Gem's Spa, he turned east.

For several days, Arnold actually thought about writing Lamar an elegy. *They told me, Heraclitus; they told me you were dead.* . . . A lament for the makers . . . the makers of Arnold's own delicate vision of the world. But no one *had* told him. It was just another thing that had—almost—slipped by.

• ◆ •

One mid-April day, as he was walking down Eleventh Street, Arnold Hawley stopped and removed his glasses, because the aging phenomenon by which elderly farsightedness corrects congenital nearsightedness had for more than a year now been apparent—at least in his right eye, though not so much in his left. But Arnold was struck all over with the unfamiliar sharpness of the milled striations on the garbage pails beside the stoop, the granulation of the mortar between the red bricks, between the tan bricks rising by them, the dogwood blossoms hanging above the streets. Just then, as a breeze stirred those fallen over the sidewalk, Arnold realized Eleventh Street was awash in dogwood petals, which, at once, swirled—thousands of them!—into the air. They scarved and unscarved the street, the lamppost's base, the trees, the metal post of a no-parking sign that tried to throw its shadow futilely to the sidewalk's sand-colored paving. They coiled in ribbons, uncoiled in streamers. As Arnold looked about, he saw other trees, days before denuded by winter, touched now with spring's greeny ghosts.

Thicker than bubbles in soda water, petals were above him and around him. (Odd, that year he'd not yet seen a single spear of forsythia, but he hadn't been up to Central Park or Van Courtland, or yet out of the city.) Through a sunlight patch on the pavement beside him, a *thousand* shadows rushed under petals whipping above! Even as so many white flakes seemed to fall, slantwise, they lifted Arnold's eyes. They tickled the backs of his hands, hit his ears and eyelids, so that he thought he'd better put his glasses back on; and did—a petal caught in the frame against his nose, to struggle like a moth. Arnold laughed.

It tugged free, and Arnold walked on in whirls of white, while sunlight winked and glimmered, catching flicks of yellow and pink. From petal-washed pavement, to window frames behind the passing rage of blossoms, to the trees with up-thrust branches—Champagne flutes overspilling silver wines—and above the cornices to the aluminum clouds, immobile and deflecting enough sunlight to keep it from blinding all, urban blue and urban beauty (Arnold thought) lift the eye. Arnold lifted not only his eyes but his hands.

Dozens of poems had choired such states. *My heart leaps up when I behold*—but there was no rainbow. Did it matter when the air was full of flowers? *The earth stands out on either side, no wider than the heart*—a nineteen-year-old girl had written, not all that far from where Arnold had been born, and for the length of her life had remained famous for it. But here were no long mountains, no wood to reinforce the feelings. Only the fabulous day, the beautiful street—to rival Patchin Place or Pomander Walk—that, with the number eleven alone to name it, still spilled raptures.

About him, men and women, boys and girls, black and Hispanic, were swirled around with ivory. They looked up and turned their heads. Now and again one looked at Arnold. Petals billowing between, they gave one another awed smiles.

Arnold dropped his hands and, head still high, wandered, happy enough for the hour, toward what awaited in evening.

•◆•

Yes, *Dashes* had come out from Copper Canyon back in the spring of '92, and over the next year and a half had garnered eleven reviews, ten of them good and three actually intelligent.

For a while, Arnold had thought, Why do I *need* to go on writing? But now that, too, was something to remember tranquilly and smile over.

In '96, three weeks after his sixtieth birthday, Arnold stood in the shadowed hallway of his apartment, looking at his books.

There beside *Dashes*—

Beleaguered Fields (1987), by Arnold Hawley, his Alfred Proctor Prize-winning volume:

Four hardcover and four trade paperback copies stood on his "brag shelf," across from his bathroom. Arnold didn't remember which writer friend had first used the phrase to him, or how many years ago. (*Had* it been Bobby, who'd hung out with all those people who wrote mysteries and pornography and westerns and actually published them, all of which rather terrified Arnold?) Arnold worked a copy half loose, till he realized the cover was cushioned on one of the Cleveland roses, dried inside.

Cleveland—land of cliffs . . .

Arnold pushed it back. No sense damaging that last flower. (If Aunt Bea ever visited again, he'd show it to her.) To the right stood eight copies of *Dashes*, one of the fifty that Copper Canyon had had bound in hardcover, and seven of the handsome paperbacks, which had received general trade release—and which, after four years, had sold about nine hundred copies, till it had been remaindered. (Pretty paltry compared to *Beleaguered Fields*.) Before the *Fields*'s eruption of relative accessibility, there was his fifth book:

High-Toned Homilies with Their Gunwales All Submerged (1984), with its subtitle (his *only* book with a subtitle): *Meditations on George Jones, Giovanni da Palestrina, and Bonnie Tyler*—the single volume put out by the brief-lived Croaton Press.

Yes, his Fifth Book: five had always seemed to Arnold an important number. A single book-length prose poem, it had received only two reviews, neither good (". . . unreadable . . ." ". . . tedious . . ."), neither intelligent (". . . makes you wonder why somebody would even . . ." ". . . finally art-as-ordeal is just dull and, anyway, who . . ."), with a promise of a third (". . . next month I'll be discussing Arnold Hawley's impressive new work, though obviously it's one you have to live with awhile . . ."). The promise had not been kept. The California reviewer had never gotten around to it. Or hadn't lived with it enough.

Or, perhaps, she simply hadn't liked it.

For Arnold there'd been ways in which *High-Toned Homilies with Their Gunwales All Submerged* was the work he himself had learned most from. Robert Graves had declared all true poems to be about love, death, or the changing of the seasons. Well, this was the poem of Arnold's that he most doubted *was* a poem, since it was about music—music that lived in language, and what instruments might wring from it. It was the work which taught Arnold that, while sexual love, however unrequited, might flog him toward poetry, for him it could never be the topic of the poem. As a boy he had lived too long and closely with Aunt Bea, and, more, had loved her too deeply.

Even more than *Dark Reflections*, it was Arnold's most painful book.

One hundred eighteen pages of solid print, arranged to correspond only to the pages' margins, his greatest formal *coup*, unrelieved by period or paragraph indentation, *High-Toned Homilies with Their Gunwales All Submerged* was also his most difficult. For a month in the midst of writing it, Arnold had walked about, mumbling, "Come on! This makes *When the Sun Tries to Go On* chopped liver! Hey, Koch! 'The New Spirit' and 'The Recital' have nothing on me, Ashbery! Move over, Caliban. *I've* got the audience, now!" Personally Arnold was convinced it contained passages as gorgeous as anything in Tolson's *Gallery* or Johnson's *Ark*. But had any reader other than himself ever burrowed through to them?

The spine and the cover were black. The lettering was silver foil—Croaton's attempt to make it look elegant. In a very, very few readings (two? one . . .?) just after *High-Toned Homilies* appeared, Arnold had included a number of selections. But when, afterward, the third person came up to say, "It sounds so nice when you hear it out loud. It's just so hard to read. On the page, I mean. Maybe you should sell it with a cassette . . .?" (CDs were just coming in.) Well, Arnold's rising anger meant he had never read from the book again. All public pleasure in it had been leached.

Croaton had distributed 140 of the 500 printed before they went out of business—though Arnold only learned of it four years later, when a belated wrap-up letter arrived. How few of those 140 had actually sold, Arnold would simply *not* flay himself by imagining.

(Twelve? Fifteen? Six?)

In what cellar—or Dumpster—the other 360 had ended up was anyone's guess. They hadn't even offered him copies. But there it was.

His major work, in his hallway—Arnold did *not* take down one of the seven—and otherwise unknown.

The sixteen Lark & Dove volumes, hardcover and paper-back, still looked nice—even if they were a bit overpowered, as was everything else on the shelf, by the red spines of the seven copies of *Pewter Pan* (number four) from Yellow Star, back in '79.

After eighteen years, three cartons of *Pewter Pan* still sat under the kitchen table, up against the refrigerator. Though that was the one he had the most of, he only kept seven out. It had actually sold about four hundred—not bad. . . .

Through overenthusiastic gift giving or friends who'd sworn they'd return it next week—then decamped for Sweden or Bogotá—*Dark Reflections* (number three: 1974) was down to a singleton. An old Harper Torchbook, it had appeared only in paper-back. The title should have been *Pretenses*. But the editor, Sam, had insisted Arnold change it. It told the story, as much of it as he'd dared, of Arnold's catastrophic marriage to the insane Haindel girl.

As a delayed response to that marriage, once it was a year or so behind him, Arnold had finally gone to bed with—well, had sex with—a man. Three men, actually, and, all when he was between thirty-eight and forty: first Eddy, then, ten months later, Tony, who'd turned up again, and finally, a year and a half after that, Big Ukrainian Mike. He'd paid each twenty dollars—and had found none much fun or interesting. He'd run into the last one, the very drunken Mike, with his single eye and the sleeves torn off his sweat-drenched flannel, that Indian summer, at two in the morning in Tompkins Square, coming unsteadily from his job at the Odessa's kitchen, where, apparently, at that hour, they didn't mind if he kept a flask in his jeans. Rarely was the park deserted—but that night it was empty. After they'd talked for five minutes, practically using force, which, oddly, Arnold had neither liked nor disliked, Mike had made him do it up against the gate beside the comfort station's side wall. Mike hadn't *asked* for money, but, after managing to stand up, Arnold had handed it to him. Mike took it, turned, lunged forward, nearly tripping over his own feet, and sprinted west. Even drunk as he was, only Big Mike had come—which, yes, had been what Arnold had hoped the others would do.

But they hadn't.

Arnold walked east, back to his apartment, holding Mike's semen in his mouth, thinking he ought to spit it out. He didn't particularly like the taste. But it was *so* close to something he had fantasized about so many times before, he couldn't. By the time he reached home, it seemed to have become a slightly bitter part of him, something he'd grown one with, words in a poem he might keep or discard. Diluted with so much of his own saliva, by now it felt like—if it did not taste like—his own waters. Aware he would probably never do *that* again, Arnold swallowed, pushed opened the glass door, and went upstairs. . . .

He had to get a *few* more copies of *Dark Reflection*s, even if he had to pay rare-book prices. He'd been telling himself that for more than a decade. Would a rare-book dealer have it, after all these years?

Though officially his second volume, *Air Tangle* (1968) had been Arnold's first *real* book. Old Stone Press. What had *happened* to those people? Without turning on the hall light, Arnold pulled one free—to heft it on his fingertips. He still felt it was the best looking, with its enameled ivory cover, its pale picture of a sunrise over farmland, its black deco lettering: eighty-four pages and, like the others (except *Dark Reflections*), dedicated to Aunt Bea: "For Beatrice Carmentha Hawley."

For years Arnold had wondered what misappropriation of "Carmen" had produced "Carmentha." Aunt Bea knew only that it had been the name of a woman friend of her own mother's— not Sara Alice. (Aunt Bea was his father's *half* sister.) But because he'd grown up with the name, it had never really struck Arnold as odd until he'd finished college and moved away from home.

Nice as it looked, the book did seem oddly old-fashioned. It hadn't when it was published. How had *that* happened?

And number one?

That was his chapbook, *Waters*—done while he'd been at school in Boston, in '63.

In public Arnold considered *Air Tangle* his first.

Alone in front of his brag shelf, at night, *Air Tangle* was his second.

Hadn't there been six copies of *Waters?* But he could feel only four spines. . . . Where *were* the other two? Somewhere in the apartment, he hoped.

Waters—he slipped one pamphlet out and opened the cover—was still the one he returned to most, with its epigraph from Xenophanes. In darkness, Arnold recited it:

". . . For not without great oceans would there come to be
in clouds the force of wind blowing out from within,
nor the streams of rivers nor rain water from the upper
sky . . ."

At Boston University (when Brown hadn't really . . . worked out), Arnold had found the quotation in a book someone had left on a bench in a library carrel. He'd picked it up, read it almost by accident, and decided that it would be perfect. At twenty-five, Arnold had had no idea who Xenophanes was—some little-known but impressive Greek. The day he'd copied the passage into his notebook, he'd read neither the entire page it had occurred on, nor even the paragraph the writer had quoted it in. Nor, indeed, who the writer citing it was. Three days later, he could not have told you the larger book's title. It had been green—and old. The print on the cover and spine had been gold leaf.

That, Arnold remembered, even today.

A month after *Waters* appeared, Professor Cohen, who taught history, had said he'd read it—and that he'd liked it. And that he was surprised he had. Professor Cohen had a short beard and spoke Greek, Latin, and Hebrew, as well as Italian, German, French, and Aramaic, with his Brooklyn twang and his dark neckties. He also said something to Arnold about "given your interest in the presocratics . . ." so that it occurred to Arnold to look Xenophanes up—in the eleventh edition of the *Britannica*, suggested a helpful librarian: that was the last one that still had all the classical articles.

Thus, months after the chapbook had come out, Arnold discovered that Xenophanes was a presocratic poet-and-philosopher (apparently the distinction between them hadn't settled into place until Plato), born on the Ionian coast about 570 BC, whose dates had him overlapping with the early Milesian trio, Thales, Anaximander, and Anaximanes—not to mention Heraclitus, whom one ancient claimed Xenophanes had taught. Actually he'd outlived the Obscure Philosopher by a decade. As well, Xenophanes had survived the devastating invasion of the Persians under General Harpagus, left Asia Minor, and probably gone to Elea in Italy, where he may have been an early instructor of Parmenides, who, along with Empedocles (*he* dressed superbly, claimed himself immortal, and had or had not ended his days by leaping into Etna's lavid cone), was another poet-philosopher.

It had started Arnold on a year of reading.

Anaximanes was pretty soon Arnold's favorite of those early thinkers, because the least was known about him. Still, imagine the conceptual jump, the historical upheaval, discovering for the first time that *air* was a *thing* and not a *nothing*, a *being* rather than a *nonbeing*—Anaximanes's contribution to that combination of science and abstract thought that was philosophy before Plato—that there could be more of it, less of it, that it could be thinner, thicker, and that, invisible as it was, it moved about, and could, in itself, be cold or hot. . . . (It's why he'd named *Air Tangle* "Air Tangle.") Wasn't that the first *real* vault into the unseen world Parmenides had later pictured and that had produced modernity, unto radio waves, electricity, and atomic energy? Anaximenes had first discovered the fundamentalness of the medium they moved through.

During the months when he was despairing of *Air Tangle*'s ever actually getting accepted, Arnold had written his one extended prose work, that embarrassing gay pornographic novel about the adventures of some Sicilian youth in the reign of the emperor Hadrian. It had been Bobby Horner's idea.

Horner had outlined the thing, all fifty-one chapters. Then, sitting at his kitchen table from September through December, working at his portable electric typewriter, Arnold had strained his imagination—and his sense of prose—to fill up the pages. Eventually, taking a break to sit on the living room couch, the only way he'd managed to get through it was to divide Bobby's absurd and abhorrent outline still further into lists of separate paragraphs, each with its narrative task.

Back in his kitchen, one after the other, rhapsodically Arnold had written them out.

It had been supposed to take him three weeks. He took four months, spending the last one lapped in sweaters because the heat had gone out.

Three weeks after Thanksgiving—that year no one, including Bobby, had invited him over; though Arnold hadn't noticed because he'd been too busy writing—when Arnold completed and delivered the thing, Bobby asked: "Come on, Arnold—didn't you have fun writing that? It reads as if you did."

"Good Lord," Arnold (who was, by then, an atheist, though occasionally during the writing he'd found himself in honest fear of hell) answered honestly, "who could have 'fun' writing *that?* I just turned my mind off and *did* it!"

"I think"—and Horner had laughed—"the reason your sex scenes are so passionate is because you're a virgin."

"Oh, *please!*" Arnold had protested. "Spare me!" But, for the first time, it occurred to Arnold that possibly Horner had actually thought there was something *to* the incomprehensible narrative— that, indeed, Arnold's friend had considered it meaningful and not just something nasty whose only excuse was, in the air of legal laxness pervading the decade, penury.

Arnold's single copy—it had arrived with a check from Bobby Arnold took six weeks to cash—was hidden behind the magazines that stuffed the upper of the four magazine shelves. How Bobby had figured out how to divide the $750 they had gotten for the whole horrible thing, Arnold didn't know and wouldn't ask. He was honestly surprised he'd gotten more than half.

Once, after owning the published copy over a year, Arnold took it from behind the magazines, wiped the dust from the cover with the heel of his hand, sat, and read twenty pages. Appalled and finally unable to go on, he stood and put it back.

For years the possibility that Aunt Bea might discover he was gay needled at Arnold, till finally he'd realized she probably knew—at least she knew he was different. But by now he also knew she'd never bring it up—because, till now, she . . . hadn't.

Indeed, it was the center of the trust between them, Arnold thought, "coming out" be damned. You didn't change your central trust with the most important person in your life, even for a nationwide political movement, at least not if you'd survived with it till you were over forty, fifty, sixty. . . .

Or did you?

That Bea might learn about his part in the porn book, however, was an actual nightmare that had shattered his sleep at least five times, when Arnold had been particularly worried or stressed.

Relatively complete, his magazine publications on the shelves below the books ran back to Arnold's first published poem in '58 (because, when he'd come down from Pittsfield with some other college friends, he'd met the editor at a party: an extremely mature white kid named Peter, who'd worn a sports jacket and must have been at the time an elderly nineteen or, who knows, even twenty . . .) on the City College's *Promethean* staff: a cascade of morbid quatrains about a dead dog, never reprinted.

"Roxbury Leaves," "Loud Children," "Moritat," "Paradise Hill"—the first of his intermittent Vision-of-Hell poems; Arnold had written one practically every decade—"Pittsfield," "Blackmailers"—still his favorite from the chapbook: its twelve stanzas began respectively with B, L, A, C, K, M, A . . . each an impressionistic evocation of a different Roxbury house. The one thing it was *not* about was blackmail!— "Clouds" . . . After paging through *Waters* for the thousandth time in forty years Arnold closed the blue cover with its etching in white of a seaside. Back in '89, the second year of his Proctor stipend, he'd added two names to the dedication, in case it should ever be reprinted, though he seldom thought about them today. With its flaking corners and edges, he returned it to the shelf.

Because of these, and these alone (sixty-year-old Arnold Hawley thought in the narrow dark), I exist.

•◆•

Fog filled the street. Bare trees lay their shatter lines on milky glass. The lamppost down from the house, the dimmed facades across from him—all rose and faded into . . . nothing. Shoveled and shoved to the curb, November snow grounded this 8:00 A.M. obscurity in soot-laced white. In a night, winter mist had fallen over the autumn city Arnold had expected, when he'd pushed from his East Ninth Street glass door (thinking for seconds that, because of some incomprehensible work, they'd covered it with tissue), so that he could no longer remember what urban autumn looked like.

Left and right, Arnold could see neither corner.

Muffled, parka'd, and leaning into the damp, a man hurried forward from, passed through, and vanished away into fog. Arnold looked at the black garbage bags heaped at the curb, wedged with snow, the plastic wrinkled and droplet speckled. He looked about this limitless heart of darkness, this forward edge of winter, as yet unleavened by harvest or solstice holiday.

Turning to the west, Arnold walked on wet pavement—and did *not* vanish. Rather, he carried his sphere of reason, of vision. (The "heart of darkness," as Conrad had known and Arnold had pointed out to his students only last month, was white, not black—a mist at the river's head, pale billowings, an ethical hollow, in which any and all atrocities might be perpetrated, and the only measure against which to judge them was aesthetic. They were vulgar, unseemly, as blood trickled between the ferns down the bank into the river's ripplings.) A block and a half later, an aching right foot made Arnold realize that, within his shoe, his sock was soaked and frozen.

It was the crack in his right sole. Six weeks ago, when it had last rained, he'd realized it was there. Arnold stopped, thought about returning home, trudging upstairs, sitting at his table, pushing off his shoe, tugging his sock from his wide, wet foot . . .

But these were the only shoes—and the only clean socks—he had.

Arnold had about three hours of Saturday morning errands—bank, drugstore, hardware, stationery store. He'd planned to reward himself with a stop, over the way home, at St. Mark's Bookshop, where he would browse over the philosophy shelves among the volumes he could not afford. (In the store, two weeks ago, he'd read in a journal Badiou's essay on Brazilian poetry and Rimbaud, and found it uplifting.) But standing around in a bookstore in November with a wet foot was only so much fun.

(A wet, frozen foot? It was vulgar. It was unseemly. So you smiled at the Duane Reade clerk, at the bank officer, at your own reflection in the ATM—and at the book clerk who pointedly did not look up when you left without buying.)

Arnold's hypertension medication was a necessity. With this evening's dose, he'd run out. He took a long breath. Once he got home, he'd take a hot shower—if he was up to it. Or go to bed. It was not the first time this had happened—forgetting a hole in his shoe. Standing straighter, he took another wet breath, and, preparing for hours of discomfort, walked into foggy winter and morning.

●◆●

On a fall day in '97, returning from the supermarket, in his mailbox Arnold found a folded manila envelope. When he opened it and slipped out the pages, they were a set of galleys, index numbers across the bottom and registration lines in the corners. The cover letter read:

"Dear Doctor Hawley—"

Where people got the idea that, if you taught in a university, you *had* to have a doctorate, he'd never know. . . .

"We apologize, but we didn't have your address till now." (Arnold *humphed*. He was in the Manhattan phone book; he'd never been unlisted.) "Indeed, we hope this is the right one. I'm Fred McManus and, with my coeditor Bull Holden"—it said "Bull"—"we are putting out a volume of 24 interviews with 24 poets, *New Poetries, New Voices*. We don't mean new in the sense of young-in-years but rather poets whose work is new to a certain order of critical attention we hope to stimulate with this book." Well, that's nicely put, Arnold thought. "Your piece is not exactly an interview, but Bull"—so it wasn't a mistyping of "Bill"—"sat in on the seminar you gave when you visited the SUNY Graduate Center nine years ago and recorded what you said on his pocket recorder. Since there were a fair number of question" [*sic*] "that prompted your answers, even if only from students, it's easy to fit your work into our interview format. Of our twenty-four contributors, five are African American poets (including you), and four are women. But that's only one reason we were particularly eager to have you represented here with us."

Light slipped down the gritty marble steps from the airshaft window halfway up. (Arnold's single bedroom's window looked out on that shaft. In picking which room to sleep in, his choice had been between light and noise; and long ago Arnold had decided that, in *his* bedroom, he wanted quiet.) Colored panes were set around the rim, though they were dusty enough that one could miss their orange, red, and green, if you didn't know they were there.

"We've tried to be very careful with the transcription and editing. We're sending these so that you can catch any mistakes we've inadvertently made. Please try to keep corrections to a minimum and avoid any that add or subtract a line of type (or more). At this point it is too costly to move type from page to page. Alas, we are too far along to sustain any major additions or omissions. But that's because we didn't know where to get in touch with you till now. We are including a full list of our contributors and hope you will find it as exciting a collection of poetic talents as we are." [Encore *sic.*]

Upstairs, when he sat down at his kitchen table and read over his eight-page piece, Arnold rather liked it, though two sections—one a paragraph and one a whole page and a half—he wished he could drop. Both were repetitious babblings in response to a dumb question from a young man (identified as "Emil") who'd been paying no attention to anything—and who had thrown Arnold off.

Still, there were passages such as—

Remember, most poets live very ordinary lives. Yes, now and again you write a poem, and perhaps six, eight, or ten, or twelve times in your life if you're lucky, you collect them into a book and then there'll be worries about acceptances and rejections—what an editor will think—galleys to go over for errors, and finally presentation copies to give your friends—even some reviews, and maybe some readings, or a guest appearance, such as this one. But for every one of those, there are hundreds—

there are *thousands*—of nights when you go to bed and lie there, once more, thinking about things you'll never remember in the morning, and hundreds—thousands—of mornings when you'll get up, still tired, and put up a pot of coffee and wait for it to drip through and decide it was silly not to have washed those dishes last night because you have to do it now. That's what poets do. That's what their lives are like. . . .

Among his various opinions on the *Dreamsongs* or Sandover's *Changing Light*, some of which he recognized and some of which sounded not *quite* like what he'd say, Arnold was rather taken with the point—though, for the life of him (probably because no one had said it was being recorded), he had no memory of any single sentence.

He recognized none of the names on the contributors' list—though (predictably) Fred and Bull were represented with the last two interviews. Arnold mailed back the galleys later that afternoon—but never received a copy.

Perhaps it never came out.

• ◆ •

At the end of his first three-year extension beyond normal retirement age at SIS, anxiety over his coming joblessness precipitated Arnold into a breakdown. At the beginning of the last week of May 1999, he'd received the news of Bea's death. ("Dear Arnold Hawley," Mrs. Polk had written, "I am so deeply grieved to tell you that Beatrice Carmentha . . ."). But there'd been no way he could have gotten to Cleveland. Bea herself would have been the first to say it: "Honey—once I'm dead, I'm dead. You can come or not. It won't mean nothin' to *me!*" He'd even asked two friends at school if he could borrow two hundred-fifty dollars, both of whom had politely, even sympathetically, said no. But it was not just because it was *his* Aunt Bea, that made it so important to go. A woman had died who, when she was ten years old, had snuck into the back of a New Hampshire town hall to watch the great Sarah Bernhardt play Madame X in her eighth and farewell American tour. A woman was dead, who, though she'd never written anything herself, had taken two courses with Margaret Walker, whose *For My People* had been the first volume by a black poet to join the Yale Younger Poets Series. A woman was dead who had gone to hear Sergei Rachmaninoff premiere his Fourth Piano Concerto, in G minor, with the Philadelphia Orchestra. ("It was spring of 1927—I'll never forget it—when I was in Philadelphia. I tell you, that concerto, in the composer's own performance, changed my life. Arnold," Bea used to tell him, pretty much once a year, as they were leaving for the opera in Lenox, "it took me completely to pieces and put those pieces back together in an entirely new way, so that when I came out of that Broad Street concert hall that night, I was *not* the same young lady who had gone in, I can *tell* you!" as though she were hoping the singers waiting for them in the Lenox Opera Rotunda would accomplish such reconstructive miracles with their *Figaro*, their *Forza del destino*, their *Tosca*. "And of course," she'd explained again, chuckling, as they walked through the summer afternoon, down by Mrs. Winterson's roses, toward the Pittsfield bus stop, "the next day, I read in the paper how the critics *hated* it. They called it derivative, incoherent noise—and I realized for the first time that critics were not the people whom, necessarily, you trust." Back in 1976, a pop singer named Carmen (male) had turned some of the Adagio from Rachmaninoff's Second Piano Concerto, in D minor, into a hit single, called, rather poignantly, "All by Myself." In general, the Second was more Arnold's speed, among hopelessly advanced romantic compositions. But it had been years before he'd learned how . . . well, eccentric Bea's tastes had been.) How many black people were still alive who had heard Bernhardt and Rachmaninoff?

Nevertheless, Arnold missed the funeral—indeed, he didn't know for sure if Bea had *had* one.

That Thursday night, going up to his roof and letting himself out the door with its red-and-white "Open Only in Emergency" sign, Arnold wandered onto the black tar paper, took off all his clothes, threw them down the air shaft, then sat on some old newspaper for four days, naked, not eating, only occasionally sleeping, terrified to go back to his four rooms on the third floor, so that he would not have to be there when the City Marshal came and asked him to leave.

Someone in a taller building had spotted him, naked on his newspaper, and called the police. (But nothing had *really* taken him apart, and the reconstruction process was rather catch-as-catch-can.) Arnold had spent six sweltering summer weeks in the Mount Sinai psychiatric ward up at 102nd Street and Fifth Avenue.

Certainly that was mostly why, as yet, there'd been no eighth book.

But how, at sixty-six, do you go on writing poems when you're sure you'll be homeless in another three weeks? Then he learned, from a letter he'd never opened—it was part of his breakdown—that the Powers That Be at SIS had decided to let him go on teaching for another year.

Poets from Drayton and Hölderlin to Sexton and Lowell had turned *their* madness, more or less successfully, into art. But it was a topic Arnold felt too uncomfortable mining. A poet under thirty cracking up had a romantic tinge. (Isn't that what Plath and Sexton had lived—and died—off of?) A pudgy black man, well over sixty, losing his grip for a couple of months, even if he *had* published seven books of poems, was pathetic.

•◆•

While the city, the nation, the world outside celebrated the coming of the faux millennium, that New Year's Eve Arnold sat in his apartment on his couch, reading the opening chapters of William Stanley Braithwaite's *The House Under Arcturus*. He read about how, at the end of 1900, the twenty-two-year-old writer had celebrated the new century's coming, as Braithwaite had begun his own struggles as a black poet in Boston and New York. (". . . the stirring old nineteenth century had passed into history. The new twentieth century had come to birth, and in the hearts of men were hopes of an approaching millennium! . . . Not in the history of human affairs had one been so fortunate as those of my age, whose lives, bridging the generations between boyhood and the present, became the witness of and the participants in events and their effects, which had so profoundly changed the foundations of civilization. . . .") All those glimpses—even just mentions—of figures Arnold's readings had now and again given him—William Dean Howells, Thomas Wentworth Higginson, Edward Everett Hale, elegant Mrs. Humphrey Ward, blind Phillip Burke Marston, Arthur O'Shaughnessy, whom Braithwaite had bumped into, or known, or met in passing (as, indeed, Arnold had said hello to this one after a reading or that one who'd come to speak at a fellow writer's class)—were somehow reassuring. Even young Braithwaite's distress, on arriving in Boston, at learning Charles Chestnut was known in Boston literary circles as "Page's darky"—because Page was the white editor who had championed him—and Braithwaite's own pain at the realization that his chances at literary success depended on becoming some other white man's darky, gave a solidity and grounding to Arnold's own uncertainties a hundred years hence.

Pope's couplet returned to him, something Arnold had read only once but could never shake from memory. The hunch-backed poet had written it to be inscribed on an eighteenth-century royal dog collar:

> *I am his Highness' dog at Kew.*
> *Pray tell me, sir, whose dog are you?*

Dog and darky: what had history written behind the two metaphors that came together now? Yes, his first published poem had been about a dog, dead, he'd seen lying in the street beside a curb. Arnold reached over, picked up his notebook, then had to go into the kitchen to get a ballpoint, but came back and began to write. (He'd had to look for the pen five minutes, until he found one that worked.) A poem, yes: "Dog and Darky." It was the one that had the line about "that Pope's chestnuts"—a reference no one would untangle from the air, but so what? Writing a poem on New Year's Eve—especially *this* New Year's—seemed auspicious, even if there were no friends, no descending ball, no Champagne. Somewhere fireworks were going off, but he would keep all such clichés out of *this* centennial project. Arnold sat for several hours, happily working. Dr. Dahl in Russia had helped Sergei Rachmaninoff. He was the dedicatee of the Second Concerto. And Dr. Engles at Mount Sinai had helped Arnold Hawley. Maybe, whenever an eighth book *was* finished, Arnold would think about dedicating it to him.

"Who let the coon in?"

Arnold stopped and put his ballpoint down on his open notebook. So far, it occurred to him, no one had, yet—and he was sixty-four. But perhaps that was a fact to cherish. I am writing a poem (he thought) and, no, while I am not yet happy with it, I am certainly interested in it. Perhaps I am a lucky man.

He went into the bathroom and, from the back of the sink, took his toothbrush from the blue plastic cup and laid it on the sink's side. Lifting the cup, he smelled remnants of toothpaste and looked down at the white line, inside, circling the bottom. Gossamer gray and violet; auburn hair . . . This could have been Judy's century, Arnold thought. Some of it. But now, perhaps, she was safely confined in the last. Surely, back then, she had spent as little time thinking about it as had he.

Then Arnold went to bed, while the century's end, with its contentments and annoyances, dropped—quietly? No, outside it was a noisy night—noisily into the past.

•◆•

Arnold had taught without a sabbatical for thirteen years—with only three summer vacations (the first two had been before he realized it was financially impossible; the third was the summer of his hospitalization).

In 2002, the year Arnold officially retired (the slight edge in social security payments he'd get by working till sixty-six he simply couldn't afford to give up), he had a distressing encounter with one of his colleagues. Some of his students—black and white—had started turning in papers with "Black" capitalized. He'd put together what he thought was a nice explanation, that, in conference, he'd given to a number of them now. "A capital letter is something we reserve for a name. Black refers to our race, yours and mine. But does 'black' *name* you? Your name is Akesha Rhanda Jones, correct? But any name I give you, if it isn't one you accept as yours, demeans you. Because it's your race, not your name, that's why black and white get small letters at the head."

One boy actually said, "But we capitalize Caucasian—and Asian and Indian."

"And those aren't races. Those are adjectives of place—like Hispanic. And Chinese. Caucasians are people from the area in and around the Caucasus Mountains, which is where, at one time—erroneously—white people were assumed to have originated."

"Latino . . .?"

"And that refers to the language spoken. So it gets a capital, like English and French. There is no country—or language—called black or white. Or yellow."

But when he told this to a much younger, tenure-track colleague, the woman looked uncomfortable and said, "Well, more and more people *are* capitalizing 'Black,' these days."

"But doesn't it strike you as illiterate?" Arnold asked.

In her gray-green blouse, the young white woman shrugged as the elevator came—and three days later left an article by bell hooks in Arnold's mailbox—which used "Black" throughout. He liked the article, but the uppercase "B" set Arnold's teeth on edge.

A month later he ran into another article on his own in which "White" carried an uppercase "W" as well.

At least, he thought, Lamar did not have to leave the country. . . .

When Mrs. Fulmer was walking him back through the glassed-in skyway from the old library to the new Humanities Building, after the little reception she had thrown for him (potato chips, pretzels, Coca-Cola, and orange juice; twelve people had told her they were coming, she confessed to Arnold, but only six—*including* Arnold—had shown up), he said to her, "I guess it's a good time to retire, though. I don't feel as if I have anything left to teach."

After a moment, Mrs. Fulmer said, "That doesn't sound like a very satisfied note—I mean, to leave on."

Arnold sighed. "It's not."

Since adjuncts had no benefits, he'd gotten nothing from his teaching. But a pension from the eight years he'd worked for the City Employment Administration, and had thought he'd lost, kicked in as soon as Arnold left off at SIS, along with social security. (He really missed the morning and evening trips across the waters in the gray-blue passenger hall, the rising gate on the upper deck, snow on the black railing, ice clunking the hull. . . .) And apparently ms. hooks didn't think enough of capitals to use them on her *own* name.

Today Arnold Hawley was sixty-eight, and some eighty pounds overweight. He'd lived in the same apartment more than forty years. He owned a radio but never turned it on. He'd had a nervous breakdown less than three years ago—but had more or less recovered. He had a phone but no television.

Arnold Hawley considered himself a very fragile man.

•◆•

"Arnold, what in the world *is* this?" Beside his bookshelf, in the lacy summer dress she wore to visit Mrs. Winterson on Saturday mornings, Aunt Bea held not the "by Anonymous" Essex House volume, but a new edition on which letters bigger than the cover itself blurted "ARNOLD HAWLEY!" Below that, in the tiniest black sans-serif type, it said in parentheses, "(after an idea by Robert Horner)," which suddenly faded from the cover as the other letters grew even larger. They were going to be interviewing him about it tomorrow. . . .

As she turned pages, Bea's eyes glittered more and more brightly with misery and outrage, while Arnold protested, "Oh, Bea! It was *Bobby's* idea—and the *idea* is what's important! *You* know that! The language wrote it by itself—not *me!*"

Aunt Bea's voice broke like thin slate: "Arnold—*don't* 'Oh, Bea!' me, honey!"

Arnold's fourteen-year-old's cheeks stung with the lie, since what he'd blurted contravened everything he'd been telling his Staten Island State University students for years: There *were* no ideas without words, without writing, without the language to dramatize and stabilize them. Otherwise, there could be no poetry—

Trying to remember his age, Arnold drew in a great gasp—and woke.

He coughed.

He swallowed.

The back of his head tingled, deep in the pillow's indent. Moving his chin, he felt the sheet against his neck—it was damp. He pushed sheet and blanket down from his naked chest. Sliding over on the mattress, he realized that the entire spot he lay on was damp—though the room was cool and dark in the end-of-September night. What in the world would give him night sweats? Arnold rolled to the side, pushed himself up, and sat on the bed's edge. I'm . . . fourteen, he thought again. No, that's absurd. I'm forty-four. I mean . . . sixty-four. No, sixty-eight. He knew the space quite well enough that the light from the door, the light from the airshaft—the tenants in the apartment above and across from his had burned their kitchen light all night long for three years now—oriented him in the bedroom.

Sliding to the bed's edge—he had to change these sheets—he stood. Even to stand up was to journey through a dozen small pains: hip, back of the neck, inner arm, behind the ear. Rotating his head, Arnold raised his hand and pushed it across his chest to rub his shoulder, only to realize—again—he couldn't quite reach it. Must cut out the . . . but, then, he should probably cut out a bit of everything. But wasn't that what time, in his rush through it, was doing quite efficiently on its own?

At the back of the bureau, the clock's green numerals read 3:18. Somewhat painfully he took a breath and thought: Were it closer to four, I'd stay up. Barefooted, Arnold walked across the rug to the door: two steps, then a shorter one, swinging his hips to the left (so as not to collide with his bureau's corner) then turn right. His soles felt his bedroom's knobby rug become the hallway runner's pile: he had stepped through the doorway.

Arnold turned down the hall, where he could see the ghost of books and bookshelves to his left. There should have been a night-light in the bathroom, but the bulb had burned out three, even four months back. Remember, when next at the super-market. (But I won't, if I don't jot it down.) He stopped, turned, and looked at his brag shelf in the dark. Beneath one foot was something like a fold in the rug he'd felt dozens of times, standing here, with his shoes off, but which he'd never managed to spot visually in the green runner during the day. Here he was, bone naked in the hallway, when only moments back Bea had been wandering the same hall, in her summer dress. He *must* get on his pants . . .!

Then he remembered that had been a dream. . . .

Then he remembered Bea was dead. . . .

Next time I'm in class I must tell them how dreams can. . . .

But he hadn't taught for two years. . . .

Chills overcame Arnold.

As if the tingling were a cocoon to tear through, Arnold reached for the books and felt two fingers fall on the top of the copies of *Dark Reflections:* he knew it from its height, its thickness. Moving his hand quickly left, his fingers dropped the three quarters of an inch to his second, *Air Tangle*. ("To Beatrice Carmentha Hawley.") In the nighttime hallway, he squeezed his eyes closed. Then he let them open.

With the electric pattern aflicker before him, Arnold remembered the many instances he had stood here, day and night, pondering time, fame, all the vanished chances (fewer than his books, really), death. . . .

•◆•

A month later, in mid-October of 2004, with its brief Indian summer a week in the past—neither fog nor snow as yet outside—Arnold stood in his lobby, reading down the column of names on the left-hand side of the Proctor Trust's creamy laid, listing its supporters, the Trust's officers, its advisers. Fifth from the bottom was . . . James Farthwell.

Had Farthwell been there before?

Had Arnold *seen* his name there before? Under his thumb, he could see the envelope's torn edge sticking from beneath the others. The red postmark circled two of the three 9/11 firemen staring up at the dangling flag against the gray background of Ground Zero: the date was unreadable. James himself Arnold hadn't seen in more than eight years—more than ten, actually.

Perhaps, now, it was a dozen. Or . . .

Someday, Arnold thought, I'll open one of these and it will be James's signature at the end of one of their form letters, asking me to contribute money for the upkeep of the arts. Arnold let his hand with the paper fall and, with his other, grasped the banister, thick with dark paint, took a breath, and started the steps to his third-floor walk-up. Halfway, he stopped, took another breath, then started the flight's second half. Why did he always walk up these things holding his breath? Surely that was the way to kill yourself. But it was hard to breathe and climb stairs at once. At the next flight's top he stopped and looked down at the letter still in his hand.

". . . due to the paucity of entries over the last three years . . ."

Apparently they were changing the Proctor's rules. Paucity of entries? Perhaps he should phone Jesse to check whether *Grants, Awards, and Prizes* was still running the incorrect Chicago address. Or maybe call James. (Would Jesse still be with them?) Slow as he could be, James was more likely to remedy such things than Jesse was. How many years *had* this been going on? Since before he'd gotten *his* Proctor, anyway. Surely it had been corrected by now.

Each few steps, he read another paragraph or two, while he got his breath back. By the time Arnold reached his dark brown door, he'd learned that the Proctor was now expanding its sights to consider *not* just published work but also poetry *manuscripts*—books the poets themselves could submit directly to the judges' committee.

In which case Phoenix Press—yes, Farthwell's company—would publish the winner.

Well, *that* was interesting.

Arnold got out his key, which, as usual, he had to jiggle in the tarnished barrel before he could get the lock to turn. (Thank God he wasn't running upstairs from a mugger.) Pushing open the door and stepping across the little indentation that had once housed the metal foot of a vanished police lock, Arnold thought: Another Proctor might be nice.

I was just over fifty when I won that prize—practically a kid. And I didn't know it!

The pressure under his bladder that had been with him through the whole climb turned suddenly—in anticipation—to pain. Without even closing the door, Arnold hurried down the hall to the bathroom. Hiking up his overcoat, unbuckling his belt, he let his black jeans drop, turned, and sat on the commode's loose wooden ring.

More and more, these days, he sat when he had to pee: it was too uncomfortable to stand that still that long—and too depressing to feel his bladder burning and to listen to its splatter while he wanted to pour. After nine or ten seconds, his weak flow began.

Arnold looked down over his wrinkled shirt and listened to his meager waters. On the street, he had seen male dogs, lurching at their leash's end, too arthritic to raise a leg, squat like bitches. Old dogs? he thought. New tricks? Well—he leaned his forearms on the black cashmere bunched on his thighs—at least sitting was comfortable.

For some years, Arnold had called himself putting together another book. For those same years, he'd been averaging between three and four poems per twelve-month. (Four—no, five—years ago, Nathan Corner had published six of them in *Spectacle*—at which point Arnold had stopped sending more in. It was just a feeling.) Well, that wasn't bad. From somewhere he remembered that, for an extended period, the French poet Paul Valéry had written only two poems a year. And Valéry was not a bad poet to beat out. Of course Arnold suspected he was not working nearly as hard on his three or four as Valéry had worked on his two. Still. His most recent poem had been written last July.

No—it had been written the July *before* last. It was almost November, and the fact was, so far this year, there'd been no poem at all.

That *wasn't* good.

What he had garnered so far *could* make a volume, though. A slim volume. Slim volumes were good. No one wanted to read a hundred fifty pages, two hundred pages of poetry. Still, you needed something spectacular to open with.

Those bits of *journaliere*, those haiku-like musings inflated to sonnet size, sometimes larger, filled with the specificity of his observational skill—slices of life (and *his* life, after all)—*were* good. "Dog and Darky" was good—though he'd sent it out to no one yet. It was *very* good. But it was not . . . spectacular. The last poem in a collection. But not the first . . . You wanted something that would catch a reader's attention, right at the start, especially if you were gunning for a prize. Neatly typed, the last dozen years' sheaf was in the kitchen drawer beneath his typewriter.

Arnold was *pretty* sure he was finished peeing—so he stood up from the toilet. From where it was bunched on his knees, his overcoat fell too quickly. Drops had lingered in the channel, only to shoot out on his rising. Yes, he'd *felt* them shoot. (However worn, it was a goddam cashmere coat.) Soon he'd have urine all over the inside of the thing. He had to remember to be more careful when he went in to take his just-on-entering-the-apartment pee from now on—or to break down and get the damned coat dry-cleaned. Probably *that* had been more than three years. . . . Surely, over the next day or two, he could summon up some energy, put some thought to it, set it as a goal—and write a poem.

Leaving the john, he went back to lock the apartment door, then walked in and hung his coat over the back of the kitchen chair. All right, he decided, standing before the table, looking at his ancient portable electric. I've got to take out the new poems—well, the most recent poems—from the drawer and go over them again, carefully, decide which ones stand up; count pages; reread; see if they'll push me on to something wonderful, new, marvelous. . . .

The phone rang.

Arnold went into the other room and picked it up. "Hello?"

"Arnold—Arnold Hawley? How are you doing, there?"

"James?" Arnold frowned. "Is this . . . James Farthwell—?" But of *course* it wasn't James! He'd been thinking of James out in the hall, had seen his name on the Proctor stationery down on the stairs, so that now he was confusing someone who sounded halfway like James for James himself. Embarrassment seized Arnold—

But the voice said, "Yes . . .! It's James. I'm surprised you recognized me. Though *you* sound the same—pretty much."

"That's so funny!" Arnold laughed. "You won't believe this, but I was just thinking about you. Really. I saw your name on the most recent Proctor mailing—minutes ago. Not forty minutes. And guess what! I've decided to enter the Proctor contest—again, I mean. Because you've started accepting manuscripts as well as books. Again—this year. I just got the letter, about you folks changing the rules. So I said to myself, *I've* got a new book. I'm finishing it up in a day or two. Why *shouldn't* I send it in?"

"*Really . . .?*" James's voice held enough disbelief that it might have been rhetorical.

"No kidding," Arnold said. "I'm serious."

"That's great!" James said. "A new book. Yes. I guess you can't keep an old poet down."

"I'm close enough to actually *being* old," Arnold said, "to where that's a dangerous compliment." But Arnold felt relief. Till then he'd been floundering on, feeling he was getting deeper and deeper into something more and more unlikely—something that could only have an awkward end. "But why are you calling?" he thought to ask.

"Well, I . . . *Um*, I . . . didn't really have a reason. I just thought it would be . . . nice to say hello."

"And it's very nice indeed!" Arnold said.

"I mean, it's been a few years. Well. More like ten or eleven. And I just wanted to . . ." Then, on the pause's far side, James's voice gathered itself: "Tell me, do you ever get out to Brooklyn?"

"Not a lot!" Arnold laughed. "Why do you ask?"

"I'm having dinner with some people, the Saturday after next. At a restaurant—it's not far from my house. I live in Park Slope, now."

"I haven't been there for ten—dear me, *fifteen* years! But, yes, I know the Slope."

James laughed now. "Well, I've only been here for three. The restaurant's been there for two—so I know it'll be new to you. If you're not doing anything in two Saturdays, come on out and join us. I'd love to take you to dinner."

"Why, that's so nice of you, James!" Arnold felt sudden warmth for this man who'd phoned out of his past.

"Nate Corner and Michael Newman—they'll be there."

"Nate? You mean Nathan Corner? Who edits *Spectacle?*"

"That's him." James laughed. "Have you seen it recently? It's twice as fat and comes out *three* times a year. Just before they changed format, didn't I see something of yours in there?"

Arnold smiled. "Yes, he did a few things of mine." He hadn't known about the format change. "I know him. It *would* be nice to see him again."

"Then come on, Arnold. I'll tell them you're coming. At six. And I'm sure you'll like Michael, too. Got a pencil?"

While Arnold was taking down the address, the subway stop, the instructions, again he was hit by the feeling that something about this was not wise. But he *was* going to enter the Proctor. As well, James was now part of the whole Proctor complex. And James was his friend. The submission, the dinner, they went with one another. Not to go would be silly. "James," Arnold said, when he had finished writing, "would I sound like an odd old creature if I asked you to leave it open? I mean, I really *will* try to come. I'd love to see you. And Nathan. But the truth is, I *don't* go out that much anymore. Sometimes, it's a little hard for me."

"Oh, of course," James said, solicitously. "I understand. I'm forty-*five*, after all—will be forty-six in two weeks. And it's hard for me, too." (Arnold heard James chuckle.) "That means you've got to be . . . what, sixty-six?"

"Sixty-eight," Arnold said. "Pushing seventy. Really, I don't want to give you the whole litany, arthritis, sciatica—I broke a rib five . . . well, six years ago, now. I took a bad fall. You know, they don't bind you up today the way they did with those things when I was a kid. But I'm certain of it, something there went really wrong. Half the time, especially on cold days, it's *still* sore. Sore as a boil."

"No apologies necessary, Arnold. You come on if you feel like it."

"I really *will* try to make it. It's wonderfully nice of you to think about me, and invite me like this. Really. But if I *shouldn't* make it, you mustn't take it personally—"

"Of course," James said. "*Only* if you feel like it."

"Thank you, James. That's nice of you. And if it looks like I can't for some reason, I'll try to call. All right?"

"You don't worry about it one way or the other. You come. Or you stay home and soak your feet in Epsom salts or whatever. It'll be fine. Just know that we all—all three of us—would love to see you."

"Thanks, James. Really." When he hung up, Arnold turned from the table and said out loud, "Arnold Hawley, you sound like a fatuous, fucking asshole!" He wandered from the room, remembering he'd been about to do something in the kitchen. "Sixty-eight . . ." he mumbled. "It isn't," he said, "*that* old, for God sakes! It's not like eighty—or eighty-eight! *What* in the world was *that* all about?" Mentioning the rib, he thought. No, you don't talk about things like *that* with people James's age.

That was an anecdote reserved for friends over fifty—over fifty-five, really. More and more of his self-presentation was compartmentalized by age. The comic anecdotes about age itself were for the truly young, the high school and college students. That's what they loved to hear. From how many high school podiums had he managed to work into whatever topic he was speaking on, most effective if he could deliver it without a hint of irony: "When I was your age, you understand, I had to walk back and forth to school—uphill . . . in *both* directions!" It always got a laugh. Graduate students up to thirty-five Arnold could generally impress with his downright encyclopedic knowledge of the Beats, Bukowski, Black Mountain, the Berkeley and San Francisco Renaissance, and the confessionals—all of which he'd done nothing in particular to absorb, save a little reading (Johnson, Watson, Chartres; Hamilton, Dubermann, Perloff . . .), a little gossip. (Thirty years ago, it had been Pound and Eliot. Sure, today most of the kids had read them. But there was nothing mysterious, nothing magical left in them.) He'd breathed in that information from the same air of time that had aged him. But it never failed to put them in awe. Indeed, the work he actually loved from that era, the rough poems and angular stories of Paul Goodman, even Goodman's dry, dry *Empire City* and *Don Juan*, the soaring intellect of his literary, psychological, and educational essays, Orlovitz's *Milkbottle-H*, the pyrotechnics of Davenport and Gass, Sontag's offhand excellence, the poems of Frank O'Hara, Lorine Niedecker, James Schuyler, Richard Howard, and Mona Van Duyn, these he'd learned he'd best not mention, or he would receive dull stares. To praise them intelligently only called up embarrassed, bland silence—the hostility the ignorant always displayed when faced with knowledge that carried no validating mark of any current trend.

Though few of the younger people knew it, the children from thirty-five to fifty (basically they were predisposed to him because he had joined that strange tribe who knew that they *were*, indeed, children, no matter what responsibilities they'd been lumbered with), while they'd listen politely enough to any intellectual performance, really wanted the curtain to come down and the actors to come out and mingle, indulging what they called an exchange of "human information," and what Arnold thought of as some ancient Nichols-and-May routine. Then, as one moved between fifty-five and sixty-five, this segued seamlessly from the complex of problems, issues, and relationships into the valetudinarian's traditional litany of untreatable physical ills—one of which Arnold had inadvertently dropped on James, in his enthusiasm at having rediscovered him.

But James was a kid of forty-five. No, the broken rib *wasn't* for James—yet.

Arnold wandered back to the kitchen, to stare at the typewriter on the table: his Remington electric portable. (Remington—the old Remington Rifle Company—had used its ballistics technology to make the very first commercial typewriter—probably why *this* 1966 object still worked after thirty-eight years.) Now, what *had* he come in here for? It had something to do with the Proctor, and his plan to submit. But for the life of him, he couldn't remember what it was. Finally, from somewhere the words *wonderful*, *marvelous*, and *new* rushed back.

"What I was *going* to do, I don't remember. What I *need* to do," he said, out loud, "is write a fucking poem." A good poem. A new poem. Then, on Saturday, I'm going to that dinner in Brooklyn. Jesus, I *am* hopeless!

But he knew that wasn't it, exactly.

Like a sand grain under his foot whose position he could not quite define, the suspicion was, however, that if he *could* remember whatever he'd just forgotten, it would tell him why he kept feeling, now and again, this was a bad idea. That afternoon Arnold began to worry seriously over how long it had been since he'd written anything—even a book review.

Two weeks later, on the day of the Brooklyn dinner, Arnold still hadn't written anything. But now the radiators had started to smell, as they always did the first half-dozen times they wheezed on for winter.

Carrying his notebook and wearing his overcoat, Arnold went out to Tompkins Square Park—it was cold enough to keep people in—and sat on a bench under bare November branches.

Where, Arnold wondered, had time dispersed so many of the people he'd known? What had it done with Max—his mailman, for Arnold's first decade in the neighborhood? Each Christmas, Arnold used to leave ten dollars in an envelope for Max in the mailbox. Then the post office had distributed those cards asking people not to leave any more tips for the carriers—Max himself had stood with his gray canvas cart between them and explained to Arnold how carriers with lots of wealthy apartment houses on their routes made out like bandits, while men and women who delivered only to poor tenements got nothing. During the holiday season, it built up major resentments at the station. It wasn't fair. "So you make things fair," Arnold said, "by making sure no one gets anything."

Max had chuckled. "Yeah—basically."

But somehow, pudgy Max himself had vanished along with the custom of Christmas tips—assigned to another route, or, more probably, retired. In his gray blue uniform and ratty postal sweater, he'd been lugging his mailbag up and down Ninth Street a good while, even back then.

Or what about tall, white-haired Officer MacCormack, who'd come to Arnold's apartment that night to help with Judy? For years afterward, Arnold had seen him in the neighborhood—practically forever—now on the streets around, now patrolling the square. They'd always smiled, always spoken. Only somehow even forever had finished with. It was done by the time they'd first locked the comfort station, there.

Forever had gone the way of Miss Evens, the teller whose jokes about her aunt Selma had once made Arnold's weekly trips to the bank up at Nineteenth Street so amusing, before a plastic bank card—with his very own PIN—and an ATM screen had come between them, severing the acquaintance.

It was convenient to get money after three in the afternoon. You could do your bank business at three in the *morning*, if you wanted! But what were any of them doing in this brave, new, and so much more convenient world, where you hardly had to speak to a soul? Were any of them, Arnold wondered, sitting around wondering about *him?*

A boyish-looking Hispanic madman—forty-five, fifty (but so

many men, up to and sometimes over sixty, looked to Arnold like faintly wrinkled, gray-haired boys)—certainly homeless, wandered vacantly along the path. James's age, Arnold thought, as the man took a few steps in one direction, spoke quietly, heatedly, then moved on in another, to stop and argue intensely, passionately, but *sotto voce*, with an absent auditor. He wore a filthy jacket, lined with sheepskin, open over a naked chest. The waist of his ragged workpants hung down far enough to see the slope of his clear girdle of Apollo. Unlike Arnold, the man had an astonishingly good body, given his obvious age. The microknot of his navel was sunk behind stretched skin. His flies gaped, the darkness between suggesting a vaginal cavity displacing all penile presence. As crinkled leaves scratched the pebbled macadam, the man turned again and dropped to a squat. He pulled apart his runners—one shoe had no laces at all—and staggering erect, kicked one soiled and cracked foot free, then the other. Barefoot and unsteady, he flung his hands again and again toward his feet and continued his silent imprecation with barely-moving lips, a muscle leaping and laxing under a pitted jaw—scars carried from what adolescent shames and teasings, as was the gift of his body itself—as if he were explaining: *Can't you see? Must I go on entreating you? Isn't it obvious, now that my feet are finally on the ground?*

Suddenly the man staggered backward. The bench hit the backs of his knees, and he sat, hands out either side on cold, colorless planks. (When was it they'd last painted them? For years they'd been green . . . then, somehow, for a decade they'd been no color at all.) The man sucked in a great breath and, as he let it out, sagged. The wide, hysterical eyes closed—then half opened. His shoulders sagged more. He took another breath and leaned to the right. His long lashes—when younger and saner, Arnold was sure, he'd probably received compliments on their glistening black—flicked over discolored globes, then closed again, like those of an anti-Antaeus, who, when his naked feet pressed the earth, was drained of all fortitude, sense, and vitality. The man dropped sideways to the bench. As he got his bare feet up, one arm flopped forward and over.

He seemed to have gone to sleep.

Behind the filthy fleece lining the side pocket, Arnold saw the copper cap on the green glass neck of a flat pint.

Arnold looked at the old runners—one on its side—still in the path. Pushing himself from the bench, he went to them, looked back at the sleeping man—who, just then, took another loud, laboring breath, before, eyes still closed, he let it—loudly—out. Bending stiffly, Arnold picked up one shoe, hobbled two steps away, without straightening, and picked up the second in the same hand, while, in the other, his fingers tightened around his notebook's wire spiral. Standing now, ignoring the pain like a slow drum beating in his side, Arnold brought the shoes over to the bench and placed them on the slats by the man's filthy feet.

Then he went and sat on a second bench across the path and a little down.

The homeless man shifted. His face twitched.

Arnold opened his notebook and wrote four, five, six words. . . .

Three barriers sever us, fellow: your language, your poverty, your insanity. Now and again, I've stepped to the far side of all three. Then Arnold realized: here was his poem. Aristotle had said that great art had to be about kings and generals and people of power. Well, it could also be about the homeless—even the *twitch* in the face of a homeless man, asleep on a bench in November. Wasn't that face as worthy of aesthetic immortality as, say, that of a fourteenth-century merchant's wife in Florence— with a husband who could pay the painter's fee? *And been a diver in deep seas.* The spider veins in the nose's slope were a legible map. Wind-burned wrinkles before his ear and across the fore- head encrypted mysteries just beyond reading. It was a dry, brown face. But unlike the face of the woman Rilke had once seen sitting on the bench in the rue Notre-Dame-des-Champs, this one would not come off—not even at midnight, when the other guests at the masquerade at last removed theirs.

Something in Arnold began to churn. (He turned the page in his notebook. He was writing again. He was *writing*.) Art could be about anything. And this was the anything, the whatever, that Arnold's poem would force, would forge, would *name* into art.

An hour and twenty minutes later, as he finished his second fair copy—twenty-three lines—with rewrites, it came to him, at once, what he'd been about to do three days before, standing in front of the kitchen table, when James had phoned.

He'd been going to look in the drawer under the typewriter and reread the poems he'd finished.

But why had he been certain that would reveal the secret reason this was all such a poor idea? Perhaps because he would see the other poems weren't really good? Certainly they weren't as good as *this* one, just completed! But that's how he felt with every new poem. No, that couldn't be it. Really, it was time to go get on the subway and start off to Brooklyn, if he was going to make it by . . . looking at his watch, Arnold realized that even if he left now, he would be twenty minutes to a half hour late. Oh, *shit*, he thought. Shit! But there was no helping it. Behind some trees, through the chest-high gate before the bushes, away from the rest room, Arnold urinated. (After a flurry of construction in 2000, which had left the men's and women's rooms as new extensions on opposite sides from where they'd initially been, while the old floor-to-shoulder-height urinals had been pulled out and replaced by the usual white porcelain catchalls—indeed, the old bathroom spaces had been turned into offices for the park attendants—after its having been locked more than a decade, they'd reopened the comfort station. Only, for some reason, today it was locked again.) Waiting to finish his endless dribble, Arnold glanced back at the three high windows in which, behind the screening, were already sheets of plywood. *Sometimes* people actually used the damned thing to pee.

Then he started for the F train down on Second Avenue at Houston.

Had *everything* gotten more inconvenient?

•—•

That night James Farthwell, Nathan Corner, and Michael Newman went to dinner at a Brooklyn boite in Park Slope and immediately began to talk of where each had been on September 11. When they'd given twenty minutes to what, for three years now, had been the obligatory opening for all conversations with anyone new, between his first and second fork of carpaccio, thin as red tissue, James explained: "Oh, Michael—I forgot to mention. I phoned Arnold Hawley last week and asked him to join us—that is, if he felt like coming. I told him seven. I would have thought he'd have been here by now."

Young Michael paused in his peroration. "Hey, you mean I'm going to meet Arnold Hawley tonight? The poet?" Two weeks ago Michael had shaved his head again but was a dozen days into a light brown beard and faint growback. "You mean the black poet? That's awesome!" Ten rings of different sizes hung from Michael's right ear. A quarter-inch thick ring through a brass barrel distended his left lobe. Six more rings stuck baldly through his right eyebrow and a seventh from the left side of his lower lip. "Arnold Hawley? That's amazing! *Wow!*" From under his black collar, black spikes from a Japanese tattoo gripped Michael's neck.

"*If* he gets here," Nathan said. "James said he might not make it."

For the next twenty minutes, through zucchini spears, garlic bread, olives, radishes, and roasted red peppers in oil, they argued about art.

"*There* he is—outside!" James put down his wine glass—he was drinking red. With a gesture and a grin toward the restaurant's window, he stood, smiled, raised his hand.

Collar up, one shoulder badly frayed, and, below the hem of his long black overcoat, his runners warn along the outer edges down to the insoles, Arnold pushed through the restaurant door.

From the podium, with its small light shining over the lectern's reservation sheet, the hostess (herself black), in her high-necked dress, started for Arnold, then hesitated, unsure whether the fat, odd-looking black man belonged there. But Arnold hadn't seen her. Only after three steps across the floor, did he look up, smile, and recognize standing James, with Nathan Corner seated at one side—and the unfamiliar skinhead on the other.

"Arnold!" Nathan leaned to pull out a chair, while James reached over to the empty table behind them and from the pristine cloth swept a glimmering glass. Stem in his fingers, he hesitated between the three-quarters-full bottle of white and the all-but-empty red. The cloth was already droplet stained. Crumbs and wrinkled napkins lay about.

"We're in the midst of an argument, here," James went on, as Arnold sat. (Nathan patted Arnold's shoulder.) "Some woman entered her bed in an art exhibition"—now James sat, too—"in London, at the I.C.A. There was an article in *Art News* about it— a rumpled bed, littered with used condoms and panties soiled with menstrual blood, urine—perhaps worse. None of us have actually *seen* it. But Michael here thinks it's funny. Nate does not."

Michael picked up the white bottle, reached up, and poured wine into the glass James held, inclining dome, cheek, and chin of his velvety egg. As the young man watched the rope of wine unraveling in candlelight, Arnold wondered if the metal hanging about his head wasn't pulling it to one side. Now Michael took the glass from James and passed it to Arnold. "I *also* think it sounds like a very interesting piece—*besides* being funny, that is. No, I *haven't* seen it, of course. But just from the description, I'm willing to say that sounds like—possibly—good art."

Arnold took the wine. He felt his overlong nails tick the globe. Arnold sipped. It *wasn't* cold.

James and Nathan wore sports jackets—though not young Michael. All three of them wore black open-necked shirts, however. And (how, Arnold wondered, did he know this without looking? When had male bohemian fashion become so predictable?) black jeans.

Arnold was wearing black jeans.

Putting down his glass, shrugging his coat off his arms, Arnold reached quickly left and right to pull it back up over his shoulders. The restaurant *was* chilly. Did it look odd hanging down either side like that? It was still a warm coat.

Nathan Corner was wider, jowlier, softer. Farthwell had lost a certain fleshiness, which had been part of his boyish attractiveness, Arnold reflected. He was gaunter and his forehead was notably higher—and lined. And, of course, he was gray. But that hadn't even been surprising. Already the differences that had registered in the first moments were vanishing with acclimation, save when, for a second, James leaned back, or Nathan sat forward, or James spread his hands out beside himself on the cloth.

"And I say you just can't let any old piece of crap into a museum and call it art." Nathan sounded grumpy, even as he went on: "*Even* at the I.C.A. Arnold, if you'd prefer red, we can *get* another bottle—"

"Or ask them to turn the heat up," Michael said. "People Mr. Hawley's age always drink white. It really *is* better for you—it's only got a third the sugar. This bullshit about red wine being healthier is just a wine growers' scam." (How in the world, Arnold wondered, did you get a job looking like that? Michael could have been the cleaned-up and slightly older cousin—twenty-eight? twenty-nine?—of any of the grungier Goths who hung out inarticulately cadging money and cigarettes in Tompkins Square.) "We drink red for the same reason winos in the street do—for the sugar rush."

"Don't bother them," Arnold said. "This is fine. And do call me Arnold. Now, you're Michael . . .?" He glanced down to the side at his coat again. Really, he *had* to get it cleaned.

While James declared, "Oh, *I'm* sorry!" Quickly he went through a formal introduction.

There was a quarter inch of red in the bottom of James's glass. Smiling Michael *couldn't* have been twenty-seven. . . . *Thirty*-seven? *No* . . .

"Really, white is fine," Arnold said. He smiled at Michael. "I prefer it."

Michael smiled back.

"All right," James said. "Which side are you on, Arnold? Michael's or Nathan's?"

"Well—" Arnold picked up and put down his glass again— "art has to have formal constraints, standards of quality, a sense of tradition. Without any of that, there wouldn't *be* art."

"There, you see, Nate?" James picked up the bottle of red and emptied it into his glass.

Till the last time he'd seen him, Arnold remembered, James had been a manic nailbiter, his fingertips a ruin of gnawed-away chitin. Apparently, though, he'd been working to overcome the habit. Obviously manicures were one way he'd been fighting it.

Arnold thought James's hands now looked ridiculously effeminate. But he'd known half a dozen people who'd gone that route.

As well he saw the wedding ring on Farthwell's left hand. Married? *James . . .?* Arnold wondered if marriage had anything to do with breaking the lifetime habit.

"It's the tradition," Michael shot back, "that *makes* that woman's work good art! Potentially good—this all hinges, of course, on liking it when I see it. But it's *precisely* the tradition I'm talking about! The most important thing about the modernist tradition—I'm not even starting in on the problems of *post*-modernism—and by modernism I mean from the revolution of 1848 on, the last hundred and fifty-six years, is that art has to be *new*. It has to be original. *'Mach neus!'* That's Wagner. 'Make it new.' That's Pound. *'Etonnez-moi!'* That's Diaghilev to Cocteau, back in the twenties: 'Astonish me!' Well, scandal astonishes. *Ulysses* was a scandal, after all. *The Rite of Spring . . .?* When Monteaux first conducted it in Paris in 1913, the audience rioted. Hell, before Wagner got to it, in the 1849 Easter performance of the Ninth Symphony in Munich the audience booed and walked out, because they thought it was 'just noise'! And *that's* modernism. So now we have a bed with some condoms and panties? And here we are, an ocean away, scandalized—right on the beat!"

"I'm *not* scandalized," Nathan said. "I'm disgusted."

"That's what the Easter audience said, walking out on Beethoven. After Mozart, it didn't sound to them like music. And it was insulting and disgusting to take people's money, then submit them to an hour of orchestral and choral *noise*." Michael smiled.

Would they let you teach if you looked like that? Arnold

wondered. Certainly this was an odd century they were moving into—were *already* four, almost five years into. It had been an unsettling thought since the first time he'd had it, when, just home from having his tonsils out—he'd been twelve and lying on his back on the peach duvet on Aunt Bea's high four-poster in the third-floor bedroom—he'd realized he'd likely live into it. Still, it was a century that, Arnold already knew, was not his.

"Have you ever taken a look at Theweleit's two-volume study, *Male Fantasies?*" Michael was saying. "I'm afraid *that's* where you'll find the reasons menstrual blood and female liquids in general disgust you."

"And what," asked Nathan, "does Mr. Theweleit have to say about menstrual blood and . . . lady pee."

"That fascist social groups," Arnold said, who had actually read Theweleit, though back in the late '80s, "tend to figure social decay and the fall of society in terms of the flooding and inundation of female liquids, particularly menstrual blood—and urine."

Now Michael gave Arnold a wonderfully youthful smile, which, at its end, he turned on James and Nathan, as if to say, *See*, he *knows!*

"Good God," Nathan said, "you mean I'm a whole fascist social group? All by myself? And here I thought I just edited a literary journal. Well, I suppose that's *some*thing."

"Probably all men are," Michael said, "at least underneath. I think that was Theweleit's point."

Arnold decided he liked Michael. Maybe he was older than he looked. Still, the idea that someone so young had actually *read* something in his decade of adulthood was encouraging.

"I used to see that upstairs all the time on the second-floor table at Books & Company." James passed his glass from one hand to the other, then back. (A decade ago, Arnold thought, he'd have gnawed at a nail.) "But I never picked it up. My God, how many years has Books & Company *been* gone, anyway—?"

"I'm sorry," Nathan interrupted. "I mean, if only on the question of . . . I don't know: of genre. You've got to make *some* sort of exclusions. There's too *much* work now for us to go along with those sweepingly inclusive gestures that characterize modernism— the last hundred and fifty years, as you say. We'll let anything and everything in. Anything can be art. Now the *necessary* question, the *social* question for art—if there's going to be any art at all—is how to keep things *out!* In 1848 we didn't *have* a world population of six billion: it probably wasn't even a billion, yet—"

"Nor did the hundred eighty million in Europe," Michael added, helpfully, "really know that the *billion* over the rest of the world existed—" When Michael's lips pulled back from his teeth for the first "i" in "billion," Arnold saw a stud pierced his tongue.

"Nor did we have jet flight or the Internet." Nathan sighed. "People tell me that I'm supposed to take rap music, science fiction, Chicana political poetry, and every little megamillion committee-constructed action-adventure film seriously, as though it were real art—not to mention the crud the kids in the MFA programs turn out by the carload, then send to *Spectacle* in the hopes I'll publish it. *You're* a publisher, James." (What *would* it be like to go to bed with Michael, Arnold wondered. Would you get all that metal caught in your teeth? Somewhere he'd read that the average male thought about sex once every ten seconds. With Arnold, these days, it was more like once every three or four hours. At an occasion like this, that could be a blessing. Now, at least, he'd done it and it was out of the way.) "You can't tell me you don't know what I mean," Nathan was going on. "The democratization of the arts—in all directions: *that's* your modernist legacy, too. That's why we have a *post*modern problem in the first place. Well, I don't want to have to take all that crap seriously. I have neither the interest nor the time—not to mention the energy. The point is, we need a *new* tradition—and the new tradition has got to be exclusive, not inclusive. Otherwise Babel's tower will topple from its own weight and flimsy construction, Atlantis will sink into the sea, and Ozymandias's statue will come crashing down in the desert—and no one will care."

That someone Michael's age *knew* something about the history of art, or anything else, was warming. James—at forty-five?—was a product of some graduate school committed to theory back in the early '80s. While he could distinguish the modern from the postmodern to a fare-thee-well when he had to, James (Arnold recalled) had not an iota of knowledge about anything that had *happened* in the world of art before his own rather lackadaisical PhD from Stanford in '84 (and in the social sciences, at that). This had come home rather startlingly to Arnold how many years ago when, in a similar argument—then, the table had been filled with Arnold's friends and contemporaries and James had been the junior member—people had been talking about Burroughs's *Naked Lunch*, and James, for all his put-down of the movies and while claiming to be talking about the novel, had described something from the Cronenberg film, clearly under the impression all those insects and lascivious ladies had something to do with the book. There'd been two chuckles; the subject had been quickly and quietly changed, without ever bringing it to James's attention that what he'd been saying had been patently uninformed.

"Come on, Arnold," James said. "Tell us, now, what *you* think."

"Well, among other things I think . . ."

The argument went on for another bottle of red—and finally a plate of cheese and fruit for the table. Only then did James remember to ask: "Arnold, are you hungry? I mean, I *did* invite you to dinner, after all. You can still get something, if you'd like." So Arnold ordered a plate of fried calamari, with two dipping sauces. It was a healthy portion, but he felt as if he devoured it in five minutes. Art can be anything, he thought. Van Gogh's *Peasant Shoes*. Andy Warhol's *Diamond Dust Shoes*. Why not the collapsed runners he'd retrieved from the park path and laid by the cold feet of a homeless madman—only the latest installment in the Jamesonian argument. Arnold had actually thought the topic of conversation had changed. At one point Michael was saying, "Grimké, Braithwaite, Cullen, Tolson—I can really get into some of those lyric black poets."

Arnold asked, "You can? I was reading Braithwaite's autobiography not so long ago—on New Year's Eve, actually—" New Year's Eve *several* years ago, Arnold corrected himself silently.

"What a great time to read it, too!" Michael exclaimed.

Arnold raised an eyebrow. *Was* the boy black, perhaps? The possibility only occurred to Arnold now. But—no—he didn't think so.

Amidst metal and tattoos, Michael confessed, "I took a lot of black studies courses, when I was at Princeton. *House Under Arcturus* isn't a great book—but it's an awfully interesting one."

"Yes," Arnold said. "It is." He was totally impressed by this gawky little tin-man, who, otherwise, had all the sex appeal of a be-ringed can of mushrooms. But things managed to swing back to the first topic, and Arnold found himself listening to James— who, for a few moments, now seemed to have drifted around to the other side of the argument—accuse Nathan of trying to put art in a box: "You're starting with values and traditions and standards, but only a step away lie censorship and institutional limitations set out on topics, subject matter, even form. And you just can't *do* that. That means art stultifies. You strait it like that, and it loses its vitality and dies."

At that point, from his side of the table, Michael said (listlessly, as though Nathan's bluster was beginning to tire him and he'd lost interest in the debate): "Of course a *box* is only a step a way from a *frame*. And the frame is the thing that gets put *around* the artwork—whether it's made of gilded plaster, or carved wood, or simply the museum or the gallery walls themselves. It's what lets you *know* it's a work of art you're looking at. It's an indicator. This way to the art, ladies and gentlemen."

Arnold smiled at the Borowski allusion ("This way for the gas . . ."), sure he and Nathan had caught it. But not so sure about James . . .

"A frame, you say." As Michael sounded listless, so Nathan sounded drunk. "Well, a frame is just . . . just a permanently pointed forefinger."

Arnold leaned back in the folds of cashmere and said, as oracularly as he could muster: "Art can be anything—but I'll add, along with Michael here, anything as long as it's *good*." It didn't sound oracular. It sounded banal.

Nathan and James split the check between them, with Corner paying his half in cash—which went to James—and James putting the whole thing on his Visa. So Michael was a guest, too. The very young, the very old . . . Well, Michael wasn't *that* young.

"You must say hello to your wife for me," Arnold said, smiling.

James paused with the platinum card in his hand, which, as he'd been about to hand it to the waiter, the waiter reached across the three inches and took. "Oh, yes . . . certainly. Have you ever actually *met* Wendy . . .?"

Pleased with his guess, Arnold busied himself with his coat.

"You know, she really wanted to come this evening," James went on, "but she's leaving for a conference tomorrow. Her flight's at seven thirty tomorrow morning, out of Newark. And she . . . well, she would have loved to have been here, but she was exhausted."

And probably has no patience with your odd literary friends and the nasty things they talk about, Arnold thought. Condoms? Really . . .!

The card and the bill came back, and, as he signed, James said, "It just makes me aware how long it's been since I've seen you, Arnold. Wendy and I have been married for seven years, so it's got to be *more* than ten," which was actually a little shock to

Arnold. *More* than ten? After the phone call, he'd decided James had been exaggerating.

Then they were all up and moving between the mostly empty tables toward the door.

This was the first new group in three years he'd been with where Arnold hadn't had to explain what he'd been doing on September 11. If anything, it was a relief not to have to tell again how he hadn't known about it till the next day at eleven, when he'd gone out to his local bodega for a quart of milk and noticed the lack of traffic, the American flag already hanging from the side of the grocery's awning (for the last five years the bodega across the street had been run by a very nice pair of Punjabi cousins, the younger of whom always smiled at him and called him "Professor," even though he was only an adjunct—but Arnold still thought of it as a bodega from the thirty years when it had been owned by a series of Dominicans), and *finally* seen the headlines on the papers strewn over the green-board counter by the door—though he'd smelled the burnt plastic and rotten stench all the previous day and night that covered the city. He'd thought, at first, it was something in his cellar—

They were actually leaving, when, in the confusion at the doorway—James and Nathan had been outside for moments, so couldn't hear—Michael said, suddenly and clumsily, "Mr. Hawley . . . uh, Arnold—your . . . uh, prose poem *Their Gunwales All Submerged* is one of my *favorite* books of the last . . . well, thirty years! In *any* genre! Really! It's just an . . . an *amazing* performance!"

It stopped Arnold like a blow, like a fall. "You mean *High-Toned Homilies with Their Gunwales All Submerged*. There's no 'the' or 'a' at the front—I don't use articles in my titles. But then, *you* didn't. No 'a's, no 'the's"—he pronounced them to rhyme—"even when I was a kid, like you. But people don't notice that . . . maybe *you* would have." He frowned at the boy with the rings all over his face and the tattoos on his neck and forearms. "It can really change the meaning, you know: like Spencer-Brown's *Laws of Form*. If it were *THE Laws of Form*, it would be restrictive, totalizing. Or Spinoza's *Ethics*. But just *Ethica*, because it's in Latin, it does the same as . . ."

Michael began to smile.

Arnold had no notion if it were recognition of a linguistic nuance, or condescension at Arnold's making so much of it. "Anyway, it's more like thirty-five years—anyway. . . ." Abruptly Arnold turned from the neoprimitive face that refused to yield him the meaning he wanted and pushed at the door. "Well, yes . . . thank you, of course," he went on. "Certainly. Thank you." But the door opened inward, not out. Finally, he tried pulling—and rather staggered into the November cool. Arnold waited only a beat to determine which direction the others were heading. Though, seconds before, he'd been envisioning a pleasant stroll to the subway, especially with intelligent, well-spoken Michael, now Arnold whirled in the other direction and lurched off, eyes filling with tears. "Good-bye, James. Thank you. Nathan—good night." Why did such compliments *always* make him so *fucking* angry! (By a species of ethical force, Arnold had taught himself to take compliments, sincere or feigned, with some graciousness, about *all* his other books. All of them. Just not *High-Toned Homilies with Their Gunwales All Submerged: Meditations on George Jones,*

Giovanni da Palestrina, and Bonnie Tyler. Not *that* one . . .!) At the block's end, Arnold slowed. He took a breath. Probably it was because he'd gotten so little practice.

Looking around at the narrow street, the stores all closed, the corner lamppost with its street signs and their names that yielded no information at all about where he was, the few windows with lights, the many dark, Arnold found someone to ask for instructions to the subway.

Once he got his bearings, Arnold realized he knew enough to work his way—again—through to his embarrassing failure to γνθι σεαυτόν: it was only because he'd wanted *so* much more. ("The fact is, there *is* no praise as great as the praise I want." He'd said it with tears welling. "That sort of praise doesn't exist—I *know* that," Arnold had told Dr. Engles, on his side of the chipped table in the small blue room at Mount Sinai. "It doesn't stop me from wanting it, though—wanting it *so* much!") Couldn't he have an entire evening without someone like Michael, sneakily and without warning, reminding him how little he'd had, who could keep his fucking mouth shut?

James lived out here, already. (Arnold took another four, five, six calming breaths.) If he ran into Michael or Nathan in the station, he would ask the boy some questions about himself, show some interest, generally make amends. (The boy liked it, after all. . . .) Only, coming down the stairs to the platform, scattered with Styrofoam cups and cigarette butts and newspapers, gripping the banister, Arnold didn't see either—and rode back to the Lower East Side alone.

Next morning at six (no matter how late he stayed up, Arnold was always up by five or five-thirty), with a mug of coffee beside the typewriter, he got his poems from the kitchen drawer, retyped a few whose edges had become frayed, including his new one, and the next day packaged up his manuscript (*That Pope's Chestnuts*), took it to the post office at four-thirty in the afternoon, and sent it off Priority to Jesse Kolodney, who, though now she worked for Doubleday-Bantam-Dell, rather than MOMA Pubs, was still, after all this time (as James explained, when Arnold phoned him at Phoenix to make sure), doing Proctor office duty.

•—•—•

A week after Arnold sent off his Proctor submission—with its (glorious!) opening poem about the fellow on the bench—in the Second Street supermarket under the fluorescent lights set in the deeply groined ceiling, a black woman behind him in line started talking to Arnold. It seemed she was a high school teacher and the adviser of her school's literary magazine. No, she hadn't heard of him. But although she'd met one fiction writer before—another teacher who'd had a story in a neighborhood throwaway tabloid—she'd never known a published *poet*. Not one with an entire *book*—one who had won a *prize*.

"Actually," Arnold said, as modestly as he could contrive, "it was nominated for the Drew-Phalen." He added quickly, "It didn't win, of course," as another black woman in front of them lifted her kid up from the shopping cart seat and sat him on the counter edge, for all the world as if she were waiting for the luminous red hairline scarring the square of glass in the scale's steel plate to sweep him and price him, so that the heavy Puerto Rican bagger with the gold earrings, one in each ear, and a green base-ball cap at the counter's end, could add him to her purchases. The bagger wore a black sweatshirt with a color picture of some bald, hulking wrestler and spoke in accentless English: "Okay, which would you like, paper or plastic?"

(Goldberg . . . ? A wrestler named Goldberg?)

The bagger's sweatshirt collar was limp. Its black was really gunmetal gray. One cuff was torn. The rubberized picture had flakes all through it. He put Arnold's three cans of tuna fish, package of celery, Spanish onion, and two cans of Redpack toma-toes in a plastic bag without asking and didn't look at him when Arnold smiled his thanks.

(Goldberg . . .?)

Why, Arnold wondered, hadn't he mentioned *Dashes?* Really, it *was* the better book—certainly closer to what he was doing now.

The teacher, whose name was Mrs. Greene, remembered the name *Beleaguered Fields*, though—and went to the Strand and found one of the thirty-five hundred hardcovers.

Someone had decided he or she could live without it.

Mrs. Greene paid four dollars for it, took it home, read it, and liked it enough to look Arnold up in the phonebook and call. Did he remember her? They'd had such a nice conversation in the supermarket line. Would he mind meeting with some of her students on the Washington High School literary magazine? Dutifully, at two-thirty that Friday afternoon, Mrs. Greene and seven teenagers rang Arnold's downstairs doorbell, then trooped up, knocked, and came in. Four were white. Three were black. Of the girls, three wore glasses. One was fat and one *extremely* fat. Of the three boys, two looked like anorexics, one of whom was *certainly* gay. Besides Mrs. Greene's copy, they'd found three more *Beleagered Fields*, a hardcover and two paperbacks—also at the Strand. Would Arnold sign them?

Of course.

In the kitchen, Arnold wiped out the carafe with a paper towel and made coffee—half from the green tin of Folger's decaf (poor Abigail, poor Jay . . . he never filled the pot without a momentary memory of the August '69 headlines), half from the all-but-black powder in the red and yellow Bustelo tin. For more than ten years, even twenty, now, Bustelo had been making decaf, but that still seemed to Arnold a contradiction in terms.

Only Mrs. Greene and one of the girls took some in his mismatched mugs.

After stirring in a lumpy tablespoon full of sugar from the two-pound yellow carton he'd kept in his icebox how long now, Mrs. Green sipped: "*Mmmm*, this is very good."

Then, in the living room, they all asked repeatedly how he managed to do anything without a computer. When, after fingering loose copies from the hall shelf, he was showing them his books, the Proctor came up. (How could it not have, as it was all over *Beleaguered Fields?*) "What's the Drew-Phalen Award?" the heaviest of the boys wanted to know. (*He* was probably straight.) Arnold and Mrs. Greene smiled at each other.

Then Mrs. Greene explained, "That's a very *big* prize—that Mr. Hawley was nominated for. It's quite an honor."

Arnold told them (again) about the Proctor competition—and its three-year stipend.

Everyone (again) said, "*Ooooooh . . .!*" You'd have thought it was a MacArthur.

As if confessing a long-held secret, Mrs. Greene blurted out that Wally Franklin here actually *had* a book of poems in manuscript. Certainly *enough* for a book, at any rate. Of poems. Surely it would be a good idea if she submitted it. What was the address again?

Arnold looked at fat, cocoa-colored Wally (the child's gray-brown skin was unhealthy looking), with her pink-rimmed glasses, the lenses thick enough for cataracts, a pair of white beads on the end of each of her two dozen minidreads.

Hazel-eyed behind her lenses, a white girl wanted to know: "Do they ever make films out of poems?"

But before Mrs. Greene had finished her dismissive laugh at such an absurdity, Arnold explained: "Well, there have been film versions of both the *Iliad* and the *Odyssey*—even bits of Dante's *Commedia* have made it to the screen, not to mention Stephen Vincent Benét's *John Brown's Body*. The greatest poet in the English language is Shakespeare, and many of his verse plays have been filmed. Pushkin's great Russian poem *Eugene Onegin*—he was black, by the bye, like us"—he smiled at Wally Franklin, who, for a moment, smiled back, then glared into her mug in atonement for the slip—"has been both an opera *and* a film. And Roger Corman *named* some of his films after poems by Poe."

Mrs. Greene said pensively, "Now, I'd never thought of it that way. . . ."

Wrinkled silver paper stuck from the Camels pack in the breast pocket of Wally's man's green plaid shirt. Politely, she'd refrained from smoking. With a boy on either side of her, one white, one black, Wally sat on the edge of Arnold's collapsed sofa, her new orange work shoes crossed on Arnold's foul gray rug, playing with her mug, clearly mortified at having been singled out as a poet with a distress Arnold understood entirely.

"But you," Mrs. Greene said, "were telling us about the competition—the prize. Where should Wally send her manuscript?"

"Actually," Arnold explained, "I don't *know* the exact address." He longed to say it was in Chicago. But such a level of prevarication he couldn't reach. "I'm sure at any local library," he explained, "you can find this year's *Grants, Awards, and Prizes*. The Alfred Proctor Prize. Just look up 'Proctor'—or 'Alfred Proctor,' in the index."

"*Grants, Awards, and Prizes*," Mrs. Greene repeated. "Now you remember that, Wally. The Proctor Prize. Write it down."

And Wally got out a very stubby pencil from beside her Camels and a wad of paper, which, folded up behind the pack, had been thrusting it forward, and, on her broad denim thigh, drew—that's what it looked like she was doing—each letter in a minute handwriting, which, nevertheless, was clear enough for Arnold to read, upside down, from where he was sitting on the other side of the green glass coffee table:

GRANTS, AWARDS, AND PRIZES

Mrs. Greene put her cup on the table's glass and rocked back. "Now, I'm not going to let you forget it, either, Wally!"

Ten minutes later, Wally, Mrs. Greene, and the other children left—and Arnold wondered if he'd done a *really* bad thing;

or if, in misdirecting them, he'd only taken what was certain to be adolescent drivel and sent it awry. Surely, after all these years, someone had fixed that misprint—James? Jesse? The people at *Poetry?* Wouldn't one of them, eventually, have made that telephone call? Of course, the address didn't give *Poetry*'s name. Maybe the submissions never made it into their mailbox. Really, he had to put it out of his mind. Probably Mrs. Greene—and certainly Wally—would never get so far as to look up the address.

Of course, Wally *might* be talented. (It kept wheedling at him.) Hadn't Marina Tsvetaeva published her first poems at fifteen, Hart Crane at seventeen? Keith Douglas had been *dead* at twenty-four, Sidney Keyes at twenty. . . .

Finally Arnold decided that, however unlikely it was that she'd follow through, the chances were far greater he'd done Wally Franklin—and the Proctor judges—a favor. Still, he decided he'd best not mention the incident to anyone. If it was a joke, let it stay a private one. Certainly he wasn't trying to avoid competition—with a sixteen-year-old black bulldyke. . . .

Or was he?

Still, he felt uncomfortable, as though their naive student smiles in return for his own jibes and jokes through the afternoon ("Uphill—and in *both* directions!" Mrs. Greene and Wally were the two who'd laughed) had been mostly polite; and as phony as the *Grants, Awards, and Prizes* address.

• ◆ •

The next Proctor mailing told Arnold that the Proctor Prize was a week away from being announced. This year's five judges included James Farthwell and Nathan Corner, and three other names Arnold didn't know.

Nathan? James?

Which just made the Park Slope dinner feel odder. At least he hadn't known they'd be picking the winner when he'd gone out to see them, so no one could accuse him of currying favor.

They hadn't told him.

He wasn't sure exactly what their reticence had kept sacrosanct, what integrity it guarded, but whatever it was, it was intact.

A week later, James phoned again. Would Arnold mind dropping by the Phoenix Press office?

"Sure," Arnold said. "When would you like me to come?"

"Could you make it this afternoon?"

"I'm on my way."

All the way down the steps, Arnold turned over fantasies of winning his second Alfred Proctor Prize for Poetry. I mean, why else would James ask him up? If it was anything like last time, he'd have his first twelve-hundred-dollar-check in hand within days—last time it had come in the same envelope with the announcement he'd won.

Last time.

As cold as the first week had been, the third week in November had grown absurdly warm. Arnold had to stop and unbutton his overcoat.

On the subway uptown, Arnold began to get it together. Of *course* he hadn't won. James was a bit thick, but he wasn't a torturer. Had Arnold won, James would have told him on the phone; or at least said, "I have some good news . . .!" James wouldn't let him dangle. No. Come on. Get ready for the letdown. Someone else had gotten it this year, as probably they deserved. His skimpy forty-two-page manuscript would look ridiculous in hard covers. The first poem was the only thing in it worth reading, anyway. And even that . . . Contests like this *didn't* mean anything. Thanks to that misprint in *Grants, Awards, and Prizes*, no one had even *heard* of the Proctor—at least not since Vikki had slathered it all over the cover of *Beleaguered Fields*. Be reasonable. (Who else might be interested in *That Pope's Chestnuts?* At that length—forty-two pages!—not many.) The truth was, *he'd* done more for the Proctor than the Proctor had done for him. And he'd done it much too long ago. No, James wanted to break it to him, in person, like a friend.

In the beige plastic subway seat across from the glassed-in "Coney Island" sign, Arnold took a large breath—he was having trouble breathing, as he often did these days when he got excited. Really, this wasn't the time for it. Look. A measly thousand just didn't make that much difference. And after twenty years' inflation I bet if I asked James for a loan, he'd probably give me more than that. And who knows, he *might* want to publish my book in *spite* of the fact it had lost! If poets could be said to *have* fans, James was one of his biggest.

Supposed to get off at Twenty-third Street, Arnold started to stand, but a burning swelled within his nasal cavity to squirrel up behind his eyes, so that they filled with water. Starting to cough, he had to sit again, blinking, unable to see. He rode a stop beyond.

By Twenty-eighth, though, Arnold had wiped his eyes free of

tears. He walked off the subway, went upstairs (holding on the railing tightly, stopping by the new, yellow-tiled wall to breathe at the halfway point), then walked back down five blocks by Madison Square to the Flatiron (né the Fuller) Building and beyond.

It isn't fair, he kept thinking, as he hiked along. It isn't fair. When you get this old, every little thing makes you cry. It *just* isn't fair. . . .

•◆•

Phoenix Press was two small rooms on the seventh floor of an office building two blocks south of Twenty-third. James was both the publisher and its single editor. Really, it felt odd waiting for the secretary—an intern, James had told Arnold, at some point during the Brooklyn dinner, whom he'd acquired through an arrangement with the Parsons School of Design—to pay attention to him and announce him. (Why should he recall *that* . . .?) Odd, too, that he'd never actually been in here before, given what a good friend of his James was—or *had* been, a decade or so ago. Phoenix put out about six books a year—rather nice-looking books, too, Arnold had always thought, when now and again he'd spotted one on the front wall at St. Mark's. Good production values—even stunning, at times—but rarely anything he wanted to read: theoretical meditations on the World Wide Web, or on contemporary architecture, or on modern weaponry and industrial warfare. The rare work of fiction tended to be written in the present tense and filled with punkish illustrations, meticulously reproduced, while, in the nonfiction, words such as "inscriptive," "graphological," "discursive," and "paradigmatic" abounded on—bounced across—the pages. The one thing he was now sure of, looking at them on the three shelves along the Phoenix office's pale orange wall: James published them because he *believed* in them.

Did James publish any poetry?

But James would be publishing the Proctor winner. The mailing had said so.

There were more Phoenix Press books than Arnold had thought, too. When was the last time he *had* looked at a Phoenix volume?

"Oh. You can go on in," the pudgy intern said, with a German accent, putting down the phone. She had little cloth rollers in her blonde hair. It had taken Arnold a moment to realize this was fashion—an attempt to turn her Aryan cuteness into that of an antebellum pickaninny—and not just ancient hair curlers. "Jimmy iz inside."

Wondering why he'd had to wait the five minutes, he went in to see . . . Jimmy.

"Hi, Arnold." James got up from his desk and stepped from behind it. He was wearing blue jeans today—and a sweatshirt across which swam, in their different directions, the three stylized fish of Farrar, Straus & Giroux. They were surrounded by the names of poets: John Ashbery, Joseph Brodsky, Elizabeth Bishop. . . . "I called you to come over, of course—about the Proctor." The sweatshirt looked as old as the Spanish kid's in the supermarket with that wrestler on it.

"I figured it had something to do with that." Arnold would be eminently civilized—and not ask.

"You know, we had less entries this year than any other. It was a bit disconcerting."

"*How* many?" Arnold asked, tentatively.

James sighed. "Three."

Three? Arnold's hopes vaulted. Only three? Then *certainly* he must have gotten it. With *only* three submissions, his must have been—by far—the best.

"It was a very hard choice. We didn't make it easily."

"Look"—Arnold laughed—"an hour ago, back at home, I said I *wasn't* going to ask you this. But I'm only human. James, who *won?*"

"Well, one of the submissions was pretty obviously high school stuff. 'Moon/June,' 'my heart leaps in painful protest of all that is real and unjust,' that sort of thing. It's laughably awful. I always wonder how she managed to get the address."

Arnold thought: The man *is* a torturer! Fifteen minutes ago, I was on the subway, crying! "James—"

"So there we were, with you and Michael." James took a large breath. "We gave it to Michael."

"Michael?"

"Michael Newman. You met him at dinner . . .?"

"I didn't even know he was a poet." Arnold had started to feel confused again.

"For such a talkative young man, he's really very reticent about his own work. I rather respect that in a writer."

"Yes, of course." It was a reticence that had come hard to Arnold, but one that—*years* before he'd met James, he was happy to say—he'd mastered. Except when it concerned *High-Toned Homilies with Their Gunwales*—

"I knew you'd be a mensch about it. You've won your share of contests, and you know how little they mean. Here's Michael's manuscript." James turned to the desk. He pulled what looked like a shoebox to the desk's edge and indicated it. "Take a look. I'd really like you to tell me what you think."

(Arnold hadn't even had time to say that he'd only won *one* contest. . . .)

The box was in his hand.

It wasn't the right proportions for a manuscript. (*Boxes*, it said on the top.) Arnold took the lid off, expecting to see a sizable sheaf of paper, nevertheless. Of course such a manuscript would win over his forty-two pages of poems. How could he expect someone to publish what was, after all, only a chapbook or—

In the shoebox were lots of . . . they looked like oaktag rectangles. On each, in dark letters, was a printed word. Among the ones lying clear enough of the others, he could read:

WHISPERED

AGO

BEEN

TEMPORIZE

YEARS

TONKA

FRIABLE . . .

"What do you mean?" Arnold said, putting the top down on the desk. "This isn't a manuscript." He picked one up. "What are these—words you tack up on your refrigerator door?"

"Oh, it's better than magnetic refrigerator poetry. Believe me, this is a serious experimental text."

"You know," Arnold said, looking up, "if I had known you and Nathan were on the judging committee, I wouldn't have come out with you that evening. Or that I was up against Michael whatever-his-name-is." He gestured with the word in his hand. "That was unfair of you, James." He felt suddenly and extraordinarily angry. "Asking me out there, like a bug under a microscope— what, did you want to see if I could still wiggle my legs, or if I'd dried up and died completely?" Yes, he was angry. But that was as much as he could comfortably let out.

"Come on, Arnold. The Proctor Prize has always been an intimate and local affair. You know that. When I first called you up, the Trust had been planning to ask you to sit on this year's judges' committee. We already knew that Michael was probably our best shot—and I was going to invite you out to meet him. I wanted to see what you thought of him. He does these wonderfully experimental things. I wanted to get your opinion—to see if you thought he really knew what he was doing. Only then you told me that you were entering, too. Yes, that rather upset my applecart. But I asked you to come out anyway, and Nathan and I figured that—that is, if you actually came—we would look at both of you. Together."

"I hope Michael didn't realize I was his competition."

"No, of course not. He didn't know the two of you were competitors any more than you did. Hell, Nathan and I were hoping we'd get at least a dozen more entries by the time the actual judging took place. Three years ago we had seven, when Sally won it. And you and Michael weren't competing at dinner—you came out on the same side . . . at least in theory."

Who, Arnold wondered, in the world was Sally? "James, I

can't believe you're going to give a . . . prize, a prize like the Proctor, to a box of random words!" How many Proctor winners had gotten past him?

He looked at the tag he held: THE. Arnold dropped it back in the box.

"Oh, no," James said. "It's more than that, Arnold." James picked up a kind of spool which had been sitting inside the shoe box.

"Honestly, I'd feel better if you gave it to Wally what's-her-name."

James's frown was bewildered.

Arnold asked: "Wasn't she the third contestant?"

"Oh," James said. "No. The third entry was from Brenda Lockwood of Palm Springs. I gather she was a friend of Miss Edena's—they tell me Lockwood's been submitting the same book every three years since the Proctor Prize was established."

"Oh," Arnold said. "You'd said 'high school stuff'. . . ."

"I think she wrote it when she was *in* high school—back in the fifties. I suspect she's had her husband instruct a secretary or something to keep sending it in for her. But, look, jokes like Brenda Lockwood we don't even have to think about. This is something serious." He handed the spool to Arnold.

Arnold took it. Immediately the end unrolled, revealing numbers along the inside of the tape.

"Numbers. A string of numbers," James said, confirming the self-evident. "The way it works is that you tear off a length of tape as long as you feel like making *your* particular poem—one number per word. At random. On the back of each of those cards is a corresponding number. You go through the box, search out the words, and you arrange the cards in the order of the numbers on the string. The tear, wherever you decide to make it, as I said, *is* random. But not the *order* of the numbers. Michael has spent a lot of time putting them together. There are three thousand two hundred and twenty-eight words in the box. Does that number mean anything to you? Three thousand two hundred twenty-eight?"

Arnold frowned. "It's the number of words in Racine's vocabulary for all of his eleven plays. Shakespeare used around ten thousand in his thirty-six attributed plays. Joyce used just over thirty thousand in *Ulysses*. Why?"

"Jesus, Arnold, you really have a wonderfully classical education in poetry. I guess that's something that you and Michael share. I mean, I would never have known that if Michael hadn't told me. That's the kind of thing that only someone steeped in the tradition of world literature would know."

"Oh, for God's sake, James! It's like knowing 'antidisestablishmentarianism' is the longest word in English; or learning to recite 'Jabberwocky.' Or a Gilbert and Sullivan patter song. Either you learn it or . . . not. It's the kind of fact you either pick up or you don't. That's all."

"Still, you knew it—and I didn't. At least not before Michael told me. Anyway, that's the number of words Michael decided to limit himself to. The only thing random about it is where, like I say, you decide to create a break, you see? But this way, you practically become the writer of the poem. And your own actions decide where it begins and where it ends."

"I don't *need* to become the writer of the poem," Arnold said. "I already write poems. What I *need* is somebody to read them. Or perhaps publish them and pay me for it. Come on, James—"

"This is something very new, Arnold. It's like Language Poetry—only more so. Michael has worked on his number string, that is to say, his word string, very hard. And for a very long time. The epigraph—it's printed on the inside of the box lid—is that quote from Coleridge. You must know it. 'Prose is words in the best order. Poetry is the best words in the best order.' It's called *The Boxes*—reminds me of *The Dashes*. The truth is, I think your work is one of Michael's influences." James sat there, on the side of the desk, blinking at Arnold. (Arnold pursed his lips, teeth set behind them. But this wasn't the time to bring up articles.) "He was so pleased when I told him you were going to be coming with us to . . ." James stopped—like a man, Arnold thought, who realizes someone knows he's lying. "Arnold—if you'll just sit down and *work* with it, tear off a few strings and set them up, make up a few poems of your own from it, go through and look for the proper words, you'll see the most amazing verbal combinations open up right under your own hands, right under your eyes. It's . . . interactive."

"Oh . . ." Arnold reached into the box, turned over a card: SHOULDER. He always felt there was something hateful about the word interactive. On the back of SHOULDER it said "1,822." Arnold dropped the card into the box, sighed, and looked despairingly at James. "It's too much work, James. . . ."

"But that's the whole point." (Though could it, Arnold wondered, take any more work than *High-Toned Homilies with Their*

Gunwales All Submerged?) "You have to sit down with it yourself. You really do. Work is what it's all about—I think the word occurs in *The Boxes* more than any other. If you do—if you can *bring* yourself to do it, then you'll see that . . ." James stopped. He set his lips. Then he seemed to see another opening. "When I met you, eighteen years ago, Arnold, it was one of the most wonderful things that ever happened to me. You were a real poet. I knew you were good. Everybody else knew you were good. Sure, it was a coterie reputation. But how can authentic art have any other kind, in the world we live in today? Knowing you, having you as one of my authors at Sid's shit-stall-consecrated-to-Mammon—hell, being able to say that one of the most interesting African American poets on the East Coast, Arnold Hawley, was my friend—you made me feel like a real editor. I felt, knowing you, I was having something to do with literature—*because* I had something to do with you! You know, I'll probably be elected president of the Proctor board of trustees next year. It's almost certain." (How, Arnold wondered, had James gotten from real literature to the president of the board of trustees so stunningly fast?) "They want someone like me, a supporter of the arts, but a *real* supporter—someone who believes that contemporary literature, contemporary literature that actually matters, is possible today. Well, when I work with Michael's text here, Arnold, I have to look for the proper words. I have to fit them together carefully. I have to check and make sure I haven't made any mistakes. If you mess up on the sequence, it makes a real difference in what you get. Like I said, he's worked on the verbal sequencing very hard. The kid's got an ear—and an eye—like Nabokov's, like Davenport's, like Gass. Only Michael's a poet. And the results are beautiful. Verbally beautiful. Unless you're willing to sit down and do it yourself, you have to take that on faith, I suppose. But I'm not kidding you, Arnold. They really *are* wonderful. Well, *you* turned me into a real editor, gave me what I needed to go on to become a publisher. What Michael's text does is turn me into a writer, a *real* writer, who puts together lines as beautiful as Hart Crane's, as witty as Clark Coolidge's, as knowing as Joanne Kyger's, as passionate as Ricky Porchine's."

Who, Arnold wondered, was Ricky Porchine? He was not too clear on Clark Coolidge, either, though a least he knew there *was* such a poet.

"And I'm searching for the words"—James was beginning to run down—"finding them, putting them together all myself. Sure, I can understand how a real poet might be momentarily jealous, at first, at one of their number strewing such Promethean fires to ordinary folks like me. But that's precisely why it's revolutionary—"

"That's the most absurd bit of poppycock I've ever heard! I hope Michael didn't put *that* together. . . ." Arnold picked up three more cards. IN, LOVELY, BLUE . . . didn't some Hölderlin fragment begin like that, at least in translation?

"No," James said. "I did. I thought it was pretty good."

Arnold dropped them back among the others. "Well, it's not . . . I'm sorry. Probably I'm just a sore loser. Michael's won. I've lost. Now I just have to get on with things—"

"You know, reproducing this in a commercial edition is going to be an ambitious undertaking for Phoenix. But I really think we're the ones to do it. I was hoping, Arnold, that as a former

Proctor winner, actually you might write a blurb for us. Michael's idea was to put it on the very bottom of the box—so it was the first thing you saw when you lifted it up—"

"You didn't tell him I'd do it before I saw it, did you?"

"Of course I didn't. I mean whatever blurbs we get"—James picked up speed again—"it's going to be hell arguing with places like St. Mark's to give this kind of thing front-of-the-store display— I'm not even thinking about B-and-N or Borders. Though I'd probably have an easier time there, *because* they'll think it's a gimmick. Like a pet rock or something. But it really isn't. Michael knows some people at the Poetics Program up in Buffalo." (Arnold was thinking: if Michael already knows he's won, I've *got* to stop sounding as if I'm trying to change his mind!) "If you can hit with those guys, you've got a great thing going for you. And they're wonderfully open to anything that's *really* new, really experimental. And you have to admit, Michael is a pretty well-spoken young man. I think he'll be able to represent himself well, don't you?"

"Yes . . ."

"Come on, Arnold. Take it home. Work with it for a while. Then write a short piece on it that we can use—maybe we'll even run it as an introductory paragraph, in the little booklet we include with it that tells how it works. I mean, if it seems to work better there."

"You mean *not* on the bottom of the box . . .?" Oh, hell, he'd *meant* it to sound withering.

James didn't wither. He looked confused. "Arnold, it doesn't *have* to be on the bottom of the box, if you don't think that's the right place for it. It was only a packaging idea."

What do you think I am? Farthwell's darky? He got half the "what" out, before he realized the reference would sail over James's head, in all its offensiveness—the more so for not being understood. Arnold said, "No."

"No, what . . .?"

"No, I'm not going to take it home." If Michael had been here, he *would* have said it!

"But if you—"

"And I'm *not* going to work with it. Look. You're talking about a concept here. The whole *thing* is packaging, James. And I've *got* the concept. I don't need the thing itself. If I get stuck, I'll make up my own. Damn it, James, I'll give you your blurb. I mean, I owe the Proctor something." (He couldn't, for the moment, think what, though.) "But I don't need a silly box of words to get the feeling you're talking about, James. I just don't."

"But—"

"Because I *am* a poet, already. Don't you understand that?"

James took a breath and held it—just like, Arnold thought, an old man starting a flight of steps.

After seconds, the breath came out. James said: "Okay . . ."

Arnold started for the door. "And by the way," he said, turning back (James had picked up a folder from his desk to look through it the moment Arnold had turned away), "the title is *Boxes*. Not *THE Boxes*. It says so, right on the"—Arnold waved a hand at the work that stood, now, angled on the desk's corner—"on the box top!"

James looked up, blinking. "Isn't that what I said? *The Boxes . . .?*"

"Oh, never *mind!*" Arnold turned the door again.

And left the office.

He hadn't asked for a loan.

Nor had James offered publication.

Well, Arnold thought, I'll give him his fucking blurb—or introductory paragraph. (*The Boxes* . . . apparently the transition to an exacting poet didn't last very long!) The least he could have done was say something nice about my first poem. Or—hell!— all of them. But then, that was James. While he rode down the elevator, Arnold's mind was absolutely racing.

Out in the street, a public telephone stood on the corner. He picked it up and, blessedly, it gave Arnold a dial tone. He put in his two quarters, and James Earl Jones welcomed him to Verizon. *And* the computer voice actually gave him the number for Phoenix Press on East Twenty-first Street. It only took another two quarters to get through to the pudgy German intern. "It's me," Arnold said. "I was just up talking to James, minutes ago"—while he thought, occasionally the gods *do* smile—"but I forgot something. Very important. Something I have to tell James. Could you put me through?" (I should *probably* start by asking him to give my regards to his wife!)

"Certainly," the intern said. "Jimmy hasn't gone out, yet. Just a moment."

Then James's voice, solid and sober, came from the earpiece. "Yes . . . Arnold?"

"Look, James"—traffic whooshed behind Arnold—"while I was up in your office carrying on like a two-year-old, I forgot to say something. It's very important, now. Please. Really, it takes precedence over anything I said to you before. Would you *please* tell Michael, me, congratulations? On his winning the Alfred Proctor Prize in Poetry, for *Boxes*."

"What? Oh . . . yes. Certainly!"

"Really," Arnold said. "I'm *very* happy for him. And that it was a pleasure to meet him out in Brooklyn at dinner. Now, be sure to tell him that. He's an impressive young man. And I'll have your blurb written by tomorrow—maybe even later this afternoon. I promise. You know, writing blurbs is an art form, too. I remember, some years ago, somebody was talking about collecting all the ones T. S. Eliot wrote for Faber and Faber."

"They did?" James asked. "Did he do more for Faber than he did for anyone else?"

Arnold rolled his eyes skyward, then let them fall again to the silver phone. (Hadn't these things, till recently, been black?) "If you tell that to Michael—about what I said about blurbs and Eliot, he'll *probably* find it funny." *Could* there actually be people over thirty, Arnold wondered, who didn't know that Eliot—after he'd left the bank—had spent most of his life as Faber's editor in chief? People in *publishing?* "You just remember to convey my sincerest congratulations to Michael—on winning the . . . Proctor prize."

"Certainly, Arnold. I won't forget. That's very nice of you."

"Thank you, James. Really, now. Good-bye." Well, Arnold thought, swaying in his open coat, under the metal hood, hanging up the receiver, that, at least, was something done—and done right. *Some* gesture had been offered toward civilization. Automatically he buttoned up his coat, warm as it was, and started walking. They can't call me a *complete* vulgarian.

Of course he'd forgotten to ask to be remembered to . . . what was Farthwell's wife's name?

At Twenty-third Street Arnold went down into the subway, and had to swipe his MetroCard eight, nine, ten, twelve, *fifteen* times along the aluminum groove, while the red LED on the black glass rectangle in the steel facing repeated blandly, insistently, maddeningly: "PLEASE SWIPE AGAIN." Was this an omen urging him to try for the Proctor once more *next* year? Oh, please, he thought. Do you want to turn into Brenda . . . what was her name? Another Proctor annual joke? He was sweating inside the overcoat. A train roared in. A rush of air from the tracks pushed a whiff of urine up from inside his collar. That couldn't be *him*, could it? No, it *must* be from the platform itself. He kept on swiping while the train racketed, windows whipping by. "PLEASE SWIPE AGAIN." The train doors opened. People got out. "PLEASE SWIPE AGAIN." People got on. Arnold swiped again. And again. One middle-aged Asian in a hat and a scarf came to stand, waiting, before Arnold's style. He was of an age that, most of his life, Arnold had thought of as of *course* older than he was. But today the man looked disastrously young. "Perhaps if you do it a little faster." The Asian smiled, helpfully. Behind him the subway doors closed.

"I'm sorry," Arnold whispered, his throat painfully dry. "But I'm . . . trying, really. . . ." Arnold began to cough.

Finally the Asian stepped over to another style and went out.

And finally—*finally* it said Arnold could go through . . . while the train pulled off into its rising, then falling, roar. As he pushed down the style's metal bar (and behind him one rolled up to shove him on), again Arnold began to cry, from the frustration of having had to stand there so long, from trying so many times to get the thing to let him in—from *again* missing his train!

Jesus, he thought, at last on the platform, a tear tickling his cheek, the tears of the old just don't mean anything, do they? (The flow from the right eye was, he'd long ago noticed, three times as full as from the left.) They really don't. He *wasn't* sad. Just a little angry, a little uncomfortable, a little disgusted—with himself and the world. If only he'd stayed silent. He could always send it to Copper Canyon, Arnold thought, sniffing—though *That Pope's Chestnuts* was *so* short! And it had been more than ten years—hell, almost fifteen—since *Dashes*. (Wasn't that exactly like reentering the Proctor? What would he do when they rejected it? Of course he'd been rejected before . . . *so* many times.) Was anyone there who would remember they'd once *done* a book by Arnold Hawley?

If *only* he'd decided not to reenter!

He'd have been a judge instead of a . . . what was the opposite of a judge? A penitent? The accused? A thief? A con man caught out, condemned to write the winner a blurb? For the bottom of the box. If he'd controlled himself, he wouldn't be any *worse* off than he was now. At least he'd have been, if not a winner, then on the winning side. Now he was crying—but with nothing so rewarding as self-pity. It was only a response to frustration, the way old people cry at everything when they've had a stroke. (A couple of times, years back, Arnold had wondered if he'd *had* a small stroke—when he'd fallen and broken his rib—or perhaps he'd had what, somewhere he'd read, was called a transient ischemic attack—a sort of ministroke that didn't necessarily make you sit down while you had it. Maybe even during his breakdown . . . But he'd never gone to check.) He walked to the platform's end, away from the heaviest gathering. Frequently, fifteen or twenty-five years ago, he'd laughed at a joke—another of Bobby Horner's, reputedly Japanese—for its social and psychological acuity: *Everyone is a madman at ten, a genius at twenty, a has-been at thirty, and a criminal at forty.* But then what happened? It didn't even *get* to fifty—much less sixty. And he was almost seventy. Did you stay a criminal? Or cease to exist? The place where his rib had broken was, he realized, as it had been all day, an unremitting throb of hurt—only it *didn't* throb. It was a plate of agony screwed flat against his flank. No wonder he'd been so irritable up at James's. At the end of the platform, waiting for the next train, Arnold thumbed his itching eye.

part ii

VASHTI IN THE DARK

for Adam E. Barker

An old Harper Torchbooks volume, Arnold Hawley's third published collection, *Dark Reflections*—five years after *Air Tangle*—had been one of a short-lived series of original paperback poetry books Harper had tried to fly toward the middle '70s. The series had put out only six volumes. After Arnold's, they canceled the line. The vomitously romantic title had been an editorial imposition. It was also the book Arnold tried to think about least, since—for those who could read—it held the story of his marriage to Judy.

He still debated whether it had been such a good idea to risk the Hölderlin epigraph he'd finally placed, unattributed and untranslated, on the first blank recto:

Närret isch se worde, närret, närret, närret!

If you knew the story, you might understand why Arnold allowed himself to consider it so rarely:

The first days of June 1972 had been wet. That Saturday, thirty-six-year-old Arnold Hawley sat on a bench in Tompkins Square, looking across the park path at the men walking in and out through the comfort station's brick columns, between which he could see the playground. He was watching someone else turn in at the men's room—

—when something hit his ear.

Hard.

It hurt!

Arnold looked sharply over, while clouds pulled from the sun. As a breeze came, from the afternoon's sprinkle, drops glittered on the benches' green paint.

Arnold rubbed the side of his head.

Two benches down, three white girls were laughing. The middle one pointed at Arnold—and the other two, hands in front of their faces, turned away, ferociously giggling. The two on either side wore high-laced combat boots. One wore black jeans. The other had on a very short black skirt. The girl in the middle was barefoot and wore a gray-and-violet dress. All three were fifteen to forty pounds too heavy for the look each was trying for. Fat, hysterical crows on either side of a bare-toed pigeon: *she* was merely plump.

On the green boards beside him, Arnold saw, when he glanced down, a paper airplane rocking side to side. A breeze made it skitter to the bench's edge, then fall over, to catch on a draft and rise six, seven . . . *nine* feet!

"Oh, look!" one girl in black shrilled. "It's still *going*. . . ."

Arnold took his hand down. Folded paper couldn't hurt *that* much, could it? What had hit him had surely been a handball, or a stone. He looked up. The plane floated above more benches, finally to veer toward the bushes, where, with another windy rush, the leaves between the playground and Arnold turned over, to show more silver than green. Leaves waved. The plane rose higher. . . .

Arnold stood and turned toward the girls—he'd decided to go home. But the two at either side shrieked, lurched upright, and ran—afraid he might come after?

The remaining one looked at him, her gray eyes wide. Her dress was low, pastel, translucent. A bra strap crossed her doughy shoulder. Rather squat and faintly dirty, she seemed covered by a shadow. Was she twenty-three? Was she twenty-nine? He wasn't sure. The dress was sheer enough that he could see her underwear—and, in the gray-violet skirt's pocket, a folded paper.

Because she was staring, Arnold looked at her as he walked. At the last minute, he turned to her. "Why did you throw that plane at me?"

She blinked twice . . . three times. Then she said, "Why do you sit there looking at those guys? You should go inside, too. You know, they have sex in there. Right in front of the urinals—not even in the stalls. Why do you just watch them—instead of going in?"

Arnold's heart vaulted into his throat. He actually said, "Um . . . *uh* . . . eh . . . uh . . ." and coughed. For moments prickle points swirled on the leaves, as though he'd sneezed. Swaying, Arnold swallowed. And swallowed again. "Because I'm . . . fat—overweight . . . and I'm too old . . . and I—" he added, realizing that he sounded inane: "—I didn't shave today."

She frowned. "You're a *bear*," she said, as though that explained everything. "I saw a whole mimeographed *magazine*—with pictures of naked guys like you! Electronic stencils. A brown bear—but you're a bear. My friend showed it to me. You'd make out like a bandit."

Arnold reached up and rubbed his ear.

"*I* think you're hot." Then she said, glumly: "I didn't *throw* the plane. It was fucking crazy Judy Haindel." Vaguely she moved her hand in the direction in which the girls had run. Then she put her arms along the bench back—and immediately took them down again, sat up, thumbed the strap an inch farther out on her shoulder, pulled the translucent shoulder up over it, and looked uncomfortable. "I went in there, once. Yeah, I mean on the men's side. With my friend, Tony. I wouldn't go by myself. Tony took me in. He's pretty crazy, too—like Judy. He's got this red and purple birthmark all on his side—but he doesn't let *that* stop him! He let one of the guys in there—you know . . . fool around with him. Right while he was standing there and grinning down at him. While he had his arm around . . . me. Like I said, Tony's crazy. That was weird—but it was interesting, too. Watchin' some guy blow your boyfriend, while he's got his arm around you, grinnin' back and forth between the two of you."

Arnold asked, "Do you have any shoes?"

"Huh? Naw."

"I mean, maybe back where you live."

She said, "I don't live nowhere."

"What about your friends?"

"I don't have no friends."

"Those girls you were with—?"

"I don't even know their names—Vashti." She sat up, now. "One of their names is Vashti. But I don't really know them. And they're *really* fuckin' crazy."

"And Judy," he said. "The one who threw the plane."

122

"Oh," she said. "Yeah. Her. Judy and Vashti—those girls."

After a moment, Arnold said, "'Vashti in the Dark.'"

"Huh?"

"'Vashti in the Dark.'"

"What's that?"

"It's a story," Arnold said. "By Stephen Crane—the fellow who wrote *The Red Badge of Courage*. Did you ever have to read that in high school?"

"Naw," she said. "Naw, I never read it."

"Well, it's possible Crane never wrote the story, either. 'Vashti . . .' It was never printed and nobody's found the manuscript. Someone who wrote a book on Crane, though, said Crane wrote a story with that title. It was supposed to be about a minister, whose wife—Vashti—was raped by a great big black man. And the minister got so upset, over the next year he died of grief."

"*Ucch!*" She made a face. "Sounds like fuckin' racist crap."

"Very probably," Arnold said.

"What happened to *her?*"

"Vashti? Actually, it didn't say. She probably withered away from the vapors—or killed herself from shame. Or maybe the big black rapist did her in. Writing about women was never Crane's strong point—he was just a kid. When he was twenty-eight, he died in Germany of tuberculosis."

"Was he gay?" she asked.

"He could have been. Some people thought so. And Beer said—Beer's the man who wrote the book about him—that three people who claimed to know Crane *said* he was. Eventually, he took up with a woman five or six years older than he was. She was the madam of a Florida brothel when he met her."

"Oh." She raised her head knowingly. "*Definitely* a faggot—nothing personal, you understand. But, I mean, *that* makes it pretty certain, in my book. Yeah, he was gay."

Arnold looked down the path in the direction the girls had run. "I thought possibly your friends—Vashti or maybe Judy—had your shoes."

"Naw," she said again. "They ain't my friends—*really*, I don't know 'em."

"Do you have a family?"

"In Connecticut," she said. "In Bridgeport." There was something in her unlovely features that he would later characterize in a poem as "hectoring, hungry"—a description, he was fairly sure—today—was inaccurate.

Arnold said, "Do you want something to eat?"

She put her head to the side. "What?"

"Do you want me to take you to get something to eat?"

"Oh, man," she said. "Would you? That would be great!" Then she hunched forward: "You're serious?"

"I'll take you over to the Odessa. They have hamburgers and pierogies and stuff."

"You mean like a *restaurant?*"

"It's a diner—a coffee shop. Over there, across from the park." He nodded west toward Avenue A.

"Will they let me in? I mean, 'cause I don't got no shoes. . . ."

Arnold smiled. "Let's go find out." Perhaps, he pondered later, the hectoring, if not the hunger, had been his.

They walked back through the park and left at the narrow avenue.

With green and gray stripes, the awning stuck out over the sidewalk. Arnold held the glass door for her. She dashed in, so that she was four, five, six steps ahead, pulling out a table, slipping around it to sit, even while behind him, pressing at his hand, the door still closed.

Everything was orange.

How long *had* it been since he'd been in the place? More than three years. When still sleeping on other people's couches, Arnold had eaten at the Odessa a lot. Since he'd gotten his own place, though, had he been in here . . . three times? What he remembered was a large gray space—the gray of the stripes on the awning outside. Only they'd changed things since he'd last come.

It was now more of a restaurant than a coffee shop or diner. The counter was shorter. (*Was* it three years since he'd been in here—or five?) Propped upright between the sugar and salt, the menus were larger and thicker. Nobody said anything about her feet, probably because she held them back in the shadows under the banquet. The doors of most eating places in the area posted yellow cardboard signs with black letters:

No Shoes?
No shirt?
No Service!

Several years ago, this one had. He saw none as he looked around. The scored aluminum edging along the counter and the tables—traditional deco-diner style—was gone, as were the black flocked signs on the back wall above the counter, with their white plastic letters behind glass. On the bench's speckled cushion she sat forward nervously, feet back in shadow, and Arnold wondered what dirt, cigarette butts, and dust bolls lay under there—though, if anything, the place seemed cleaner than he'd remembered from before this renovation.

"They have *great* pierogies. . . ." Arnold slid out one menu. Another fell, knocking over the salt and pepper. (She set them quickly upright, then slid the fallen menu to the table's edge and opened it.) As he turned the large plastic covered pages, bound by a red tasseled cord, he wondered if, among those dozens and dozens of offerings, they still did. But there they were: meat, sauerkraut, and potato pierogies—boiled or fried.

"What's that?" she asked, picking hers up.

"It's kind of like ravioli—or dumplings. They're Polish—or Ukrainian. You can get them stuffed with sauerkraut. Or meat—"

"—or potato." Apparently she'd found them on the laminated page.

"They're on the heavy side," Arnold said. "Very filling."

From the big-handed Hispanic waiter, who finally wandered up, with his white shirt and black tie (*ties* on the waiters at the Odessa? Arnold remembered blowsy blondes in green smocks, age sixteen to sixty), they both ordered plates of assorted pierogies and a dish of applesauce each. She also wanted a malted milk. Arnold said, "I don't *think* they have ice cream here. . . ."

She turned to the waiter. "Can I get a chocolate malted?"

The waiter ("Manolo," white letters spelled out on his black badge) said, "Yeah. Sure. If you want one." There seemed so much . . . *air*, behind the black cloth swinging at his thigh, rising to the loops around the narrow silver belt. With fingers thick as lengths of brown garden hose, he set blue plastic water glasses full of clicking ice on the table's orange and gold. *Could* such a ham-fisted youngster be otherwise so bony?

When Manolo took the black menus away, tassels swinging from their spines, Arnold leaned back and smiled. "Come on— tell me. How come you don't have any shoes?"

But she leaned forward to whisper: "Oh, please . . . *shushhh!*"

Coming in the door, a large black woman in a purple and orange scarf pulled from the four white people with her to step over to Arnold's table. "Now, *when* are you gonna write me that verse tragedy you promised? Nope—no, it's all *right!* No. I *know* you're gonna do it *some* day!" Laughing, she turned to rejoin her friends. She was an actress Arnold had met at a cast party after some local theater event, four or five years before. It had become a running joke (however uncomfortable), when, now at two-month, now at six-month intervals, they passed on the street or met in a bookstore. Really, she'd been extraordinary; but what he'd told her was that he *might* translate a soliloquy from *Phaedra* for her. That's all. Only he couldn't remember her name. Three thousand two hundred twenty-eight—that was one of Bobby Horner's facts.

Across from him, the girl asked: "You're a writer?"

"I'm a poet," Arnold said, more softly than he'd intended. Then, to change the subject, he asked, "What's your name—your real one?"

"Vashti," she said. "I mean Audrey. My real name's Audrey. But I think Vashti is a pretty name. Don't you?"

"My name's Arnold Hawley."

She looked at him, measuring. "*You* could be a minister."

"I could also be a big black rapist." Arnold smiled.

"Oh, yeah—*that's* for fuckin' sure!" A forearm on the table, she pushed herself back in the chair.

Arnold chuckled. "Well, it's nice to meet you, Audrey."

Returning Manolo put the malted's metal carafe on the table. Condensation tracked the aluminum.

Carefully she picked it up and poured it into the tall glass that had come with it. By its paper cover a straw stuck to the wet side. Brown rose behind.

Arnold had *never* seen anyone suck down a malted that fast: she finished in two continuous draws. (He thought of his own jaw throbbing with such cold.) Immediately she turned to the pierogies on the thick plate, just arrived. By the time he'd cut into his second with his fork, she was finished. Arnold laughed. "Did you chew those at *all?*"

"Yeah," she answered with a serious look. "They're good."

"Would you like some more? You can have a couple of mine—"

She shook her head, a sharp, small shake, then stared at his plate with the nervousness of someone starving . . . while he ate the next two.

Arnold asked: "Are you *sure* you don't want this last one?"

"I wouldn't know where to put it," she said. "I'm stuffed. They really *are* filling." Hands in her lap, she leaned forward, over her empty plate—toward his.

When they left, again her bare feet escaping notice, they walked back through Tompkins.

She asked: "Do you have a phone? In your house, I mean?"

"Yes," Arnold said.

"Could I make a phone call, maybe? Long distance—to Connecticut? To my mom? In Bridgeport?"

Arnold said, "Sure, you can," and felt uncomfortable within his expansiveness.

As they passed the comfort station, its brick columns separating the men's and women's sections, she said: "You could go in there, if you wanted. Have some fun. I'd wait for you." Four bars dropped across the side wall's high window, to curve in sharply and jab the lighter lintel beneath, in the heaviest parts of four inverted teardrops of rust. "I don't mind." At an empty bench, she slowed, looking down at it, as if considering sitting. Now and again, her hand was wrapped in blowing pastels, held partly flat only by the pocketed paper.

"No." Arnold laughed again. (Really, the bars made the thing look like a small prison.) "No. That's all right. Besides, you said you wanted to use my phone."

•—•—•

Arnold's clearest memory from their meeting (he used three different parts of it in three later poems) came after they'd walked back across the park up to Ninth Street, after they'd climbed his stoop and gone through the glass door's echoing lock into his lobby. They were climbing the stairs to his third-floor apartment

(3-E). She was three steps ahead. Glancing down, Arnold saw the blackened ball of her foot land and spread on gray marble—bowed in its center with ninety years' tenants, visitors, quickly-called police, occasional delivery men—while light from the stairwell's colored glass struck her speckled calf through flowered gossamer. Momentarily Arnold thought of some large-footed peasant on the steps of castle or convent, a water jug on her shoulder, a milk bowl—perhaps—at her hip.

•◆•

In his living room, gossamer over her knees, Audrey sat crossed-legged in the corner of his collapsing once-gold sofa. (Today it was a soiled mustard, with orange blotches where, on the arms and upper back, the knap had worn away.) Hunched forward, with one hand she cupped the phone's mouthpiece. An oil portrait of Arnold's grandmother, Sara-Alice Logan, which Aunt Bea had commissioned and Sara-Alice had hated, hung off-center above the couch back on the blue wall. Dust darkened the gilt frame's lower ledge. Arnold was *not* thorough about cleaning.

On the far side of the green-glass coffee table, Arnold sat in the broken recliner (it no longer reclined and, if you leaned back too hard, would drop suddenly and awkwardly on the right) while, on the couch, Audrey finished pressing buttons:

"Mom . . .? Hi, Mom . . .? Mom . . .? Judy . . . Your daughter, Judy . . . No, not Audrey . . . Not Audrey, Mom . . . No, not Audrey. It's Judy . . . In New York . . . New York . . . *No*, I'm not pregnant . . .! *Mom* . . .! Yeah, I'm all right . . . I said I was all right . . . I'm all right . . .! In New York, I said . . . That's right, in New York . . . *Mom*, Jesus . . .! Come *on*, now . . . What do you mean, do I have a boyfriend . . .? No, *not* Audrey, Mom—I told you . . . Yeah, Judy . . . Yeah . . . Yeah . . .Yeah, Tony . . . No, you didn't meet him . . . You didn't meet him . . . no, *not* the gay one, Mom. I *said* I wasn't pregnant . . .! And, no, I *don't* want you to send any money . . . Yeah, I *know* you don't have any money to send me . . . I didn't *ask* you . . . No, I'm in New York. I'm all right . . . No, not San Francisco; New *York* . . . Yeah . . . Yeah . . . No, this is Judy, Mom. *Not* Ellen. Ellen's dead—you know that. Come on, now . . . That's right, Judy . . . To let you know I'm all right, Mom . . . To see how you were doing . . . Yeah . . . Yeah, that's right . . . Yeah, how're you doing . . .? That's nice. How's Ruthie . . .? No, Ruthie . . . How's Aunt Ruthie . . .? No, Mom . . . No, Mom, your sister—Ruthie . . . ? No . . . no . . . Huh . . .? Oh, *Jesus* . . . She did . . .? Huh . . .? Again . . .? No, I *don't* want to speak to her—*especially* if she tried again last Saturday . . . Oh, yeah . . . Yeah . . . Yeah, I see . . . No . . . Yeah . . . Oh, she's still in the hospital . . .? Well, that's probably easier for you . . . No, it's not *my* phone, see; so I can't make another call . . . Los Angeles . . .? No, New *York* . . . I don't know—the East Village, I guess . . . Yeah . . . Yeah . . . The Lower East Side . . . The East *Village*, in New York . . . Okay, good-bye."

She put the phone down in its cradle on the glass, let out a long breath, and sank back against soiled velveteen. Not looking at him, she said: "I'm Judy Haindel." Her eyes came up to his. "I ain't really Audrey. That's just pretend. I'm the one who threw the plane." (Above her, he imagined Sara-Alice sighing and relaxing at the admission.) "I was trying to hit you, too. Hey, I'm sorry. *Jesus*, I wish I could get married." With one hand, she began to pull the gossamer up from her knee. "I was gonna get married a couple of months ago—to my friend. His name ain't really Tony, either. At least nobody calls him that. We got our blood tests and"—she reached for the pocket, pushed her hand in, and pulled out the folded paper—"everything." She held it up. It was a form, parts filled in with typewriter, parts with ballpoint. "But he fuckin' chickened out." With the paper in her fingers, she dropped her hand on the pastels over her thigh. "*You* ain't interested in gettin' married, are you? Some gay guys wanna do it, just so people'll stop hasslin' 'em, you know? I guess that's why I want to, so bad. So they'll stop hasslin' *me*—my family an' everybody." She produced a high, busybody whine: "'When ya' gonna get married?' 'When ya' gonna get married?' 'When ya' gonna get married?'" Her voice dropped again into its rough contralto: "You know what I mean?" She laughed.

So Arnold laughed, too—and nodded.

Then he saw she was frowning.

So he stopped chuckling.

"You *wanna?*" she asked.

He wasn't sure what she meant.

"You was noddin'. You wanna do it?"

"Do what?"

"Get married."

She said it with the meekest inflection he could imagine. Arnold sat in paralytic stillness. If it was not a hunger in her face, intense, subdued, it was—with an all but maniacal edge—near it.

Had any aggression, sarcasm, or even interrogation colored her voice, he would never have said what he said now: "Sure. Why not? When?"

"You're serious?" She spoke with a meek gratitude and wonder he found thrilling.

Arnold shrugged. "Yeah."

"Oh. *Wow!*" A strange relaxation worked through her body, so that one bare foot slipped forward, off the couch's edge.

"I've never been married before," he said. "Maybe it would be interesting."

"We wouldn't have to fuck or anything," she added, excitedly. "I mean, I said, I know you're queer. Heck, I'd probably only be here for a couple of days—maybe a week."

"Sounds better and better," Arnold said.

"We're talkin' about a convenience, here—for both of us." For a moment, she frowned: "You *are* black, aren't you . . .?"

"Yes," Arnold answered, suddenly aware that he was speaking to a very poor white woman.

"*Oh*. Wow!" she repeated. "I mean that is going to wig them *out—so* much! That's so exciting! I'm sweating, it's so exciting—see?" She held out her hands, thick palms up, shiny and perspiration-gemmed. "I mean, I just wanted to make sure. That you weren't one of those black-looking Spanish fellas or something." She pulled her hands, fists closed, back into her lap. "Some people think Tony's Spanish . . . sometimes."

"No." Arnold laughed. "You've got yourself a black man, here."

"Oh, that is so fuckin' *great!*" she whispered. "This is gonna be wonderful! Hey"—she moved forward on the couch, so that both feet went to the throw rug—"gimme twenty bucks!"

"Huh?" Arnold said.

"Come on. Gimme. I'll be back in"—considering, she frowned—"half an hour."

Arnold felt his good feelings fall. Reaching into the hip pocket of his jeans, he pulled out his wallet. One of three twenties had already been broken for the Odessa lunch. He fingered out the second and handed it across the coffee table, where the green glass reflected his arm.

She all but snatched it from him. "Okay—great!" Standing, she moved from the couch's edge.

He wanted to say, *Give that* back *to me!* And, *No, I think this is a* terrible *idea! I'm* not *marrying you!* But she was up and gone to the door.

He heard it close.

With his wallet in his hand, Arnold sat very, very still. Finally he glanced at Sara-Alice's portrait. I've just given twenty dollars to a crazed white woman—certainly a drug addict—whom I'll never see again. Well, probably I've gotten off cheap. *He* was sweating, too, around his neck, under his thighs. He dropped his hand, with the wallet, in his lap.

At last Arnold up stood up and rubbed his ear—of course it no longer hurt. As he went toward the kitchen, he thought: Oh, my God! Suppose she *does* come back—*with* whatever speed or heroine or Quaaludes she's run out to get! Oh, *no*—that's insane! Had he even told her his name? He couldn't remember!

When, forty minutes later, the downstairs bell rang, and,

in the kitchen, he was standing beside the refrigerator, he jumped enough to bite his tongue. After waiting almost ten seconds, he went over to the sealed-off dumbwaiter where the bell was screwed into the wall, and thumbed the button to let her in.

Fifteen seconds later, Arnold heard her push open the apartment door.

A brown shopping bag in each arm and still barefoot, she stepped into the kitchen, walked up to him, stood on tiptoe, and, leaning between the paper sacks, kissed Arnold's nose. "Hello, dear—that's what wives are supposed to say to their husbands, right?" She stepped back and looked at him with an appraising air intense enough to make him frown. "I bet you changed your mind half a dozen times about this marriage thing, while I was gone—*I* did." She had a faint smell that he recalled from a homeless man he'd started talking to, once, in the park—and kept talking to, for half an hour, because he'd rather liked it. With her, though, it left him indifferent. "But . . . well, that's normal. You know—I think we're doing the right thing." (He thought, surprised, *She's* not *crazy*, while she went on in quiet seriousness.) "For both of us." Suddenly, with her bags, she turned to the kitchen table. "Hey, I got all sorts of stuff—chicken, and mushrooms, and onions." She began to take things out. "And sausages. And green peppers—you like those?"

"Sure," he said, a little surprised.

"And spaghetti. I do this chicken and spaghetti thing . . . cacciatore. Well, it's kinda like chicken cacciatore. It's pretty good. And salad and a bottle a wine. I hope you drink white."

"Uh . . ." he said. (He *only* drank white.)

"And your change. Six dollars and seven cents—here." She put the notes and coins clutched in her fist on the table by the typewriter. "The wine was four bucks. Well . . . three-ninety-five. They wanted to card me at the liquor store. But I showed them my wedding license." She laughed. "I figured because we're celebrating, you know . . .?" On the table's faded oilcloth, the gray-green bills opened slowly. "You got a pot?" She looked to where one sat on the back of the stove. "Oh—" she put one of the bags on the table (actually there was little in each) and pulled up the wine bottle—"lemme put this in the refrigerator so it'll stay cold. Okay?"

"Sure." Arnold turned to open the refrigerator door for her.

"And you've got a good knife . . .? You don't mind if I move your typewriter off the table, do you? Actually, I'd like to take a shower first, before I get started cooking."

"Oh," Arnold said again. "Certainly."

He had a room, which, while he used it mostly for storage, had a daybed in it. "Would you mind sleeping in here?"

"*Fuck*, no!" she said. "I wouldn't mind! If you *have* sheets for it"—she looked around at the boxes, the piles of books and papers—"I'll use 'em. If you don't, that's all right, too. It sure beats where I been sleepin' for the last two weeks. You probably do a lot of reading, huh?"

"Yes," Arnold said. "I guess so."

"Wow," she repeated. "Can I get to that shower, now?"

He gave her the red towel, which was two down in the pile of clean laundry, and sent her into the bathroom.

As she closed the bathroom door, Arnold remembered the all-but-full bottle of Percocet on the medicine cabinet's top shelf, from when he'd dislocated his shoulder two years back. Again, he thought, Oh, *Jesus* . . .!

Twenty-five minutes later she came out, her hair's auburn gone dark as the patina inside his mailbox, tousled and half dry. She shrugged up one shoulder of her dress so that a breast disappeared beneath translucent cloth, as he realized—now—she wore no underwear at all. "Okay," she announced. (Through the pastels, Arnold could see her nipples, one a full inch and a half lower than the other—like . . . testicles, he thought inanely—her navel, her pubic hair . . .) "I'm gonna cook us a dinner that'll knock your socks off." She turned to walk, still barefoot, into the kitchen.

First thing, he went into the bathroom. Wrinkled from having been wrung out, her bra and her blue flowered panties hung, pulled into the elastic around the leg holes, over the shower curtain bar.

Above the sink, his medicine cabinet door closed with a magnet that had been losing its strength for years. The door hung a quarter inch open—as it often did when Arnold hadn't pushed it firmly. He swung it wide, reached up, and fingered among the top shelf's brown plastic bottles. He found the Percocet, took it down, and, holding it up to the stippled bathroom window and rotating it back and forth between his fingers, stared through the transparent amber either side the label. None appeared to be gone. Perhaps she'd only taken one or two—or none. He put the bottle back, pushed the mirrored door closed—

hard—and turned. She'd hung the bath mat over the tub's rolled edge—and the red towel over the shower bar, along with her underwear, at the end where it was bolted to the wall.

For a while he stood looking at the transparent shower cur-tain, with, here and there, its blotches of yellow, representing ten-inch petals of childishly painted black-eyed Susans, bunched back toward the wall tile, its bottom inside the tub. (Judy had begun to clatter in the kitchen.) I guess, Arnold thought, neither one of us will be using the toilet while the other's in the shower.

Why he pulled the damp towel from the shower curtain bar, Arnold wasn't sure.

(A week later he would wish he hadn't—deeply.)

As the red terry cloth fell open over his hand, Arnold saw, at one end, it had been torn—ripped through by a good eight inches, as though she had started to tear it in half the long way. (At first it seemed she *must* have done it, till he began to wonder why . . .) Reversing it and taking one side of the tear in each hand, Arnold frowned. But, no—it *hadn't* been ripped when he'd taken it to the laundry. Had it happened in the corner laun-dromat's machine or in one of their ancient dryers? *Had* she done it—?

Frowning, Arnold refolded it and rehung it on the bar, not quite as neatly as she had.

It struck him that he wanted a drink of water. But going into the kitchen and interrupting her industry (he heard the water go on, then off, then on again—even louder—in the kitchen sink) seemed too much.

Taking his toothbrush from the water glass on the sink and

putting it on the basin's rim, Arnold turned on the water. Rinsing the glass out twice, he refilled it, then lifted it to drink—

As, through the glimmer of water, he saw the white line of toothpaste that had sedimented inside around the bottom, he was hit by the smell of old toothpaste. A moment later, as he drank, the mint taste defused through the cold water.

It was both a surprise and . . . unpleasant.

After three swallows, he emptied the glass, set it down, and put his toothbrush back in it.

·—·

They ate in the living room on the coffee table, their salads on mismatched plates—because that's all Arnold had. No, dinner was *not* spectacular. But it was good. She drank her wine from a champagne flute he'd brought home from a New Year's Eve party a few years back, while Arnold used a juice glass. She drank one and a half glasses, exactly. Arnold killed the bottle.

She listened to him talk about poetry. She smiled when he went to the shelf and pulled out a copy of *Air Tangle* and brought it back to the couch to show her. Then he thought, what the hell, went back to the shelf across from the bathroom, and got down a copy of his first chapbook, *Waters*, which she glanced at. Paging through *Air Tangle* again, she said, "Hey—you really wrote these? They put 'em in a real book, too! That must mean somebody thought they were good, huh?"

Arnold was pleased. "I've always *hoped* that's what it meant." Was his pleasure in her naïve response the wine?

Opening *Waters*, he read her some, out loud.

After the sixth, she said, "I don't think you should read me any more of them. I mean, I like 'em and all. But that's some heavy stuff. I have to think about 'em a while, you know? But too much, and it starts to go in one ear and come out the other."

Which basically decided him she was pretty sharp. Even if it was just an excuse to get out of listening to more, it was a civilized one. He couldn't hold it against her. So, with *Waters* and *Air Tangle* on the green glass between them, they talked—about what had occurred here four years before—with Bobby Horner and Lamar and Noel, in the libraries with his friends—which had changed the nation's language. . . . "So you see: That's why *you* wanted to know today if I was 'black,' instead of 'Negro.'"

"Really—no kiddin'?"

In his bedroom, Arnold went to sleep happy.

Seeing her for the first time the next morning, coming from the kitchen at the hall's far end, was remarkably easy.

He smiled.

She said, "Hello," and smiled back. "Yeah, I'm still here."

And the books were no longer on the coffee table. Checking across from the bathroom door, he found they'd been replaced on the shelf, among the ten copies of each.

They had oatmeal for breakfast.

Judy volunteered to make it, but when Arnold insisted, she let him fix it. He phoned work to say he'd be in at noon. Then he took her, still barefoot, up to Fourteenth Street, where he bought her a pair of sneakers for $6.95 and three pairs of peds. They got two simple dresses, one for $9.98 and one for twelve dollars. And some underwear. Then they subwayed down to City Hall, to get the license thing straightened out. "Because no matter what," she explained, "you have to wait three days. Then you just show up at civil court and, when they get a minute, whatever judge is on duty . . . marries you—with the court stenographer for a witness. It's easy. That's how lots of people do it."

"Have you done it before?" Arnold asked.

"Naw, but I asked people."

Then, giving her the ten dollars she asked for as he left, Arnold went in for work among the green cubicles on Twenty-seventh Street.

On his way home that evening, as Judy had instructed, Arnold stopped at the high onyx door in the red stone Public Health Clinic on Twenty-third to get his Wasserman test. The green waiting room, the thick-set black woman in her white nurse's uniform who took his blood, the snap of the rubber tube around his dark upper arm, the shiny aluminum table on which the test tubes, with their red stoppers and bottoms clotted with what looked like Vaseline, stood in a white plastic rack—even the pure surprise when the swab was thrust an inch into his penis ("You might as well get the whole series—gonorrhea, too," a young man in a tweed jacket identical to Arnold's told him and looked up from a clipboard)—had the lucidity of things never before done and therefore things he'd never forget. (Judy still had hers from her last failed attempt. That's what the paper in her pocket had been all about.) They told him he could expect the results in five to ten business days.

Surprisingly calm, Arnold returned to East Ninth Street;

141

perhaps it was the anxiety of the medical tests, or a reaction against the good feelings of the afternoon. But by the time he got home, he'd slipped back into paranoia—and was expecting to find his apartment stripped. (She'd have friends. She'd have gone and gotten them. She'd bring them in. They'd take *every-thing*. . . .) She'd been out shopping again—and confessed she'd left the door unlocked while she'd been gone.

But nothing was out of place. He still felt rather grumpy about it. This wasn't the neighborhood for leaving doors unlocked. Even for an hour. But walking heavily up and down the hall, fingering books not his on dusty-edged shelves, he more or less held it in.

That night's dinner was to be scampi with lemon-butter sauce, over rice.

"Where'd you learn to cook?" he asked her. In the kitchen, with his second glass of pre-dinner wine, the grumpiness dissipated.

"Just picked it up." Judy looked up from the sauce pan with steam around her hair till she put the cover back down.

"How old are you?" he asked, now.

"Twenty," she said. Then she grinned. "Naw—actually I'm twenty-three." The grin became a small, harsh laugh. "Isn't it funny how women are always lyin' about their age?" (She said it without a jot of irony.) "Hey, I gotta stop that, now. That's just so"— she searched for a word—"ordinary."

The next night was pork chops and zucchini.

And the Wasserman results—in only three days—arrived. Arnold was free of venereal taint.

The morning they actually got married—she didn't ask him

to, but he called in sick that day—she went went out and, at the supermarket, purchased all the makings for a chocolate cake.

"My God," Arnold said, "are you actually going to have *time?*"

She did. Judy started mixing at twenty after eight. The cake came out of the oven by ten, only slightly higher on the left than on the right. ("You just turn 'em opposite ways, when you put the layers on top of each other to frost 'em. That'll take care of it.") Then they went down to the courthouse—yes, by now they had all the papers. As well they'd waited the proper three days. Among the court rotunda's drear columns, it was even more matter-of-fact than Arnold expected. With them, seven other couples were getting married that morning.

They all sat on the front bench of a traditional dark wood courtroom, the grooms—most in jeans, but one in a blue suit with a flower in his lapel—nodding as each new couple arrived, the brides smiling occasionally at one another. One black fellow, older and *much* bigger than Arnold, came in wearing a stained yellow T-shirt under a pair of bib denims, his great cracked feet only loosely contained in sandals. With him, a diminutive young woman, in brocaded jeans and a white lace blouse, looked as if she were an East Indian child bride. Had someone told Arnold she was fourteen, he would have believed it. Only her solemn expression strained toward adulthood. One great hand splayed over the bench back, the big fellow lowered himself heavily to sit, put his head back, opened his mouth, and, in three minutes, listing hugely left, was asleep. The exquisite girl-woman sat rigidly upright beside him. Now and again a muscle pulsed in her jaw. Some of the others smiled at her. Some did not.

Couple at a time, a clerk called them into the very small judge's office inside a door to the right of the judge's dais. Judy and Arnold were the third ones to enter. In the tiny space, crammed with papers and crowded with books up the walls, Judy Alice Haindel said, "I do."

(He hadn't known her middle name was the same as his grandmother's.)

Arnold Frederic Hawley said, "I do."

Judge Alice Hong (*another* Alice!), who was small and Asian, said, "I now pronounce you man and wife." She smiled as if she enjoyed her job. "If you'd like, you may kiss the bride." So Arnold did—on Judy's chastely offered cheek. That day she had on the freshly washed pastel gossamer, as well as underwear and sneakers.

Though they only walked quickly, Arnold felt as though they *raced* from the courtroom!

Halfway down the court's thirty-foot-wide stone steps, Judy cried, "*Whoopee!* Ain't this *great?* Oh, *wow!*" She let go Arnold's hand and threw up both of hers. The translucent pastel blew about her spotty shins. "Oh, this is wonderful. It's even a June wedding. I bet *that'll* fuck 'em up! I mean this is just so fuckin' wonderful. I'm *married!* I'm gonna go grocery shopping again, if it's okay with you—so we can have something *really* special—tonight!"

When they reached the sidewalk, they turned up the street. The act's energy, the sunny sky, and the traffic's happy honking made dropping into the subway seem absurd. Arnold wasn't sure if she were following him or he were following her—or if, in the

144

way married folk were supposed to be, they were simply at one. They walked two, three, then four blocks up bustling lower Broadway, without having said a thing about walking home. He would glance at her, and she would glance, grinning, back.

Had anyone else ever taken the time to make her happy? It seemed so easy. It made him feel wonderful.

Judy seized his hand and veered around—at first he thought she wanted to look at a store window, but it was to turn down a side street. Arnold veered with her—to show her immediately how in touch they were, in thought, in feeling—onto a street with bars and news stands and delis and drugstores. When he felt certain she was pursuing no particular goal, but merely wished to follow the Imp of the Perverse another way home, halfway down the block, Arnold said, "Hey—let's get pictures. In there." He pointed at a drugstore. "You know, just some jokey ones, in one of those fifty-cent photo booths."

Again she swung around him, exclaiming, "Photos? Oh, *shit*, man—!" Over the delivery vans and the kid in his red and blue spring jacket, trundling an empty hand truck beside them, Arnold first heard her increased volume as the same enthusiasm with which she'd come out on the courthouse steps, one with her *Whoopee!* and her *Wow—! "No!"*

Arnold was too startled to say, *Huh . . .?*

"*No*, man! What the fuck you want *pictures* for—*now?* Oh, shit! No *way*—come *on!*"

Arnold stood, blinking.

"I don't want no fuckin' photographs! I don't *want* 'em!" As though she just remembered to do it, she crossed her arms, pushing up her breasts, making them look absurdly large under the translucent cloth.

"It would be . . . fun," Arnold said, inanely (and realized he was terrified). "I thought—"

A tear wriggled from Judy's eye to track down her cheek. Though she had combed and brushed it that morning, her hair was awry. "Well, it *wouldn't* be fun! It would be fuckin' *awful!*" She sniffled. "I mean, oh, *man*—that you really went and—"

"Oh, *Judy* . . ." Arnold had no idea what she was referring to. Standing in the street, he felt desolate. "I'm so *sorry*. . . ." He was frightened. He was hurt. He was confused. Something in him pulled back from her. Something else urged him toward her, to take her in his arms. "Really, Judy, I didn't *mean*—" Arnold didn't move.

"Jesus!" She tightened her arms around herself. "I don't *want* no pictures!" Slowly she turned and started—stomping, in her sneakers—up the sidewalk.

As Arnold started to follow, he thought her shoulders looked too rounded and too narrow. He caught up to her. "Really, Judy—hey, it isn't *that* important! You don't have to do anything you don't want to. Especially today." She's very much younger than I am, he thought, a bit hysterically. More than a dozen years! "Come on, we're married now."

Her shoulder hit his sports jacket arm. He glanced to see her arms were still folded, her head still down. He had no idea if it had been a tap signaling peace, a nudge to leave her alone, or an accident.

While he walked—and she remained silent—Arnold's heart

began to slow. How absurd this was! What sort of crazed neu-
rotic had he gotten himself involved with, anyway? Or, indeed,
was *he*, to go along with it?

Was this an insane mistake that, three or five years hence,
would find them on opposite sides of a courtroom—like the one
in which they'd sat this morning—yelling and screaming that
the other was mad? He imagined a dark-robed judge—not the
diminutive Asian Alice, but a secure, craggy, white-haired Caucasian, who, when Arnold got a chance to explain his side of the
story, with only Judy's grunts and sniffles interrupting from the
prosecutor's table, finally leaned down and told Arnold: "That's
all very well, Mr. Hawley. But however deranged Mrs. Hawley
might be, the fact is, for getting involved in the whole thing in
the first place—agreeing to marry a homeless woman you met in
a park after only an hour—you are out of your *mind!*"

Judy said: "There's one."

Arnold said, "What—?"

"See?" Judy unfolded her arms and pointed toward—no,
through—the plate glass of a deli. "There. We could get them in
there."

"Pardon . . .?" Arnold wasn't *trying* to sound supercilious.

"Right in there." Judy looked at him, blankly. "In there—one
of those picture machines." She stopped walking. The tear track
lay wet and jagged beneath her eye. "We can get our picture."

"Oh, *Judy* . . ." he said. "Look. The *last* thing I wanted to do was
ruin today for you. For us. Really . . . You've been cooking, cleaning
up—trying to keep me laughing. And you're good at it, too. You're
interested in what I talk about. It's a really nice friendship. I don't

want to mess it up for you. I don't understand it—about the pictures. But I don't have to. Some people are camera shy. If you're not into photographs, that's fine. Believe me—"

She said, "But—we *should* get some pictures. Yeah. For our wedding. Lots of . . . *real* people have pictures taken, for their wedding. Isn't that right? It's not unusual. Look, I . . ." Looking down, she dropped her forearms from beneath her heavy breasts. "You're pretending to be a really good husband. I want to pretend to be a really good wife. That means I have to try to do the things my husband wants. Only, you see, I ain't never *been* married before—for real, I mean. I only dreamed about it." She looked at him.

Her blank expression held no particular sincerity.

Or either duplicity.

Something in her inflection made him sure, however, that when she'd said "dream," it wasn't a metaphor. Though how recently such dreams had assailed her, he wondered. Arnold shook his head. "Hey—we *really* don't have to."

"Naw, come *on*. Let's *do* it." Her voice edged toward whining.

"You're *sure?*"

"I mean," she said, "ain't that stupid—getting all upset because somebody might find some fuckin' twenty-five-cent photograph?"

"I promise you"— Arnold smiled—"I won't let *anyone* find it. I'll keep it with me, all the time."

"Okay," she said, already starting into the delicatessen.

Arnold followed her, realizing he was frightened again.

With its purple plastic curtain, on the yellow poster behind cracked plastic, the photo booth against the wall said: "*Four* Poses! Only *Three* Dollars!"

Arnold laughed. "You know, when I was a kid, they really *were* just twenty-five cents." He fed in three bills. One was rejected three times, till he turned it around the other way.

Still with her blank expression, she pushed the half-closed curtain aside, to slip her hips onto the booth's aluminum bench. Arnold pushed in after her. Then, before the rectangular glass on the pale blue interior wall, he brought his head close to hers and tried to smile. A three-second interval fell between each of the flashes.

Outside, still looking blank, she stood—nervously, he thought—her arms folded once more. "They sure take a long time," she told him, after a couple of minutes.

Finally the black-and-white photo strip dropped into the niche behind the aluminum gate. Arnold reached in to finger it out. "Let's see what we got."

Judy looked over, with serene disinterest.

Arnold thought they'd been perfectly centered on the bench. But Judy's face was in the dead middle of the frame. On the left, Arnold's face was up and bent toward hers. In three of them a flare of light covered one of the lenses in his glasses. Though his teeth showed, it would have been hard to call Arnold's loopy leer a grin. Judy, however, had an enchanting smile. She looked— astonishingly!—attractive. Her heaviness was neither in her shoulders nor her face, so that in the picture she looked like the second or third female lead in some teen horror movie—the first or second girl to be murdered while changing her clothes up in her bedroom or waiting in front of the gym locker or taking a cigarette in the parking lot during the school dance. There was no tear. She must have fingered it away. And she'd run her hands over her head or something—so that even her hair was back in place. (This, Arnold pondered, is a photograph of a woman who, not three minutes before, had been raving and weeping in the street!) He'd always thought of photographs as making people look older and fatter, not younger and more attractive—but in Judy's case, at least, the row of four all-but-square photos had dissolved from her half a dozen years.

It had never occurred to Arnold, when the light had flashed, she'd be smiling. She looked like a very pretty child.

"They're nice," Judy said.

"Yes." Arnold wondered what to do with them. If he just impulsively tore them up and generously threw them away, would the gesture reach her? Or would it evoke another violent response. "They are." He didn't want to find out—so, smiling, he slipped them in the inside pocket of his sports coat.

"I don't mean to make you nervous," she said. "I really don't. I'm sorry."

"That's all right. You don't, really," Arnold lied.

"I know I'm a little weird. But I'm okay, now."

Back at the apartment, Judy frosted the cake in chocolate butter frosting, and made a veal stew.

"It's called a daube or something. I saw some guy make it on television, once. I don't see how you can *live* without a television. But I guess that's because of all the reading and writing you do. I'm glad I'll be outta here soon."

Which, again, surprised Arnold. The incident on the street,

over the pictures, had almost dropped from mind: had she *not* been enjoying her time with him? Incident aside, the rest, for Arnold, had been rather fun.

Once Judy forked the potatoes to see if they were done, she came in (barefoot again) while they were in the kitchen draining, to tell him: "I've got a *special* wedding present for you, tonight." She had not mentioned the photographs since they'd left the delicatessen.

"Other than chocolate wedding cake?"

"Yep."

"What is it."

"You get out the dishes. Okay?"

While Arnold was putting down paper napkins on the coffee table, then uncorking the wine that had just come from the refrigerator (the dark green bottle, stood on its reflection in pale green glass), Judy explained, "Tonight I want you—"

He'd drunk most of a fifth of wine a day since she'd been here. Maybe it was time to cut down—

She looked up, then, and he realized he was frowning.

Judy laughed. "No, don't worry—I'm *not* gonna try to make you fuck me or anything like that." Then *she* frowned. "Well— maybe it's a *little* like that." She sat on the blotched, dumpy couch.

Arnold said, "What?"

"After dinner," Judy said, "about eight or nine o'clock, I want you to go out to the park—and I want you to sit there, near the men's room—they leave it open twenty-four hours. Did you know that?"

"No," he said. "I didn't."

"I'm gonna cut your nails first. Because I *just* don't think most guys are really turned on by men who keep their nails as long as you do—but, then, you never know. See, I want you to go in there—and find the guy with the biggest, hardest dick they got in there—and suck it! Or let him fuck you up the ass. Or fuck *him*— if that's what you want. And I want you to keep doing that till you can hardly stand up. You can even bring somebody you *really* like back up here, in your bedroom—but if you do, I think you should sit around out on the benches for a little while and talk to him some, first: to make sure he's somebody who ain't gonna rip us off or nothing. Usually if you talk to people, you can pretty much tell that stuff, if you use your common sense. I mean, you understand, if it's somebody who's all hot to come up to your place right away, a lot of times that means he's just lookin' to rip you off."

"Oh," said Arnold. "Yeah. Of course."

"But the main things is, I want you to fuck and suck your brains out—till you can't hardly stand up no more. That's my wedding present. Does that sound cool?"

At her proposition, Arnold's heart had begun beating high in his throat—rather as it had with her protest to his suggestion about the pictures. "I . . . guess so."

"I mean, it's all goin' on, outside your door, pretty much twenty-four hours a day, right in the park, over there. And *you* don't take advantage of it. That's just so crazy. If I was a guy, *I* sure would!"

"You would?"

"You try it. If you don't like it, you don't have to do it again. But I kind of feel like you're a minister, who I have to . . . you know, corrupt." She leered. "By sending you out into the dark." She did say *dark*, not *park*. "All by yourself."

Arnold was surprised that she remembered the tale. Or had she? "You remembered the Crane story. . . ." Why on earth would she, he wondered—while she answered:

"Yeah, but you said he didn't really write it—that *Red Badge of Courage* faggot."

So she *did* remember.

"Who *was* Vashti, anyway? Was she some Indian goddess or something?"

Arnold smiled. "She was the queen of the great and ancient King Ahasuerus—who ruled the world, it's claimed, from India to Egypt. The story's in the Bible. Queen Vashti refused to appear when Ahasuerus called her to come in and join him at a grand banquet he gave for all the princes of the world, in order to show off her beauty to them. She was giving her own banquet, apparently, for all the princesses. Probably she didn't like the idea of being shown off like a kewpie doll. Also, there may have been something about matriarchal religions and patriarchal religions. But that part's pretty unclear."

"Hey, right on!" Judy said. "So what happened to her? Is the king the guy who died of shame?"

Arnold laughed. "No, that's just Crane's addition, about a woman with the same name. In the Bible story, I think she just got stripped of her queenship and Ahasuerus went and married somebody else more tractable."

"Yeah," Judy said. "Ain't *that* a bitch! I mean, it's typical. Probably that's what I'd do." She laughed.

There was something interesting about Judy—even if it wasn't literary.

"Hey, I'm not going to *make* you go out and do this, I mean *all* the time—at least more than once. But I thought . . . well, you know—tonight." She smiled, for the world like a *femme fatale* coaxing a present from some moneybags businessman in a silent film. She looked perfectly theatrical, totally phony. And charming.

Arnold laughed. "You really think I should cut my nails?"

"Oh, yeah." Judy nodded. "It's the only thing that makes you look like a faggot. Actually, they kind of creep *me* out. I mean, how am I supposed to have a husband whose nails are longer than mine? Come on, sit down. I was a manicurist once—I bet you believe *that!*"

"Oh," he said. "Well, okay."

So that's what she did.

For some reason, that evening, she only ate two bites of her veal—which really *was* awfully good. "I don't know," she said. "Actually, my stomach's felt kinda funny all day. I think it's the excitement. You know—I mean, getting married and everything."

"You're sure you don't want me to stay in and keep you company?"

"*No!*" she insisted. "Not on your *life!* I want you to go out and get fuckin' laid. *I* wanna stay in, hang around on *my* bed, and . . . read a book. Like you do. That's gonna be my wedding present to *me!* In fact, I'm gonna stay in and read *your* book. No, that's all right—"

He had started to move to the shelf to get her a copy.

"I know where you keep 'em."

"Oh. . . ." He felt embarrassed. "All right. I mean, if you're sure—" It had been what he was going to suggest.

"Put on your sports jacket," she told him, "like you wore this morning. It looks great with your jeans. Believe me, you'll break hearts. Besides, it'll be easier for me to read it all the way through—the first time, I mean—if you're not here."

As he went downstairs, it occurred to Arnold—as it had from time to time all through growing up—that basically he *always* did what women asked. That's how he'd gotten along with Aunt Bea and even his grandmother. (Grandma Logan had been a ghostly presence on the second floor of Aunt Bea's house in Pittsfield, until, when Arnold was ten, she'd died.) The fact is, neither had ever asked him to do much he hadn't actually wanted. Here, out of habit, he was doing it again—though he wasn't feeling particularly sexual. True, he'd been curious about these urges that, perhaps once every two or three weeks, led him to masturbate. (What would Judy think of the several cinquains, of the enchained sestinas . . .?) But, like many less-adventurous folk, he had about decided that such intermittent pleasure was all he could expect under the burden of his perversion.

Out on the sidewalk, Arnold stopped and looked at the sky above the ragged Ninth Street cornices.

But other people did it—and did it a lot. Actually, it was rather exciting.

Within days of the summer solstice, at nine o'clock some blue still clung to the sky. (It had been six months since *he'd* read either *Waters* or *Air Tangle* end to end.) Minutes later, as Arnold wandered into the park, up one of the side paths, then down another—on the Seventh Street side, five Hispanic kids had stopped to listen to an older guy play bongos—the city's indigo covering beyond the leaves had become gunmetal black. Without their half-inch blades, his fingertips—he kept feeling them with his thumb—felt extraordinarily odd.

For a while, across from the comfort station, the caged light burning over the door, Arnold sat on the same bench he'd sat on when he'd met Judy—his wife of . . . *was* it twelve hours?— where he'd written three of the poems in *Air Tangle* Judy was reading now.

Every two or three minutes one or another man walking by left the back-and-forth traffic to turn in at the men's room. As far as Arnold could tell by the park lights, perhaps one out of four was younger than he was. But—and now it struck Arnold that for all the time he'd watched them, he'd never looked at them so analytically before—half of those entering were five to fifteen years older. . . .

And, yes, fewer seemed to be coming out than were going in.

Suddenly Arnold stood, strode across the macadam toward the stone columns with their pale stone architrave between the men's side and the women's, stepped up the shallow rise, turned right toward the brick doorway rimmed with black metal, and walked in. A step and a second step put him within a vestibule covered with small white tiles. A third took him (definitely!) inside. At the same time he realized there was no light. Across the dark room, through an upper window, park light outside dropped slant illumination. Yes, there *were* men in here!

Looking over, Arnold saw, standing before one wall, the backs of some six, each before a chest-high urinal that went down to the floor. In the three-quarters dark, as Arnold blinked, one man stepped back, turned, and moved toward another at the urinal two away from his.

(The urinal between was unoccupied. From the outside park lamp, through the window, light fell there, leaving the tiles gray.)

The man stepped into and out of the glow.

Arnold's heart hammered. He pulled his chin sharply back. In the lavatory's coolness his neck had started to sweat.

The man's fly had been open.

His penis had been in his hand.

And it had been hard. . . .

Though the light had only gone halfway up the man's orange-and-gray-splotched T-shirt (tie-dyed?), Arnold had seen that the fellow was black and, what's more, stocky. Now the two men were doing something with each other—holding each other? *Kissing?*

Then someone short and brisk rushed in around Arnold's left. "Oh, I'm sor—" Arnold began, not to the intruder but to the eight or so men standing about, whom he felt deeply, distressingly, he'd interrupted. Blindly, Arnold turned right—and thought: This place is huge, cavernous, immense! It stretched at least *twice* as far as he'd imagined.

Arnold took another step, only then realizing he was going further in. Whirling, he fled outside.

He did not remember getting to the benches or managing to sit—well, drop—onto the plank seat. His heart bumped. His breath filled only the upper third of his lungs, the rest of his body too constricted to let in air.

How could the place—inside—have *been* so big? Were the men's and women's sides somehow . . . joined within? Robberies could happen in a place like that! It was an old thought that, he remembered now, had kept him sanely out of such places for years.

Blinking, Arnold looked around at the night leaves, crisply black in the park light, shiny along their edges, with now and again one a deep green, suggesting their daytime hue.

The men's and women's spaces were, Arnold confirmed now, totally separate—the space between the columns assured it—through which he could see the playground, empty and locked for the night. No, the two shared not a wall!

Only when his breath began to work its way down, lower and lower, did it hit him: the right-hand wall had been mirrored! At least from the waist up! Yes, of course. A mirror must have stretched there.

(Did that mean there'd been only half as many people as he'd thought?)

Dragging down a breath, Arnold forced shoulders, hips, then knees to relax. From the park bench, he looked up, high on the front wall, at the two barred windows. Both were dark. Another thought came—a wholly new one, a product of his having actually entered: if robberies were committed in there with any frequency, Arnold had spent enough time in the park that he would have heard about them. Besides, the men he'd just seen hadn't been robbing each other. They'd been . . . *doing* things!

About thirty seconds apart, back under the arches, two people came out the men's room door—neither of them the stocky black man.

(No women had gone into the other side.)

Three minutes later, someone else came out—a little guy, maybe even a kid. He stopped between the central columns, both hands tugging at the crotch of his black jeans—as though he were having trouble with his fly.

Arnold watched him stand there, tugging, grimacing left and right. He wore a black denim jacket, slightly too big—and unbuttoned. A black-haired white kid, Arnold saw, as the fellow stepped into the light. Under the jacket he was bare-chested. Nor did he have on the combat shoes so many youngsters in the park wore, but rather engineers' boots, pretty scuffed up. Arnold could see the buckle on the side of the one. The boots were big enough to make the little guy look *all* feet.

Giving up on his jeans, the kid stretched, punching his fists up and out from his shoulders, so that the jacket pulled from his latticed abdomen. Around his neck he wore a dog collar, set with, no, not spikes, but metal studs. Sauntering to the benches, he turned and sat—a bench away from Arnold—and lifted his arms out along the back, a dozen feet closer to the lamppost than Arnold was . . . the position Judy had assumed, when they'd first talked.

Arnold glanced at him a couple of times, trying not to stare.

Suddenly the kid sat forward—to shrug back, then to tug off, his jacket. His naked arms and shoulders were all small, hard-looking muscle. Around each biceps was another studded band, like the one at his neck. Jacket beside him on the green planks, again he sat back, bare-chested, to cross one leg at the ankle, widely and flatly over his thigh, bare arms again along the back.

Arnold thought: he's probably half my age. And half my weight.

Which is when the kid looked over at Arnold—and smiled. At the same time, in a play of the park light over the lap of the kid's grungy jeans, from the glistening, out-of-sync brass teeth, separated by an inch, though his waist button was closed, Arnold saw the kid's flies were unzipped.

The look between them went on six, eight, twelve seconds, the kid smiling, Arnold staring—till Arnold managed to break his own maddening paralysis with the smallest nod.

The kid said, "Hey—man, how're they hangin'?" (Arnold was surprised enough to flinch.) The kid opened the fist nearest Arnold on the dark boards. For seconds Arnold had an intimation that the "kid" was older than he'd thought: the hand was thick, rough, meaty, half again as big (like his boots) as you might have expected on a little fellow—more like the hand on some six-and-a-half-foot laborer. (Briefly Arnold wondered if he were the Odessa waiter. But no . . .) The wide nails were short, but with scimitars of black at the ends of each, while the knuckles were heavy, wrinkled, and, in the park light, gray.

Arnold nodded again, tried to say something, tried to smile—and failed at both. Finally, even though he was sure the answer was no, he managed: "Your name isn't Manolo, is it . . .? You don't work at the Odessa?"

"You mean that place over on A? At the Odessa? *Me?*"

"I thought I might have seen you—"

"Huh?" The kid laughed. "Naw. I wish the fuck I did! Them guys rack up in those waiter jobs, man. Me, I'm just out here on my own, a workin' stiff." The kid nodded toward the comfort station. "You was in there, when I went in." (Once he spoke,

Arnold was again sure he was no more than nineteen or twenty.)
"Wasn't you." The down-falling inflection was all confirmation.

"The light was . . ." Arnold started to explain his flight. "You
couldn't see anything. The light had burned out. . . ."

The kid took his hand from the bench back and made a dismissive gesture. "Naw—it wasn't out." (For a moment Arnold
had a sense that the broad palms and thick fingers weighted his
muscular forearm, kept it from rising too high, slowed its swing
and sweep.) "Somebody just climbed up on the sink and
unscrewed it. If you want it on, you gotta climb up there and
screw it back in. That's all."

"But why would they do . . .? I mean something could
happen!"

"Fuckin'-A!" The kid nodded. "Man, it just ain't like it was,
back a couple of years ago. I mean, you can't make *no* money."
The nodding stopped; his head began to shake. "Two years ago,
I could come around here, meet three or four guys in a night, get
fifteen or twenty bucks off of each of 'em—before eleven o'clock,
man. But now I hang out up on Twenty-third. Most of the time,
I don't even come down here no more."

Arnold looked puzzled.

"This used to be a good place to hustle. For us workin' men."

"You mean all the guys in there are prostitutes—hustlers?"

"Them?" The youngster looked back at Arnold, his smile
disbelieving. "*Naw*, man—they're all in there tryin' to get somethin' from each other—for *free!*" He snorted. "That's why a
workin' stiff can't make no bread."

"Oh," Arnold said. "You—oh, yes. Yes, I see."

"I mean, I don't understand why anyone would want one of them old guys in there, when they could have a guy like me." The kid's face was delicate, Mediterranean, and—just this side of adolescent—almost beautiful . . . while his hands were thick and brutal-looking enough to make Arnold think of a murderer, a— yes—rapist, or at least some thief's or thug's. "You know what I mean? I mean, it don't make no sense."

"Well," Arnold said. (Or maybe just a laborer. His smallness and energy held something attractive—even the great, sluggish fingers.) "Perhaps they don't . . . want to pay for it."

"Aw, shit!" the fellow said. "*I* ain't expensive. Twenty bucks— that's if I come up to your place. If you just wanna find a bench out of the light in the park here and suck on my eleven-and-a-half-inch Polack-dago sausage . . . till it spits all over your fuckin' tonsils! Hey, and it spits a *lot*, too!" Again he nodded. "*That's* just a dime. Ten fuckin' bucks. Less than a dollar an inch, man. *Jesus*, I'm fuckin' horny!" Dropping one hand from the bench back to his crotch, the thick fingers massaged his jeans. "I just got up a couple of hours ago—and I come right out here. Man, you know how you're all horny when you wake up? Tonight I could do it for free, know what I'm sayin'? I mean, just to get off—" Looking at Arnold, he began to chuckle. "'Course I gotta make me *some* money—you understand?"

"Oh, yeah," Arnold said. "Of course."

"But that's how fuckin' horny I am. Hey—" Suddenly the kid's hand slid into the open jeans to . . . pull himself free. "*Wow!*" He frowned down at his revealed erection (Arnold thought, Good *Lord* . . . !), while he raised his hand up along its length, then pressed his fist back into his crotch, to waggle himself side to side—once, twice, a third time—and it was gone, again, inside his pants! (On the park bench, the shock of exposure again started Arnold's heart thudding. Arnold looked frantically left, right, and back.) "I guess that's why they call us guys 'workin' *stiffs*,' huh?" The chuckle became a laugh. "You *seen* that, man?" (Twenty and thirty feet off, there were people walking. But no one seemed to have noticed.) A frown mixed with the remains of the kid's smile, as though something really *had* surprised him. "Jesus! That's a hell of a dick, ain't it? Damn! Even *I* didn't remember the fucker was *that* big!" Despite his thudding heart, Arnold began to grin at how the kid had carried it off. "Hey, with me you got it any way you want. You like it rough? I can be a rough guy: 'You fuckin' sonofabitch, *get* down on your sorry-ass knees and suck my AK-47 till I blast the back of your cocksuckin' head off.' I can be nice, too: 'Come on, baby, I *know* you know how to do it for me. I ain't had no real pussy in three months, and I *know* you can make it feel good. . . .'"

It was not a quick decision, nor was it a short discussion. They sat for twenty more minutes. Then they got up and walked around the park—the kid with his denim jacket hooked over his shoulder by one Goliath of a finger—three leisurely circuits. Arnold was not sure how to cut himself loose, nor was the kid apparently interested in losing Arnold. While they were off on a side path, again he pulled his cock free of his jeans. "I gotta make sure it's still there—know what I'm sayin'?—that it's as big as I remember . . .? Damned thing's *so* big, man—that's why I can whip it out in public and"—it disappeared once more—"nobody even knows what the fucker is!" He laughed harshly. Then, on a darker path, he stopped, swung his jacket down from his shoulder, hooked it over the spike of the fence beside them, squatted, and fell forward to the ground, to begin doing push-ups. Looking up over his hard defined shoulder, speckled with lamplight through the night leaves, rising and falling while he breathed heavily, he asked, "Come on. How do I look? I bet I look *good*, huh?" And, when Arnold had again decided he *must* say that he wasn't interested, once more the kid pulled his cock loose. (Hard, too! How did he *do* that, Arnold wondered.) "Man, *look* at that thing! You *gotta* want to wrestle with six or seven inches of that. I know all eleven and a half might be a little much for ya'. Hey—yeah—it measures out at eleven-and-a-half, no shit! A solid *foot* sometimes, on a *real* warm day. And—like you saw—it's a fat one, too, not just some fuckin' soda straw."

It *was* thick.

Actually it looked longer than a foot—probably because the kid himself was so short—not over five-two or -three.

"I'm one of those little fuckers who's *all* dick. I mean, what can you do . . .?"

Arnold *did* want it, though he was not sure what he was going to *do* with it. Out here he was afraid to touch it. So, at last, he said: "All right. You can come to my place." After all, Judy *had* said it would be fine.

"You interested in water sports?" was the kid's first response to being told they were going to Arnold's.

"Pardon me?"

"You know, man. Piss. It's just another five bucks on top of my twenty for the house call. If you wanted, I could do that right out here. But a lot of guys prefer that in the privacy of their own bathtub, know what I'm sayin'?"

Arnold said, "*No!* I mean I *don't* want—"

"Oh. Yeah—Hey, I understand. That's a little complicated for you, anyway. Right?"

"Yes, I . . . eh, think so!"

"But I had to ask—'cause a lot of times guys are shy about bringing that up. You and me, it'll be nice and simple. That's how I like it, too. I'll stick my eleven and a half inches into whatever hole you want, and you can swing on it till you get happy. Okay? Simple, see? But I'm the guy who really knows how to make you . . ."

An hour and fifteen minutes after they'd met (the kid had hardly stopped talking once), on Avenue B they turned the corner at Ninth.

As they walked along the Ninth Street sidewalk, the kid nattering on, Arnold looked uncomfortably at the heaped black plastic garbage bags in front of 345 a week now (he set his mouth at the smell as they passed) and frowned at the chain through the plastic garbage-can handles beside them (they were supposed to be behind the gate in the alley) and the broken light globe across the street at the side of 352—all the things that might make someone think twice before returning for a visit: things he'd never thought about when he'd walked along here with Judy. Was the only reason for the difference in his reaction that all three times the kid had exposed his erection (*so* much larger than Arnold's that it might have been a different bodily organ),

Arnold, too, had hardened? Certainly there'd been nothing like that with . . . his wife.

The kid was saying, "You understand—I gotta go meet someone soon. And you're one of those guys who likes to ask a lot of questions, I can tell—ain't nothin' wrong with that. But a lot of guys, man, all they wanna *do* is talk." He laughed. "Though I bet *I* talk more'n you—right? So I guess I don't gotta worry."

"I guess you don't." Arnold *had* been thinking he might make some coffee for them when they got upstairs, and ask Judy at least to come out and meet him before they—well, went to Arnold's bedroom and did . . . whatever it was they would do.

At the apartment house's stone-columned stoop, Arnold got his key from his jeans pocket and put it in the lock to the vestibule's glass door. As the lock turned over, Arnold said, "I haven't even asked your name."

Behind Arnold's shoulder, the kid said, "Horse—that's what I tell most of my johns—my clients, you know—to call me. Callin' you guys clients 'stead of johns, that's more high class. Some john told me that, up on Twenty-third. Hey, this is a pretty nice building. Horse. That's my workin' name. 'Cause when that fuckin' thing goes off, it spills as much as a goddam stallion!" They moved together across the tiled lobby. Under the fluorescent lighting, Arnold saw how uneven the kid's teeth were. As they started up the stairs, wrinkles in the corners of the kid's eyes pushed him further into his twenties—his *late* twenties. As the fellow moved one, then two steps ahead on the stairs, Arnold realized that the air of youth was largely his garrulousness; and probably a daily weight-lifting workout.

Swinging around the newel, the kid started up the fourth flight.

Arnold said, "No, it's *this* floor—"

"Oh . . . Okay." The kid turned and came back down, to follow Arnold along the apartment hall to the door toward the end. "I thought maybe you was upstairs, 'cause—"

Arnold fingered up the other key, pushed it into the lock, jiggled and turned it.

The kid chattered on behind him.

Arnold pushed the door in and stepped through, while the kid followed. His apartment hall had taken on the unfamiliarity a stranger's entering always loaned it.

Arnold turned, so he could let the kid by and close the door. But, in the open doorway, the kid had halted: tossing his black jacket on the floor against the hall's baseboard, he unbuckled his belt, at the same time kicking free a boot. Without a sock, his immensely wide, bony foot (notably paler than his suntanned face, arms, and chest) was hammertoed—and hairy. He pushed his pants down over paler thighs—surprisingly hirsute, after his bald sun-browned pectorals.

Did he *shave* his chest, Arnold wondered.

The kid said, "See, you and me are gonna get down to the nasty, right away. Here it is, man—ready and waiting for you." The kid wore no underpants. His genitals were dark as a black man's and, yes . . . sizable, even soft. Behind him the apartment door still stood open. (Arnold listened, sure he heard someone coming down the stairs—not that they could see into the place from the steps.) "Hey, now don't get wigged out by my birthmark— you're starin' at it already." Leaning against one wall, he pushed down his black jeans to work them free of one ankle. On his right hip, around to within three inches of his thick pubic hair, rough flesh swirled red-and-purple, continuing down his thigh, extending even below his knee, to slather his calf's right side. "Most guys don't pay it no mind. Once you get to work on it, you ain't even gonna remember it's there. One guy, though, he makes me cover it up with my jacket or a pillow or somethin', 'fore he gets started. If coverin' it up works better for you, that's cool." He stood up, swaying from booted foot to bare. "Either way, it don't bother *me!* Okay, now—yeah, this is where I always lose a *few* guys. It *used* to bother me, when I was a kid, when some-body'd let me get this far, and then tell me, naw, I had to go. But not no more. You wanna call it quits, here? You don't like the way it looks? Believe me, there ain't no hard feelings. You gimme five bucks for my time, and I'm gone, man. Hey, go on, take a look." Raising his arms slightly, Horse turned fully around, displaying himself. "Yeah, look at the whole thing. . . ." The purple discol-oration was only on his right hip and leg. His buttocks were largely free of it. At the floor, his jeans twisted around one ankle. Again facing Arnold, he dropped his hands to his thighs. "Okay—what do you think? I mean, there it is—you seen it all. Hey, some guys even get into it. It's just a birthmark, man. It don't mean nothin'. I ain't sick or anything—it ain't catchin'. And it sure don't stop *most* of you motherfuckers"— Again he moved his hand over to waggle his genitals, which, even soft, hung almost halfway down his thigh—"you know what I mean? Hey, if it's better for you to cover it up, like I say, that's cool." He shook his other foot. His second boot—along with the second pants leg—dropped free. Both broad, hirsute feet now bare, he stepped forward from the door's sill.

Save for his studded collar, the studded bands on his upper arms—and, Arnold saw, surprised, another band nearly hidden in his pubic hair, around the base of his pendulous, gray-brown penis and testicles (aluminum studs which, just then for half a second—neck, arms, and groin—all gleamed at once)—he stood, nude, on the hall's green runner.

"Do you want to close the door behind you?" Arnold said. "Actually I was going to suggest you keep your pants on till—"

"What the fuck for?" Smiling, the kid rubbed his scrotal sack and his half-engorged penis, grasped them, shook them—half-erect, flopping, dark. "Come on, man. You're still interested—I know that, 'cause you ain't kicked me out. So let's *do* it. I don't know about you, but I'm so fuckin' horny I can't *stand* it!"

Arnold had been thinking of calling in Judy to say hello, hoping she would somehow approve his choice. But not with the birthmarked fellow naked. (How many poems in *Air Tangle*, he wondered, had she gotten through)? Then a memory—half a memory—emerged: "You're not . . . Tony, are you?" Arnold frowned, trying to recall where the name had come from, or why he associated it with . . . the birthmark. At some point Judy had mentioned a birthmark. . . .

The naked kid laughed. "Yeah, I got johns who call me 'Tony'—'cause I'm half Italian. 'Cause *everybody* calls a fuckin' wop 'Tony,' man. It's not too fuckin' original, know what I mean? What—you must've run into one of my other clients, before, right? Bet he said I was fuckin' *good*, too! Man, once you get a liplock on old donkey dong down here"—again he wag-gled himself—"you ain't gonna *think* about callin' me 'Tony.' I'll be the Horse of your dreams. Hey—you're sure, now, you don't need a little pee outta my pipe . . .?"

"Huh?" For a moment Arnold was lost. "Oh—*no* . . .! No, I'm sure—"

"'Cause, man, I gotta piss so bad I can fuckin' *taste* it! I would have done it out in the gutter, but I was savin' it up, just in case. You know, some guys are shy tellin' you about that stuff, until they actually get down to it. Look—if you're *sure* you ain't into that, how about lettin' me use your fuckin' terlet?" (Was he from Brooklyn?) "I'll be out in a minute. You get yourself comfortable—and we can get down to it."

"Oh, of course," Arnold said. "Right there—on your left."

They passed each other—Horse naked, Arnold clothed—somehow without touching. Arnold went back, pushed the apart-ment door shut, then turned the small copper bolt to lock it, above the big nonworking brass lock. (Arnold was thinking absently that both he and Judy usually left the bathroom door open when they'd finished.) Behind him he heard the knob on the bathroom door turn.

"*Achhhhh—!*"

It *could* have been a woman's shriek. It could have been a man's—

Quickly Arnold turned to look. Had the kid walked in on her—? The shout's shock again started Arnold's heart to hammer.

He saw Horse vault back from the doorway. (The birthmark stretched like a single chap down his right leg, its last sliver ending four or five inches above his ankle.) The kid's naked back struck the bookshelf edge. Stumbling, he half sat, then got himself upright, turning to face Arnold, in a crouch: "What'd you do to her, man! What'd you *do* to her? That's Judy in there! What the fuck did you *do* to her?" Whites encircled his pupils. At his sentences' ends, his mouth did not fully close—till, at once, he swallowed. "What the fuck did you do—you some kind of fuckin' *psycho?*"

Arnold took a bewildered step forward. The look on the kid's face was terror. Arnold's heart hammering grew.

He stepped forward, while the kid turned his back against the wall by the bookshelf, shouting: "Don't you touch me, man! Get *away* from me, you psycho motherfucker!" From the bathroom door, Arnold heard water slosh and rustle. The sink faucet turned on full? No, the shower . . . As Arnold looked inside, the kid bolted by him up the hall.

The first thing Arnold saw—the first thing that registered as something he could have told someone else in words—was that every brown plastic pill bottle from his medicine cabinet lay on the floor, all open, their white caps scattered about. All were empty.

At the tub's near end, by the wall, half wrapped in the transparent and yellow shower curtain, something, mostly red, especially the bottom third, hung from the shower curtain rod, down and—at its thickest—outside the tub's rim.

From the showerhead, water arched.

Red covered more than half the floor—some of the pill bottles seemed to float in it.

Just below the shower rod, beside the curtain—it was the

only thing not blotched red, although a brown smear crossed one cheek—was a face . . . on a head with tousled hair.

It leaned to the side. Behind it, water *shishshsh'd*.

Slightly puffy, the lids were half-closed, bruised-looking, greenish. . . .

It was Judy Alice Haindel Hawley.

Looking down, Arnold made out her hand, visible through the plastic transparency. Completely red, it glistened, up to a little above the fullest part of her forearm.

Later, what Arnold remembered was standing there two, three, maybe five minutes, while he tried to figure out what had happened. At last he started calling, "Tony . . .? Horse . . .!"

He stepped back from the door and looked up the hall, expecting to see the apartment door wide and Horse gone.

What he actually saw, though, made him realize (later) that he'd only stood there five, six, *maybe* seven seconds. The naked kid still stood there, back to Arnold, trying to open the locks.

"Tony . . .? Horse—please! We have to—"

Tony whirled, his back to the door, one hand splayed flat against it beside his birthmarked hip. His other came up, to shake a fore-finger at Arnold, like an admonishing teacher. "Come on, man—lemme *out* of here!" (Like Mrs. Palmer, in the sixth grade, Arnold thought inanely.) "*Now!* You tell me how to get out of this place, or I swear I'm gonna fuckin' *waste* you!" (Hysterically calm, Arnold saw that the kid's other hand, on the door, spread over more area than his terrified face.) "She tell you we was gonna get married? Yeah, I was gonna marry her! But it was just a fuckin' joke. Judy—yeah, she said we was gonna get married. But it was a *joke!*" He seemed balanced between terror and grief. "She *knew* it was a joke—why the fuck is she gonna marry somebody like *me?* You didn't have to do that to her! It was a joke! Come on, man. Lemme *out* of here, now!"

"Look, please, Tony—I didn't do *anything* to her! I swear it! Please, you have to believe—"

"If you didn't do nothin' to her, what the fuck is that in *there?*" Suddenly the kid shouted: "POLICE . . .! POLICE! MURDER . . . !" His chin went up. Ligaments tightened in his neck each side of his Adam's apple. "POLICE! *HELP!*"

"But I didn't *do* anything!" Arnold's own voice became an answering shout. "Look—you want to get out? Turn the lock!"

"I *been* turnin' the fuckin' lock! And nothing fuckin *happens!*" In frustration, the kid swung around to pound the door with his fist—beside the brass deadlock connected to no bolt since Arnold had moved in.

"The *little* one," Arnold said meekly, looking at the hollowed buttocks, the dirty heels, the shoulder blades moving in their nests of muscle, "over it."

"*Where* . . .?" The kid stepped back from the door, saw the small copper handle, the same green as the runner, and twisted at it viciously.

The door floated in an inch and a half.

Whirling again, the kid ducked to scoop up his jacket and jeans, turned once more, and was out and gone.

"Tony! *Please*, couldn't you—?"

In the hall Arnold heard what sounded like scuffling, moving off toward the stairs. A sudden silence, then, three seconds later, naked Tony swung back into the apartment, declaring, "*Shit* . . .!"

He looked around, saw one of his boots, and bent to grab it up. "Look, man—I *told* you, I was gonna marry her. But it was just pretend, I'm not *kiddin'*! It wasn't *really* gonna happen—you didn't have to go doin' shit like that to her. You stupid jealous fuck!"

"Tony, please, I didn't do anything. I *swear*, when I left, she was fine. She was the one who sent me out, to have a good time . . . to find . . . *you*—"

Which was not exactly what Arnold had meant. Tony's eyes went big again. Again he turned and ran out.

"*Tony*—!" though by now the conviction had hit Arnold that, again and again he was saying something wrong; that he was *not* saying whatever was needed to make it all clear—"I didn't *do* anything! I *swear* it!"

Outside the scuffling sound moved down the hall. Then came another three seconds of silence. And *again* Tony was back, naked, barefoot, crouching in the doorway, looking around. "*Fuckin'* shit . . .!" he muttered. "Where's my other boot?"

"There . . ." Arnold pointed.

Tony lunged for it and scooped it up.

"Tony, will you *please* stay here! While I get some help? You *knew* her—at least. I didn't, really . . . I mean, I'd never seen her. I mean, before—"

"Look, man—yeah. I fooled around with the bitch, some. But I ain't *seen* her in two weeks—*three* weeks! Hey . . ." Holding his boot in both hands, in front of his chest, Tony backed again toward the hallway entrance. "Maybe you *didn't* do nothin'—she was always talking about how she was gonna off herself as soon as we got married—like her sister or somebody done. But if you *didn't* do nothin'—and even if you *did*—what *I'd* do is call the fuckin' cops. Nine-one-one, you know? 'Cause she *could* still be alive—"

Arnold turned (breathing, "Jesus Christ . . .!") and ran for the living room. The vision in the bathroom passed on his left—white, yellow, and red, red, red. . . . He tripped on the rug, fell, and pulled the phone crashing down from the coffee table's glass. Praying it wasn't broken, he pushed himself up on one elbow, and punched buttons.

Some immense confusion was going on with the woman on the other end of 911.

As soon as he gave the number of the building, she cut him off with: ". . . you mean on East Ninth Street? Apartment 3-E or 3-F?"

"3-E," Arnold said. "3-E! Not 3-F! 3-E! That's right—"

"We've already got the call," she said. "There's no need to call twice, ma'am. Someone's on their way. They should be there in minutes."

"You don't understand," Arnold said, rolling on the floor, trying to sit up. "There's a woman in my bathroom. I don't know if she's alive or dead. I mean—I don't know what to do. Maybe you should send an ambulance."

"The police will be there in five or six minutes, ma'am. They'll do whatever has to be done next."

"But you don't understand," Arnold repeated. "She's hanging—she's *hung* herself. She may still be alive, though. I don't know what to *do!*"

"Oh—when you called before, you didn't mention the hanging—"

"I *didn't* call before—!"

"All right, all right—stay calm, now. Stay calm, ma'am. She's hung herself in her bathroom—"

"*My* bathroom—!"

"She's hung herself? Is there any way you can relieve the pressure on the neck without moving her significantly? Remember, if she's hanging, the neck may be broken. If, in moving her, you damage the spinal chord any more than it already is, she could die."

"I don't *know* . . . !" Arnold moaned, huddling by the coffee table. "I don't know! I don't know. . . ."

"All right then—you sit down, stay calm, and wait for the police to get there and help you. The police are on their way."

"Oh, thank you! Thank—" Suddenly Arnold dropped the receiver to his chest and looked around. "Tony?" he called. "Tony . . .! Horse . . .? They want us to relieve the pressure on . . ." Suddenly he sucked his teeth. Of course the little idiot was gone! When he lifted the receiver again, the woman was saying: ". . . your name and the name of the woman?"

"What? Oh . . . Hawley. My name is Hawley. H-A-W-L-E-Y. The woman is Judy Alice Haindel."

"Again?"

"Haindel. I think that's H-A-I-N-D-E-L. She's from some-place in Connecticut, I think. Bridgeport." Arnold had started to rock and felt himself nearing tears, while the woman spoke on:

"All right, ma'am. You can stay on the phone if you like. The police will be there in two or three minutes. But you can hang up if you'd rather. What's important is that you stay right where you are—if you *can't* relieve the pressure on the neck, without moving her, you just wait and stay calm. You're upset. I can hear that. So you sit where you are—and tell the police when they get there, where the apartment is—"

"It's *my* apartment!" Arnold shouted into the phone.

"Yes, that's right," the woman said. "Just sit there, and don't try to move her. When they get there, you tell them whether it's 3-E or 3-F."

"All right. . . ." Struck with sudden exhaustion, Arnold dragged in a loud breath, understanding only now that, in his confusion, his voice had gone up till it sounded like a woman's.

"Now remember, in the future, ma'am, if you have to call Nine-one-one, you only have to call once." Momentarily the voice was friendly. "Do you understand that?"

He dragged in another. "Yes. All . . ." Then he hung up.

After putting the phone back on the glass, Arnold stood.

He walked to the bathroom door and looked in. (Maybe, he thought, there *was* some way to relieve the pressure without . . . moving her?) This time it looked a lot clearer and somehow less confusing.

Stepping in to stand on the tile floor, Arnold could see that Judy had finished ripping the red towel in two and knotted its ends together. Then she'd made a noose. Even going two steps closer or moving from one side to the other (he didn't want to step in the blood), Arnold couldn't tell if it were a working slip knot. She'd tied one end around the shower curtain's rod, by the wall, at the ancient claw-footed tub's back end. Why, he wondered, hadn't the damned rod pulled loose or broken or bent? Was it the *only* solid thing in the building? One foot bloody, one not, both outside the tub and pointing down, her soles were black from going barefoot, even in the house. Her stubby toes hung some eighteen inches above the red floor.

Her color and her stillness . . . certainly she was dead. Places where there was no blood, her flesh looked like cake batter.

She was not wearing the pastel he'd met her in—that she'd married him in—but one of the dresses he'd bought her.

Clearly, she'd swallowed everything in the medicine cabinet. How many pills would that have been? he wondered. On its side in the sink was the water glass for his toothbrush, in which she'd surely put the water to swallow them.

His toothbrush lay neatly on the sink's side.

Mechanically he lifted the glass, sniffed the chalky mint, as if hoping it might smell like something else. But it didn't. My Lord, Arnold thought. Was the last thing she'd smelled his old toothpaste? Water drops still clung inside. He put the glass down. It rolled a little—loudly—in the porcelain basin. Was that, along with the shower's rushing, the last sound she'd heard?

On its side by the toilet's unwashed base was the empty Percocet bottle. After she'd climbed on the tub's edge to put her head in the noose, while standing there she must have taken one of his sharper cooking knives (Arnold had only disposable safety razors) and made three or four jabs into her left forearm. Two knives lay on the floor beneath the shower curtain's dripping edge, in the blood—one had fallen just under the tub.

For some reason, Judy had turned the shower on—perhaps because she'd thought she'd bleed mostly into the tub, and had some notion of making it easier to clean up . . .?

Sometime in there, she'd stepped—or slipped—from the tub's edge, while the transparent and yellow shower curtain, hanging outside, ran—its lower quarter now scarlet and brown—with her gore, before it fell to the tile.

Arnold thought about turning off the water. But didn't. He thought about walking out of his apartment, taking the subway up to Port Authority, and catching a bus to Appleton or Cleveland or Pittsfield. . . .

But that was silly.

One June evening, Arnold thought, the poet Arnold Hawley (age thirty-six) took a Greyhound bus from New York City to . . .

As he left the bathroom, his foot hit a pill bottle, which rolled out the bathroom door, across the sill, and onto the hall rug. Arnold frowned at it a moment, but didn't pick it up.

He walked down the hall to Judy's room. Its door was ajar. He pushed it in. On her bed, the pillowcase was gone from the pillow—at the bed's end the sheet and bedding were neatly folded, the way Aunt Bea had taught him to strip a bed whenever he left anyone's house in which he'd been a guest. On the bare pillow lay a copy of *Air Tangle*, perfectly centered on some papers, squared at the corners. He wondered about her clothing—and saw, almost as if in answer, the cardboard box under the bed's iron frame. It sat only slightly askew. Written on it in angry ballpoint letters:

GARBAGE!

with three insistent underlinings. Below that, with only one: *TOSS IT!*

Arnold bent down and pulled it out. When he lifted a flap, he saw, beneath it, the wadded pastel and one of her sneakers. He let the flap fall and, with his shoe, pushed it back under the bed.

As he stood, he saw now that the papers—six sheets, written over in small letters—were actually safety-pinned to the pillow. He picked up his book, put it back, thought about unpinning them, to preserve their neatness—then, suddenly, snatched them free. Six torn paper strips stayed on the pillow. *Air Tangle* slid over the ticking. He looked around again. Things that had once been scattered about were now in careful piles. The drenched and splattered bathroom wholly belied the order here, greater than any Arnold himself could have brought to bear.

Again the book in one hand, papers in the other, he walked back into the hall. Passing the books across from the bathroom, he saw the gap on the upper shelf where *Air Tangle* had been. Pausing only three seconds in his stride, he reached up and slid it into place . . . then went on to the living room.

With the paper-covered volume back among its fellows, Arnold felt more stable.

Sitting in the recliner on the far side of the coffee table, he looked down at the pages in his hand: Why in the *world* do I have to read this! He felt no sense of curiosity, only overwhelming annoyance and imposition.

Shuffling through them, he saw the sixth page was the wedding license.

He read them anyway.

•—•—•

"DEAR ARNOLD" it said in small uppercase letters and went on with no paragraph break, the entire text all-but-without margins, "I'm writing this at three o'clock in the morning before we go off to get married tomorrow. . . ."

Arnold looked up at Sara Alice Logan on the wall. He looked down at the pathetic couch with its pancaked cushions. He looked at the pages.

. . . to get married tomorrow. I wonder if it will really happen. Probably when we get up, you'll tell me it was a stupid idea and I should get the fuck out. And you'll see me around. And if you do, I will, too. Then, maybe you'll find this. But *maybe*, maybe, just maybe you'll actually let us do it. It will make me so happy, if you do, so happy if I can finally do it the right way, if I can finally end it. I'm not crazy, you know. Or, I don't know, maybe I am.

You're going to be very mad at me at first, because I know how mad I was when Jane (my oldest sister) did it and I had to clean it all up, because my crazy mother was too upset to mop the fucking kitchen floor. (Jane did it in the kitchen—when me and Ellen and my Mom were out at the movies, of course!) Or at the first three of Aunt Ruthie's tries. I hope I get it right on the first. 'Tries' that don't work are a lot messier. They go on and on and on for weeks afterwards, with hospital visits and social workers and counseling and mental hospitals and wondering why. (Why? Ha!) Oh, I forgot. My mom said Ruthie had tried again, when I phoned her last week. One hard day of scrubbing and cleaning and then you can forget about me. I'll just be that weird girl who went and cut her wrists in your bathtub. And you didn't even know she was fucking insane. And had spent three fucking years in a fucking mental hospital. And was fucking pregnant. And didn't fucking know if it was fucking Tony's or the fucking plainclothes detective who raped me in the back of that fucking hallway three months ago down on fucking Second Street. But I wouldn't give either one the fucking satisfaction of making a fucking kid. I'm going to kill it, kill it, kill it, kill it. But since abortion is fucking wrong and would get my crazy fucking mother upset, I have to fucking kill me, too. Right? Please don't argue. But you won't, because you don't. But at least it's nice to have a reason a few people might understand. Though I've known this was coming for years—that's why they put me in Wingdale.

I hardly ever think about Jane or Ellen (my other sister) or Kimmy either—each of which I had to clean up after they did it. Kimmy was my first roommate at Wingdale. She was black like you and we used to talk about doing it together *all* the time. But then she wigged out and beat me to it. And in two weeks, three weeks, you won't think about me either—I promise. Because we don't know each other that well. But we'll get married, for which I thank you so much, so much, Arnold.

Even though it's just pretend. But that's the only kind—pretend fun—I've ever been able to enjoy. The real kind is too awful. You let real fun go on, even for a few hours, and it just gets too horrible. I mean, *really*. [Three angrily thick lines underscored "really," though the letters themselves were in her neat print, as though the anger had overwhelmed her as an afterthought.] So, since this is all pretend, you won't think too much about me, either. You can't even let the pretend kind go on too long, which is probably the reason I have to do this. But I hope you understand how much easier you have made everything by being so nice. Now I have a lot of instructions for you. The most important part is calling my mother. But you can get them all done in a day—maybe the same day you decide to clean up. You have to promise me—

Arnold thought, suddenly, furiously, *I don't have to promise you shit!*

And something heavy knocked against his open door—a policeman's club?

Someone said, "Is this it . . .? Yes, it's gotta be. Hello? Is somebody here—you called the police?"

Someone else said, "Come on—get on in there, Tony. And put your clothes on, will you?"

Arnold stood up with the papers in his hand and, folding them as he walked, went up the hall. As he saw the policemen, he crumpled letter and license into his hip pocket.

Horse/Tony stood between them—naked—in just his boots, his hands behind his back. One of the policemen was very tall, big-hipped, and white. The other was almost as small as Tony and black. The tall one—my God, Arnold thought, he must be six-foot-four, six-foot-*six*—was holding Horse's rumpled jeans and jacket. "Come on, put your stuff *on!*" The policeman's face made him look a weathered, handsome-ugly forty-eight or forty-nine. From under his cap, the gray-brown hair was unruly.

"I can't," Tony said. "You got my hands cuffed."

Holding Tony's arm, the little black officer said, "That'll teach you to go running around in the fuckin' street wavin' your pecker in the wind—that gerbil collar on your dick? What does that do, make it look bigger? Man, that's *sick!*"

The tall white officer dropped the jeans and the jacket on the floor. "Turn him loose and let him get his clothes on."

"Suppose he runs?" the black officer said.

The white officer grinned. "He ain't gonna run—Tony's a local kid. Where the fuck is he gonna run to? Come on, Tony and me is old friends—right? He's a fuckin' punk."

"You say so." While the black officer stepped behind Tony, first to close the door, then to do something with a key, the white officer said to Arnold:

"You know this guy? You know Tony? He says he was just up here, where you got this girl . . .?"

Arnold said, "Yes, he was . . . here. Would you *plea*se take a look—at her, I mean. Maybe there's something you can do. I don't think so, but *maybe*—"

"Come on." Something about the white policeman's

towering beefiness made Arnold feel more comfortable. "Let's see what you got."

Opening and closing his fists, Tony brought his hands in front of him, looking at his fingers. The black officer stepped ahead of him while the white officer said, "Bring your clothes here, Tony, and put 'em on with us—okay?"

Arnold was surprised at his own calm. If I *were* a murderer, he thought, I could probably get away with this, at least now. "She's in the bathroom. She told me her name was Judy."

Tony said, "Judy Haindel. On the street, man, they called her Crazy Judy Haindel. She don't really live here, man. She's homeless."

Arnold said, "I let her stay here for a couple of days. That's all. When I went out, to take a walk in the park, she was fine. But when I got back here, with Tony . . . Tony, well . . . she—"

Ahead the two officers reached the bathroom. Both looked in. The little black one said, "*Shhheesh . . .!*"

The towering white one exclaimed, "Jesus, Mary, and *fuckin'* Joe!" Reaching up he snatched off his police cap and turned it around in his long hands. (There was less hair under the cap than Arnold had thought. With his baldness, he gained a decade, lost three-quarters of his craggy good looks—and all his ability to reassure.) Holding it by the visor, the over-tall cop settled his cap back in place.

Beside Arnold, Tony was pushing off his boots again, picking up his pants to shake them out, pulling them up his right leg over the birthmark, dropping them again to stick his other foot in and pulling them up both legs now, pushing his privates inside, bending to swipe up—and twisting to shrug on—his jacket, hopping on one foot, getting one boot on, hopping on the other . . . finally grabbing Arnold's arm to steady himself. The grip startled Arnold. At last Tony got the second boot back on and released him. "That's a mess, ain't it? Hey, I gotta take a wicked piss—can I go in there?"

The black officer looked back at Tony, disbelieving. "You wanna go in *there?*"

"Yeah, man. I gotta piss. I won't step on nothin'—"

The white officer said, "No, you *can't* go in there. Not until the coroner gets here."

"Aw, come on, MacCormack!" Tony said. "That's gonna be *hours*—I really gotta piss!"

"Well, you're not pissin' in there," the white officer said. "Hey—*you're* a workin' stiff, Tony. Hold it a while."

"Aw, fuck *you!*"

"I think we're going to have to use your phone," the black officer said. "We have to phone the fire department."

"Huh?" Arnold said. "You do? Certainly. Please. Go ahead."

"When they take a body out your place"—moving his foot around on the floor, Tony looked up at Arnold—"the first people to come is always the goddam fire department." He snorted. "I wish this was the first time I'd ended up some place with a fuckin' body in it. But it's more like my third. You might as well get ready. We're gonna be here a while. If they figure you really done somethin', they're gonna take us in. Jesus, man—they won't even let me take a piss!"

Arnold said, "Go in the kitchen and use the sink—but please turn the water on, will you?"

"Aw, *thanks*, man . . .! *These* fuckin' assholes—"

"Hey, Tony, come *back* here—!" the tall one called from the bathroom doorway, but didn't stop him.

Over the next forty minutes, the number of policemen, then the number of policemen and detectives doubled, trebled, quadrupled in Arnold's apartment—and Arnold's hysterical calmness dissipated. Then, though he'd heard no siren, three firemen in black rubber coats and helmets, and two in what Arnold guessed was plain clothes for the Fire Department (navy blue T-shirts with F.D.N.Y. in white letters across front and back) came in—two were women, who managed not to speak to Arnold—and, two and a half hours later, a young coroner in a sport shirt and silver-rimmed granny glasses arrived.

While Arnold sat nervously in the living room, from down the hall came a Polaroid camera flash—three, five, seven times. They cut her down. Arnold happened to be passing by the bathroom door, when he looked in and, among the three policemen standing inside, saw gangling MacCormack lean in and turn off the shower. The spray's arc became a dribble.

The coroner said, "Oh, yeah. *She's* dead!" and that it certainly *looked* like suicide. And a pretty determined one. As far as he could tell, the immediate cause was that she'd choked on her own chyme, when, in the noose, she vomited as soon as she'd begun to strangle. While she'd bled a lot, it hadn't been enough to cause death, in his opinion.

Arnold got that last secondhand from a plainclothes detective named Perez. "He said she was probably afraid of cutting herself. The cuts aren't that deep—and she don't have no other wrist scars."

To which Tony said sarcastically, "Suicide . . . Jesus Christ—ain't *that* good news!" At the other end of the couch from Arnold, back in his black denim jacket, Tony sat with his ankle crossed on his thigh, knee out wide, arm along the couch—the position he'd taken when he'd first come from the park restroom to sit on the bench, though rather than loose-limbed and adolescent, it now seemed quintessentially self-possessed and adult.

They were taking the body out the front door. Arnold heard the lock close.

Dapperly dressed Perez stood, looking down at Tony dismissively. "What's a matter, you little scumbag, you ain't got nothin' to say, now? Huh?" (Arnold thought that was excessive.) "Well, that's a blessing on us all. Hey, fuck-face, would you at least zip your goddam fly? I'm tired of starin' at the studs on your cock harness."

"I told you," Tony said. "My zipper's broken. I can't close it."

Perez shook his head.

By now Arnold was sure Horse/Tony was at least twenty-nine, even thirty. Older wouldn't have surprised him. The last of his childish air had gone with his hysteria at Judy's death. It was rather (Arnold thought) as if he'd been watching a play in which a midget had taken the part of a winning child, only he'd gone backstage to find the little performer at his makeup mirror, chomping a cigar.

Arnold was in his second version of what he, at any rate, thought of as his "statement"—Perez was taking notes and occasionally yawning (it was past one in the morning)—when Arnold realized he had actually and honestly forgotten to mention his wedding to Judy that day at City Hall!

He had been working so hard to make the evening sound reasonable—after he'd let her sleep there a few days, that night she'd wanted to stay in and insisted he go out and walk in the park (without saying she'd told him to get laid as a wedding present).

The wedding itself had slipped his mind!

Arnold stopped talking.

Lieutenant Perez looked up. "What—you remember something?"

"No." Arnold went on, "Anyway, while I was out, I just started talking to Tony—in the park, there. We were having an interesting conversation, and he sounded like an interesting . . . kid. So I asked him to come back here. I thought we'd all have a cup of coffee—"

"You know what he does for a living, don't you?" Lieutenant Perez asked.

"Huh? No—actually I don't."

"He sells drugs." Under his brown suit jacket, the Lieutenant wore a creamy gray and gold tie, which Arnold would have thought silk, had he not seen hundreds, on the vendors' racks, hanging along the curb in front of the cheap clothing stores, up and down Fourteenth, when he'd taken Judy shopping.

"Oh . . . !" Arnold said.

From the couch, Tony said, "Man, I don't sell no drugs. Not no more. You know that, Perez. That's not what I do. You know what I do as well as any of these other fuckers in here. What—I gotta tell everybody here and embarrass this guy"— he nodded toward Arnold—"who's tryin' to be a good fellow and help you bastards out? I mean, if you want, I can tell you anything you—"

"*You*"—Perez lifted up a hand—"don't gotta say *nothin'*. Don't start. Don't start, scumbag—I'm *not* up for your fuckin' bullshit tonight—or I'll turn around and kick your fuckin' teeth down your fuckin' throat. Right here, in front of everybody."

Tall MacCormack said, "Come *on*, Perez! You know as well as I do, Tony ain't sold no drugs in seven, eight years. He sells his fuckin' *ass* is what he sells. I already told you, we caught him downstairs, hiding behind the steps, naked as a jaybird, with a cock ring on and his damned Polack-Wop dick out to here. They just come up here to fuck—"

"*Uh-uh*." Perez shook his head. "I don't even wanna hear about that. I ain't gettin' involved in *that* shit! Ain't no profit in it—nobody wants to carry through. Tony sold drugs when he was fifteen—'cause *I* busted him. So as far as *I'm* concerned, that's what he does now. Got it?"

"That was more than nine, ten years ago!" The tall officer in uniform sounded disgusted. "The kid's been clean since he was twenty—and you're gonna hang that on him now? Let the punk alone, man. He don't bother nobody."

"What—he's suckin' *your* dick, now? Hey, I bet he still smokes up a storm, that's if he ain't doin' fuckin' lines like they was goin' outta style. Besides, Tony's Italian."

"Polack-Italian. That's where he gets his meat. Man, they're worse than the fuckin' . . . excuse me, sir"—in his blue-black uniform, with silver badge and, here and there, multicolored bars,

MacCormack blinked watery gray eyes down at Arnold—"worse than you black guys."

"Yeah." Perez shook his head. "So says the Irish King Kong." He turned away. "In the precinct, the big mick here'll go in the back with you and show it to you for five dollars. What I don't understand is that there're guys who'll fuckin' *give* it to 'im, too!"

From his end of the couch, Tony laughed: "If you got it and you don't show it off, ain't nobody ever gonna know it."

It all rather startled Arnold. But MacCormack seemed to find it funny, too. "Most guys I know in the foot-long club are black. But *every* once in a while, some guinea or a couple of us micks'll slip in. First time one of you PRs gimme fifty cents to see it, Perez, I was a kid out here playin' handball in the school yard in the alley up to Fifth Street between B and C. And you're right. They're *still* guys at the precinct who'll—"

"Hey, I *told* you, MacCormack. I don't even wanna *hear* that shit!"

Chuckling, MacComack shook his head.

Tony told Arnold: "We're just fuckin' with you 'cause you're gay. It don't mean nothin'."

I don't like Perez, Arnold thought.

"Yeah, you guys fuck with everbody, dontcha?" Perez stepped toward Tony. "I'll fuck my fuckin' foot up your fuckin' ass, scumbag!"

Tony actually flinched.

MacCormack said, "Hey! Come *on*—!"

Later Lieutenant Perez stopped conferring with another

plainclothesman to ask Arnold, with a surprising show of sincere-sounding concern, if he were planning to stay in a hotel that night. "'Cause a lot of guys, if somethin' like this happens in their own place, it wigs 'em out. It would sure wig *me* out! I wouldn't wanna stay here, after that. I mean I'd want to get away from it, you know—for at least a few days."

"No. That's all right." Was Arnold free to clean the place up?

"Yep." Under his suit-jacket edges, Perez put his hands in his pockets. "Coroner says it was suicide. He said she was probably pregnant—about four and a half months. So suicide is what we're putting down."

"Oh, my *God* . . . .!" Arnold said. "That's terrible!"

"You didn't know?"

"No." He'd been hoping that, somehow, the pregnancy mentioned in the letter had been more psychotic pretense.

"Mr. Hawley, you got a stronger constitution than I do—I'd sure understand it if you wanted to go somewhere else for a few nights. Stay with some friends or something. But I hope you think twice now about taking some homeless crazy in off the street. I mean—this is what can happen. We've looked around. We got the box with her clothes. But if you should find anything else, I'd appreciate you letting us know. If a note or anything like that should turn up—or maybe some stuff of hers that wasn't in the box . . ."

Along with their wedding, Arnold hadn't said anything about the pages in his pocket—with the license. The tall white and the little black officer—both had gone, along with a now all-but-silent Tony—*must* have seen him pushing them into his pocket when they'd walked in. What, he wondered, had they thought they were?

Though Arnold wasn't really supposed to know it, by now he'd figured out that Tony's story, which they'd taken down in the kitchen, pretty much confirmed his own—that they'd met in the park, decided to come up here, and things had—well, yeah— started to get sexual (no, it *wasn't* a hustling thing!), when Tony had to use the bathroom, opened the door—and freaked.

(The first 911 call—Arnold now had had time to figure it out—had been from some other woman in the building when Tony started shouting MURDER! HELP! POLICE!)

That night, Arnold lay in his bed, mostly awake, till dawn. He knew enough not to have expected some Sherlock Holmes investigation in detail. *Those paper scraps, pinned to the pillow— where did you say she slept while she was here? You're sure, now, there wasn't any note . . .?* But no one had even brought them up. By sunup Arnold had decided, probably because she *was* homeless, they didn't care. Still, they hadn't dusted for fingerprints— though what would fingerprints have shown, had they found any? What had been confirmed, of course, a bit more dramatically than he was comfortable with, was something Arnold already knew. The forensic machinery of tests and chemicals and precision measurements was reserved for cases where something was at stake. The sad fact was, with this sad homeless woman, nothing—sadly—was at stake at all. Even so, by the time his air-shaft bedroom window had begun to lighten, Arnold had decided that withholding the wedding—not to mention her letter—was the stupidest thing he'd *ever* done! At nine on the button, he was going to phone the number Lieutenant Perez had left with him and add the tale of the marriage *and* the note to what the police knew—after he had finished reading it himself. The wedding they'd find out about anyway, so he might as well tell them about the letter. The idea of her writing all that—with *instructions!*—still made him angry. Relieved by the decision, though, he went to sleep.

And woke—Lord, it was eleven thirty!—to the phone's ring.

"Mr. Hawley? Is this Mr. Hawley? This is Lieutenant Perez. The woman who killed herself in your place yesterday, her name *wasn't* Judy Haindel. That's just something she made up. It was Audrey Filbert—she's from Bridgeport. She had a history of severe mental problems. I just got off the phone with her doctor, at the mental hospital at Wingdale where she used to be a patient. He said she'd tried over a dozen suicide attempts in the last five years—it occurred to me that might make you feel better. She'd been out of the hospital almost four and a half months. He said he was surprised she had lasted *that* long!" Arnold remembered Perez's remarks to Tony and wondered where all this solicitous feeling for a single, black, gay man came from. "Apparently she was eighteen two weeks ago—lucky for you! With minors, we're usually a little more concerned. She'd had a couple of hospitalizations, actually—for several years, each. Some of this is supposed to be confidential—but: I mean, she's dead, now. She had two sisters, who both killed themselves when they were twenty-three. We might learn something more about her, now that we have her proper name. We gave an aunt of hers *your* name—*she* might call you to find out some more. Or, who knows, she might not. Still, I thought you'd want to know."

"Of course—thank you. Thank you. Yes. Thanks."

When, in his underwear, he walked back up the hall to his bedroom, Arnold thought: he'd had a *pretend* marriage to Judy Alice Haindel. The only name they'd be running down now was Audrey Filbert. First, it *couldn't* make any difference to the case, whether they'd been "married" or not, other than to confuse things. Second . . . well, the first was enough. Arnold went into the bathroom, because he had to urinate. Last night he'd mopped and mopped the floor, forty minutes at least. Between the tiles, blood still left brown grout lines on the floor around the tub. They'd taken his shower curtain. In the corner was the pail, the mop still in it. Along the bottom of the tub, wet and frayed, stretched the red towel, still with its knot. Why had they taken the shower curtain and left *that?* (Also, they'd taken the two knives.) The red terry cloth was a soggy rope.

Judy . . .

And two sisters . . .

And black Kimmy . . .

Looking down at the cloth, Arnold remembered when he had first opened the towel to find the tear she'd begun—and felt himself start to cry . . . it was the emotional overflow from it all. Yes—but only starting. Before tears spilled down his cheeks, the sadness subsided . . . though what remained felt far deeper and more uncomfortable.

Eight days later, on a Sunday morning, Arnold sat in Tompkins Square, not far from the comfort station, writing the fifth poem in a series whose working title was *Pretences*. He was drafting one he'd already titled "MacCormack," when he *saw* the tall policeman coming along the path from Avenue B, going into the comfort station, ducking his head to the side, so that his cap was shoved from its secure position over his curly hair by the black metal door frame. Within the next five seconds, two elderly men and five younger ones—rather suddenly—left, at their different paces, one of the younger turning toward Avenue A, the others toward Avenue B. With sympathetic guilt, Arnold looked down at his notebook, to continue writing and crossing out words in his poem.

Was it a full minute, a minute and a half before Arnold became aware that a shadow had fallen on the blue-lined page? He looked up, to see a slab of darkness, which said, "Hey, Mr. Hawley."

Come from the john to stand directly before him, cap in hand, tall MacCormack raised it to fit it back on again.

Arnold started—and found himself with chills. Reflexively he dropped his hand across the paper, though there was little chance of MacCormack reading his name at the head, in Arnold's slanting cursive. It was uncharacteristically breezy for June, so that— uncharacteristically—Arnold was wearing a sweater Aunt Bea had sent him, among several over the years, under his sports jacket. "Hello, sir," Arnold said. And smiled.

"Everything okay, over at your place?"

"Oh . . . *um* . . . yes. No, everything's fine."

"That was some evening, wasn't it?"

"Yes." Arnold squinted up. "It certainly was." He wondered which would call least attention to itself—leaving his hand carelessly over the page, or picking up the notebook and closing it?

MacCormack said, "I sure wouldn't want to come home and find something like that at *my* house, I can tell you! But that's the problem with takin' in crazies like that. Never know *what* the fuck they're gonna do!"

"*Mmm.*" Arnold nodded. (Perez had made it sound bigger than Tony's. I wonder if *I* offered him . . . well, five. *Absurd* . . .!) Then, both because he was interested and because the silence had stretched the edges of discomfort, Arnold said, "I was wondering, if you'd seen our little friend, since then—you know, what's-his-name, Tony . . . Horse, whatever they call him."

Above Arnold, MacCormack began to smile, a kind of bigger and bigger grin, that at first seemed welcoming and friendly, but, after moments, passed through knowing into the accusatory. When Arnold was about to say something else, MacCormack said, "Yeah, I seen him . . . in the Jefferson Theater—you know the Spanish movie, on Fourteenth?—maybe last week. But— naw—you ain't gonna see that cocksucker around here no more, for a while. Especially after what happened at *your* place. He hangs out up around Twenty-third and Lex—there're some bars up around Gramercy Park—they're his stompin' grounds, today. Maybe he comes down here at night sometimes. But not during the daytime, know what I mean?"

With no idea at all *what* MacCormack meant, Arnold nodded. "I was just wondering."

"If I run into him again, you want me to tell him you was lookin' for him?"

"Oh, no . . .!" Arnold said. "*No*—not at all! I'm not . . . looking for him. Really."

"Didn't think you were." MacCormack shifted his weight. "But you never know. Well, it's good to run into you. Nice to know everything's going well—especially after something like that." While a roar gathered in the leaves around them, louder and louder, MacComack turned and stepped away from the sun, which fell now over Arnold's hand, his face, his notebook page.

•◆•

A month later, on the last Thursday evening in July, just after a drizzle had stopped, Arnold came home from the Employment Administration, sure now that he had a pretty final draft of all fifty-seven poems in the sequence. They'd erupted practically like Rilke's *Sonnets to Orpheus*. That night, in his hot apartment, he took Audrey's five-page suicide note from the drawer in the kitchen table—for the first time since her death—to read the rest.

Yes, instructions were pretty much what they consisted of.

He should phone this one, write that one, tell them she'd killed herself, but the most important thing was to tell them they'd gotten married. *If* they actually went through with the marriage, she explained, he was supposed to get nine photocopies of the license and mail one to this one and to that one (". . . *especially* Dr. Stevens at fucking Wingdale, who said it was fucking unrealistic of me to fucking even *think* about getting fucking married. It will be so great to show him what realistic *is!*") and the other. At the end, there was a space. Then, in black ballpoint (the rest had been in blue), the writing went on:

All right, we did it. We even had some wedding cake—a wonderful pretend wedding cake. With chocolate frosting—in honor of the big, black rapist you like to pretend to be. It was good, too. You've gone out to have some fun in the park. To do your raping and fucking. So I figure I have about an hour. Maybe an hour and a half. Really, I'm going to try to keep all the mess in one room—in the bathroom, I mean. Ellen tore up our whole house when she did it. That seems *so* unnecessary! It just makes people more angry than they have to be— and I don't want to do that to you. Because I know you'll do everything I asked—you're that kind of person, Arnold. And I don't want to seem completely inconsiderate. Because you're really good. And a poet, I guess. I only pretend to understand your poems. But even that's fun—more than if I really did, I bet. 'Cause that's how it is with everything. If you weren't so nice and smart, there wouldn't be any point to it. And you wouldn't have said yes. No—that's not true. Because the main point, after all, is that all this awful, awful, awfulness will be over. Really over. That's the reason. But please try not to leave anyone out—especially the ones who need copies of the license. I'm still wondering about the wrists— 'cause you don't have anything really sharp in the house.

And I've never cut myself before, the other times I tried. But this is special. I've got an idea. Okay. Good-bye.

Oh. One other thing.

You probably thought I was fucking crazy with those pictures this morning. But about a year after fucking Ellen offed her fucking self in the fucking kitchen from the fucking light fixture, I was looking through one of mom's drawers and I found her picture, and I started crying. I cried and cried—and I couldn't stop, I was so frightened! That's because I knew, then, I had to do it, too, and there wasn't any getting out of it. And my mom came home, and I couldn't even talk I was crying too much, so after about ten hours they came and took me to the hospital again—for the next three years. I don't want that to happen to you. That's why I didn't want any pictures. That's all. You're too nice. But I realize you don't even know me enough for that—not the way I knew Ellen. But I'm not frightened anymore. I've lived with enough people who've done it to know it's no big deal, really. It just seems that way at first. And it won't be me finding it. It'll be you. You just have to do everything like I say. And I'm sorry.

It wasn't signed—so how was he to know whether he was to tell them about Judy or Audrey? Of course, *she'd* put "Judy Alice Haindel" on the license—

◆

There were poems in *Pretences* called "Tony," and "Horse," and "Dr. Stevens" and "Perez," and, yes, "MacCormack." There were poems he'd titled "Judy" and "Audrey" and "Ellen" and "Ruth" (he had started to call it "Ruthie," but it just *wasn't* a pretty word) and "Manolo" and "Kim" and "Odessa" and "Vashti" and "Bridgeport" and "Jane." And there were *dozens* of references to the events of that week. But, at the same time, there was no way you could actually *read* the events themselves from the poems. (That's not the kind of poetry Arnold wrote. . . .) Nevertheless, it was interesting to think about some critic, perhaps a graduate student somewhere, who'd gotten a hint of the whole thing, somehow, phoning him up for an interview to find out what the story actually was. How did Kenner learn that Pound had been sitting on the steps of St. Mary's in Venice, looking out over the waters, when he'd drafted the opening of the second *Canto* ("Hang it all, Robert Browning, there can be but the one 'Sordello.' But Sordello, and my Sordello? Lo Sordels si fo di Montavana. So-shu churned in the sea. . . .")? How did Perloff learn Silliman had been watching the door across the street at the Bank of America when he'd begun *Ketjack* ("Revolving door . . .")? Trackle hadn't left a note—so how did anyone really know *why* he had taken his own life, among all those sick and wounded soldiers with their staph infections, stinking enough to make your eyes water? Would such knowledge add its particular highlights and tonal colorings to the abstract and tasked constructions that were *Pretences'* fifty-seven lyrics?

•-◆-•

On a hot August 6, he was coming home through the park. When it happened it seemed inevitable. Arnold wondered why it hadn't occurred before. He saw the heavy young woman with short black hair and black jeans rolled up over the tops of black combat boots. Though it had been almost two months, he was sure it was her. He veered sideways to reach her: "Excuse me. Please. I'm sorry, excuse me . . .?"

She turned to him, her face round and with an all-but-domino of black eye makeup. Holes here and there on her black jeans' thigh were bridged with safety pins.

"Excuse me. Did you know someone named Judy? Judy Haindel? Sometimes they called her Crazy Judy Haindel. . . ."

Her look became more and more puzzled. "Naw, I don't think so."

"Your name is—Vashti . . .?"

She smiled. "Yeah. That's right."

"And you had a friend named Audrey . . ." though, even as he said it, Judy's propensity for fictions filled Arnold's memory. Audrey *had* been Judy's real name, after all.

"Yeah—that's right."

"Because I saw all three of you sitting out here, once—back in June. . . ."

"Yeah, I used to come out here with Audrey, back in the spring. I don't no more, 'cause I'm waitressing over on Second Avenue, now."

"Well," Arnold said, "I thought you might want to know. Judy . . . died."

"Oh . . ." she said, slowly. "That's too bad." She stepped back, smiling. "But I don't think I knew her."

Arnold said: "It could have been Audrey, I mean, who died—"

"Audrey?" The young woman frowned. "No. I don't think so—unless you mean . . . recently. You don't mean *today* or something, do you? I spoke to Audrey last night on the phone. Her and Phil are down in Coconut Grove, being vegans and drinking orange juice and stuff—"

"Oh, no—" Arnold confirmed. "I just meant sometimes Judy said . . . her name was Audrey. Audrey Filbert. In fact that was her real name. You guys threw a paper plane at me. And when I came over, you and . . . Audrey got up and ran away."

"Audrey Barker," the young woman—Vashti—said. "Audrey and Phil went down to Florida, 'cause Phil's uncle or something has a place down there and said he could work for the summer. No, I don't think that was us. Unless we were *very* stoned . . . which is possible. But I don't think so. It's too bad your friend died, though." Vashti stood in the middle of the sweltering macadam. August heat was a hand pressing against Arnold's forehead. Weeks ago the leaves on the bushes and trees around had lost their spring brightness and mellowed into smoky green-gray. Vashti asked, "Do you go out?"

Arnold said, "Pardon?"

"I don't go out a lot anymore," Vashti said. "But I thought, maybe, 'cause you knew my name, that's what you were lookin' to do. I don't do it now, 'cause I'm waitressin' over on Second. But I thought maybe you'd been talking to some of the guys out here, Fink, or Smoky, or Joey, or Little Irish Mike, or Big Ukrainian Mike—Ukrainian Mike is the fellow with all those *really* bad burns on his face and chest and arms? He's only got one eye. He works in the kitchen at the Odessa—in the back? You'd know him. Just three fingers on his right hand. . . ." She raised one of hers, two fingers bent over, and held her wrist with her other. (Nothing identified him for Arnold.) Vashti's short nails glistened green. "The others were burned off—in the accident when he was a kid. He don't go out much or let too many people see 'im, 'cause he thinks people are turned off by the scars. Yeah, he's built kind of like a bowling pin. But he's got a terrific, hard body—rock hard, *all* of it. It's like doin' it with a scarred-up Ukrainian giant—*I* think he's cute! It don't bother me. I could even have a regular thing with him. But *he's* too embarrassed." She smiled. "You lookin' to go out, later— maybe when I finish waitressin'? I'll be back through the park here—"

"Oh!" Arnold said. "Oh. I'm sorry. No. Really, I didn't mean that. I just thought you might have remembered her."

"Well," she said, without a smile, "if you're here when I come back through at about midnight or twelve thirty, I'll say hello. I may be waitin' around for one of the Mikes . . . but"—she winked—"if I see you first, well, we'll see what happens." She slid her hands in her pockets, practically like a boy, and walked on.

That evening, at his kitchen table, with the window wide, though doing little to relieve the heat, Arnold added two stanzas (and heavily revised four others) to the poem "Vashti."

He even wrote a whole new poem, "Mike." Finally, though,

because fifty-seven was a prime number, he decided to save it for his next book.

"Mike" became the third poem in *Pewter Pan*.

·—•·

Eighteen months later, Arnold made the mistake of mentioning Judy's death when Sam, the Harper Torchbooks editor, was trying to come up with another title because *Pretences* was *too* flat, and *too* unyielding of, really, anything.

Arnold's palms on the leather chair arms felt moist. "But Sam, that's the *point*." The blinds in the waiting room window were slightly slanted. The red flowerpot on the side of the sill held no plant.

"I don't *care* if that's the point," Sam said. "So put it out of your mind, Arnold. You have to *forget* it." That there had to be *some* change of title had been decided in editorial: if Arnold wanted them to do the book at all, he *had* to think of something else. "You wrote it, and we think it's a wonderful collection." The rug was dark red. The ceiling fan was not turning. "We really do. But it's our job to publish it, and publish it properly—and make it as successful as we can. We're not telling you how to write your poems—but book titles are something we *know* about. Arnold, we *do* want something true to the book. I can't say it enough times. Really, everyone likes it *very* much. Look—let's just think a minute, you and me. These poems are . . . your own very *personal* reflections, on some painful, personal experiences—that poor girl who killed herself, who you just mentioned. But, because of the pain, purposefully—and by beautifully artful means, I might add—you've obscured them. You *don't* want them to be transparent . . . as who would? Okay. What about . . . *Dark Reflections?* I mean, that's what they *are*, aren't they? Now *that's* a title that will speak to people—I mean, poetry readers. *I'm* a poetry reader. It would speak to *me*."

Arnold felt he was melting in the leather chair on the other side of the Harper waiting room table—the conversation hadn't even gotten him as far as Sam's manuscript-cluttered office. "Okay. I mean, if you really think—and, I *don't* have a choice, anyway . . . I mean, *really*—"

"No." Sam smiled. "Really. You don't."

Perhaps Sam's curiosity would be piqued—maybe Sam would phone one day to ask Arnold a few more questions, and even write that article which would nudge a few people—a few scholars of modern poetry—toward a greater curiosity.

Eventually, though—once Torchbooks nixed the poetry line—Sam went on to Home Repair books at Simon & Schuster (the job had been given him as a favor), where he shortly had a nervous breakdown, was fired, and over the next year and a half drank himself to death, someone eventually told Arnold.

The same day, at two in the morning (three years after talking to Vashti), Arnold actually ran into Ukrainian Mike, drunk . . . in the park.

They'd spoken Russian.

It was the rare Ukrainian who didn't also speak a good deal of Russian, Arnold had learned a long time back—though a good many did not like to.

Only a year before, coming through Tompkins Square on a Wednesday morning (at school, they'd told him a while ago, Mondays or Fridays free were no longer an option for adjuncts), Arnold had run into Tony again, who had started off the conversation, "You wanna take me up to your place? It's still twenty if I come up. I ain't changed my prices, man. I'm probably one of the few things that *don't* cost more, these days." They'd gone to Ninth Street. In a slightly uncanny replay, moments into the apartment Tony was again out of his denims, all blue this time, before the door had been shut. For all Tony's chatter, there was no mention of Judy—though Arnold thought of her constantly. This time, however, Arnold got him into the bedroom and also got down to his own underwear. Tony lay on the bedspread, while, next to him, one arm over Tony's hard, still chest, Arnold held those impressive genitals—though there was no cock ring on them now. In his hand, scrotum and penis felt like soft, liquid-filled rubber. After not three minutes, Tony said, "Hey—you come?"

Arnold hadn't even gotten hard—nor had Tony.

But, surprised and intimidated by the question, Arnold had said, "Sure—I guess so."

Tony bounded off the bed—"Good!"—was asking for his money, was getting back into his clothes—"Hey, that was nice, man. I like you. Maybe I'll run into you again."—and, moments later, was gone. Back in his slacks and still in his undershirt, standing in the apartment hall, Arnold thought, Why did I do that?

Back in his apartment, the night he heard of Sam's death—the same night as his two-in-the-morning encounter with scarred, one-eyed, three-fingered Mike—Arnold decided he would throw Judy's suicide letter out the next day. He was never going to show it to anyone, after all. Who in the world would care—and would he want them to? It had been years, now.

He'd been in his middle thirties. He was now forty.

He'd gotten as close to the real thing, he knew, as he was ever going to get.

And suppose something happened to him. And someone shipped all his papers to Aunt Bea. No.

Keeping it in the kitchen table drawer was just . . . well, it was going out. Tomorrow.

About 9:40 P.M., *three* nights later, just before taking down the garbage—somehow another couple of days had gone by, but that's how these thing turned into years—Arnold opened the kitchen drawer, took out the pages (for some reason a few sheets of music were on top of them that he had no memory of putting in there or where, exactly, they'd come from) and the "pretend" wedding license, beneath them—

Beneath that were, yes, three of the photographs from the strip, of a slightly younger Arnold and a smiling teenaged girl. (What had happened to the fourth . . .? For the life of him, he couldn't remember.) All he felt was blankness. He pictured a young woman coming across a photograph of her dead sister and crying and crying—for years. . . . Leaving the pictures, he pushed the drawer closed.

Without rereading them—after four and a half years in the drawer, the pages looked extraordinarily brittle—he pushed them down into the black plastic sack, carried it downstairs, and put it outside in one of the building's three cans.

part iii

THE BOOK OF PICTURES

for Rikki Ducornet

Sea is the source of water and the source of wind.
For not without the great ocean would there come to be
in clouds the force of wind blowing out from within,
nor the stream of rivers nor the rain water of the upper sky,
but great ocean is the sire of clouds and winds and rivers.
—Xenophanes of Colophon (DK 21B30)

In December '58, when he was twenty-two, Arnold Hawley took a Greyhound bus from Providence, Rhode Island, to Appleton, Ohio. It was the end of his second term since transferring to Brown, and, when he thought about it seriously, he was pretty sure he was *not* settling in. (The only class Arnold attended regularly was Russian.) This was the Christmas the Donaldsons/Hawleys were visiting the new house for one of Cousin Anita Donaldson's holiday dinners, since she and Harold had moved from western Massachusetts to try life in Harold Donaldson's hometown.

In the basement, in a shoebox atop a pile of framed and glass-covered photographs, some of which had hung on the walls at Anita's old Maryland place, in an envelope full of snapshots Arnold found one of himself, pudgy, in white shorts, T-shirt, and white loafers, sitting on a railing, head raised in laughter—probably at the idea of someone taking his picture. The photograph's edges were scalloped, the white border almost a full inch. The black-and-white image was practically square and in the center, rather than the three-inch by five-inch prints, to within a quarter inch of the edge, which thirty-five millimeter film, become popular over the last couple of years, produced.

Arnold brought the photo upstairs into the suburban kitchen, where by now almost everyone had a cut-glass cup, heaped with spoon after spoon of eggnog, this year as it had been the last time they'd gathered in another city, too thick for the glass ladle whose familiar swan's neck (in the unfamiliar kitchen) rose above the silver bowl's several peaks to lean at the rim.

By now each cup's white hillocks bore brown speckles from the barrel of Anita's silver nutmeg grater.

"Does anyone know when—or where—this was taken?"

After three aunts and four cousins came up to look over his shoulder, pondered, then shook their heads, Anita finished sliding the eighteen-pound turkey ("That should be enough for the sixteen of us, don't you think?") from the rack in the green oven to set the navy blue enameled pan on the stovetop. Wiping her hands on a red-and-green dish towel, in her gray silk blouse, she stepped over and glanced down. "Oh, you know—my friend Gordie sent me that a few years ago—my white friend, Gordie, who I used to work with, when we were in Maryland. Remember, he lived down the coast?" (Arnold remembered nothing.) "You found it downstairs, didn't you? He must have snapped you the afternoon he invited us all to drive down and have that barbecue . . . on his houseboat? The summer in Virginia—? At Diamond Harbor . . .?" Anita inquired of each of Arnold's blanker and blanker looks. "Back when we lived in Maryland? You don't remember?" Then, though Diamond Harbor was meaningless, memory welled: the sapphire sea, the island's gray-and-green scratch along the horizon, a boat rail pressed to his belly, hamburgers charring over the grill's coals while someone with a wooden-handled spatula pried one and another patty from the ashy tines.

Moonlight had turned damp dock boards velvet.

Ready to leave, the station wagon settled lower on its tires as each aunt or cousin crowded in—

Though *who* Gordie was or *what* he'd looked like left Arnold at a loss.

Through the kitchen, Uncle Harold's cigar cut the smell of sweet potatoes, creamed onions, kale, and giblet gravy, thyme and green peppers from the stuffing, the odor rich as food itself. "Negro"—Harold sat by the heavy wooden table, and Arnold looked up, since he was the only person Harold addressed that way—"your aunt tells me you're *still* foolin' around with that writin' nonsense and rhymin' foolishness. Remember, you and I are colored men. We don't have to be triflin' with no whitefolks' trash."

Arnold smiled. "You mean poetry?" (Arnold's poems used rhyme only sparingly.) When, two years before, he'd realized Harold hated the word—didn't like to hear it or say it—Arnold knew he had a dazzling weapon with which to cut free. "I enjoy writing poems, Uncle Harold. Besides, poetry is the most important thing—yes, writing poems—a person can do. 'Movers and shakers of the world forever,' you know. Poets. Yep, Uncle Harry, that's me. Saving the race with the purified Word of the tribe." His garage-owning, thirty-eight-year-old, cigar-wielding cousin by marriage (whom Arnold called "uncle") winced each time the word fell. "You have to remember, too, the tribe is a *lot* larger than Appleton."

"Aw, *shoot*—!" Harold said.

"Harold"—on the far side of the scarred oak, Aunt Bea paused in her polishing, a knife gleaming in gray cloth—"have some eggnog and leave the boy alone."

"You know I don't drink spirits." (By and large, at least back then, neither did Arnold. But the similarity did more to hold him and Harold apart than join them.) "Still, I *have* to say it, at least once." Harold leaned back, a dark forefinger along the rolled tobacco over the ashtray's cut glass. (Only thirty-eight—four years younger than long-suffering Anita—still, to Arnold, Harold could have been sixty.) "His parents would have wanted me to. Boy, get yourself married to a good woman and study to be a lawyer or a salesman—somethin' that'll make you some *money!*"

"Well, now"—Aunt Bea polished harder—"you've said it. And puttin' money ahead of God and all other things sounds pretty white to me." Bea—Arnold's dead father's half sister—was a very black, tree-branch gaunt woman, who, back in Pittsfield, had raised Arnold and encouraged him to pursue his own goals and be anything he wanted—the opposite of almost-as-dark Harold. With her summer trips with Mrs. Polk to Dar Es Salaam, her Second Thursday of the Month Ladies Reading Group, where they read William Demby and C. L. R. James and John O. Killens (and—years later—Martin Bernal), Aunt Bea had managed to learn Italian and Arabic and Japanese—she spoke the first two fluently and the third with wild ineptitude, but doggedly ("Otherwise I'll *never* improve")—and, on her high school history teacher's salary, had managed to take Arnold to the opera, at the Rotunda over in Lenox, summer, fall, winter, and spring, every year from the time he'd been twelve till he was nineteen. Now she pulled loose another spoon from the mahogany chest's purple velvet clutches. "For God's sakes, Harry. It's Christmas."

"Poetry . . ." Arnold looked idly at the ceiling.

As if struck, Harold said, "*Unnn . . .*"

Through the arch, Arnold could see the holiday cloth, already spread on the dining table—though, besides candlesticks, no silver was yet laid.

A minute later, Arnold took the picture down the cellar steps, back to the basement shoebox. Before he picked the box top up from where it had fallen on the cement floor, he took out his ballpoint from his shirt pocket and wrote across the photo's back:

The poet Arnold Hawley,

Summer, c. 1947, Diamond Harbor,

Virginia, approximately

11 years of age.

• ◆ •

On the bus back to Rhode Island, rushing toward a sea, Arnold read a confusing newspaper story on page sixteen of the *Boston Globe*, with no pictures, which explained that the FBI had recently broken up a "vice ring" covering three northwestern states, including Idaho. At least seventeen young men "of college age or under" had been involved, and already six prominent businessmen had been arrested. A number of the youngsters had been sent to reform school. (Among those a bit older, their colleges had expelled four.) The writer anticipated more arrests.

The ring had used blackmail photographs.

As the snowy landscape passed the bus windows, Arnold only wondered how you could have a "vice ring" without "vice." The article mentioned *no* women! That the article ended in the midst of a sentence that did not continue anywhere in the paper made it no clearer. Arnold read the column-and-a-half account three times and hunted for half an hour, even checking successive page numbers, to make sure none was missing.

•◦•

Things had been whispered about in Arnold's Pittsfield elementary school. Also, things had been done by a group of boys, all from Dr. Josephson's science class, in the elementary school basement after gym. While Arnold had not directly taken part, he'd nonetheless agreed to be a dirty little Jap—Japs were usually colored; Germans were just small white kids—for an entire week in the war games of blackouts and MiG bombers, in order to be allowed to watch. (Arnold remembered blackouts. They'd terrified him. Why, he always wondered, would anyone want them in a game?) Then their math teacher, Mrs. Palmer, had suddenly rushed down the steps, one fist whipping back and forth across her felt skirt, the other sliding in jerks down the pipe banister's flaking orange, to catch them in the middle. Arnold had heard her chastise one boy, yanking him from his knees in front of another: "Don't you realize how dangerous what you're doing is?" Her voice echoed under the basement conduits. It was November. "Now fix your clothes! This instant! You could grow up to be a homosexualist!" Though he hadn't—really—*done* any-thing, Arnold knew that he would have—eagerly. It started him on a series of dictionary and encyclopedia searches, skims down book indices in psychology volumes, normal and abnormal, in his elementary school, high school, and town libraries.

(By ten, Arnold had established himself with the Pittsfield librarian as someone allowed to read any book he wanted.)

At twelve, when he went into the hospital to have his tonsils out—Arnold was three or four years older than most kids, but till then they'd never bothered him—yes, he knew he suffered from homosexuality and that it was a dangerous perversion.

The morning after his operation, Aunt Bea had been in to see Arnold at eight o'clock, then withdrawn, smiling through the white enamel bars at the foot of his bed, with a promise that, when she could leave the high school, she'd return at one. At ten o'clock, a young white doctor had come in to check on Arnold—the one who, when he'd last been in the room, was so surprised to see Arnold reading *Of Human Bondage* ("That's about a doctor, isn't it? You can actually . . . *understand* that?" Arnold had nodded), and been even further surprised when Arnold had called something "preposterous."

While, after feeling under Arnold's throat, the man went on to listen to Arnold's chest, Arnold asked suddenly: "Are there are a lot of homosexuals?" He tried to make the question sound as innocent as possible.

From his ears the doctor took the stethoscope, whose rubber buds already had collars of cracks around the bright steel tubes that came together through the brace. "Excuse me?"

"I was just wondering"—Arnold pushed himself back in the hospital bed—"if there were lots of homosexuals."

Standing half in and half out of a patch of sunlight coming through the window into the yellow-painted pediatric ward, the blond resident said: "What in the world would you want to know *that* for?"

"I was reading an article. And it mentioned it—homosexuality. So I was wondering"—Arnold shrugged—"how common it was."

"Oh. Well, you know," the doctor said, "sometimes kids fool around." He chuckled. "But, as diseases go, I can assure you, it's *not* very common at all."

"Would you say"—Arnold slid a brown foot over the bed's edge in his blue pajama pants and reached up to rub his sore neck—"one out of a hundred?'

The resident chuckled. "I doubt if it's anywhere *near* that frequent."

"One out of a thousand?"

"Maybe"—the doctor looked pensive—"one out of five or *six* thousand."

"Oh . . .!" Arnold said.

"So you see," the doctor concluded, hanging the stethoscope around his neck with pink, heavy hands, "the chance of that one-out-of-five- or one-out-of-six-thousand turning out to be *you* is pretty slim."

"Oh, that isn't why I was . . ." Arnold sat up sharply and swallowed hard; his throat throbbed, painful enough to bring him near to tears. "Really, I—"

"Also," the young white man went on, "smart as you are, you

are, after all, Negro. As far as I know, there's never been a case of Negro homosexuality—at least that *I* know of—in the annals of medical history. It has to do with your race's extraordinarily high constitutional level of . . . *ahem*, libido. Inversion, onanism, things like that, on the other hand, are all sexually degenerative conditions." He smiled. "Now, bookworm that you are, I'll bet you don't know what any of *those* words mean!" (Arnold was surprised. Thanks to his reading, he knew them all—but said nothing. Nor, later, did he say anything to Bea.) "Anyhow, that pretty much lets *you* off the hook. All right—why don't you try sipping some more of that ice water the nurse left you on the table, there. Really, it'll make your throat feel *lots* better."

"Why"—Arnold picked up the striated plastic glass, in which the ice cubes, grown small, all floated on the top—"would you think I was worried about *me?*"

The resident walked toward the door, then smiled back over his white uniform shoulder. "Why *else* would you possibly want to know?" He left Arnold alone in the room, with its other, unmade bed. No other Negro children were in the hospital that weekend, so they'd allowed Arnold to stay, reading his volume of Maugham, till Aunt Bea could bring him home.

· ◆ ·

Throughout his Pittsfield years, while he lived with Aunt Bea, Arnold had had a series of crushes on conveniently distant fellows. First was the big-handed basketball player, Junior Johns, one of the six Negro seniors in the high school when Arnold was a sophomore. Then it was a Hispanic bulldozer driver—Arnold never knew his name—on the construction site beside the White Castle, who, as Arnold passed, stopped astride his machine to haul his lemon-colored T-shirt up from a streaming abdomen across which each muscular band and, above those, each pectoral lay like a mahogany plaque. The driver worked the sopping canary cloth over his shoulders, to shake out wet hair and grin—unshaven—down at Arnold. Once it was the nineteen-year-old painter's apprentice, that second May weekend, with the guys painting Mrs. Winterson's house, three away from Aunt Bea's: a broad-faced Irish kid with green eyes and paint-grayed hair, who also spent most of his time shirtless, while his drab pants and thick wrists became more and more ivory splattered over the job's four days. Arnold rode his bike back and forth on Warbler Road, trying not to be too obvious about staring in at him over the weathered pickets. Arnold even talked to him once, on the job's last day, when, as sunset layered copper with violet behind Mrs. Winterson's yellow roses, again in his shirt but with only the bottom two buttons closed (both in the wrong holes, which dissolved Arnold in tenderness toward the taciturn young man, two years his senior), Doogie Mallone carried the wooden ladders and paint cans back to the truck. Then Arnold never saw him again, because Doogie wasn't a Pittsfield boy.

A year after his Appleton Christmas, however, Arnold was no longer at Brown: his scholarship had been forfeited. ("Yes, I know—*you* think you're a poet. But I hope eventually you'll realize how unrealistic that is for anybody, much less a colored boy like you. And whatever you want to be, if you don't put your schoolwork first, you're just another darky moron, like any other running around out there. And that's all, Hawley—I'm sorry." Arnold's ears stung. He clenched his teeth in the dean's carpeted office. Why, he wondered, had he even *thought* about Brown?) But after three months back with Bea, he was again in school, in Boston.

•◆•

At BU and even as far away as Tufts, Miss Merelda's place was popular with the growing number of Negro students at the Boston colleges. Behind its linoleum counter and its gilt cash register—with its cherrywood drawer, its diminutive marble counter under the round-headed tabs, the rococo crank on its side—Miss Merelda did fried chicken, pulled pork, and an array of auxiliary dishes in stainless-steel tubs held up over a blackened gaspipe with triple-flame burners every eight inches: green beans, candied yams, corn-off-the-cob with cut-up red and green fried peppers, and one sort or another of greens, cooked with hamhocks, pretty much every night—collards, kale, turnips, or mustards, along with a wooden bucket of potato salad and another of slaw. No one called it "soul food" yet: Vinny the truck driver, who was scheduled to change the 78 rpm records on the jukebox behind the two tables at Miss Merelda's once a month (though Vinny's actual visits were closer to once every three) took the ten-inch rhythm-and-blues disks from a set of double-thickness corrugated cardboard bins in the back of his truck still labeled "race records" rather than the fiberglass ones which, three years later after the presidential assassination and provided free of charge by Detroit's Hit House, in red stenciled letters would read "Soul Music."

So far, at a malt shop with mirrored walls closer to BU, Arnold had seen one jukebox, surmounted by a back-lit tortoise-shell arch around the window showing the turntable and the thick spindle, which actually played the new seven-and-a-half-inch 45s, though there was nothing on it anyone, white or colored, could possibly want to hear unless they were over forty.

On the second floor of the A-frame house two from the block's end, in Arnold's East Roxbury room that warm April evening, instead of Old Chinese Sam—with his crooked leg, his gray woolen army socks and leather bedroom slippers, and his knitted cap, worn year-round—the delivery boy who knocked on Arnold's second-floor door with Arnold's fried chicken, sweet potatoes, and ginger ale, was a huge, muscular man, darker than Harold.

The sleeves had been torn from his white shirt.

With cannonball shoulders and ox-sized arms that shamed the Charles Atlas ads for Dynamic Tension in the back of the comics Arnold still occasionally looked through, the man stood solidly in the doorway. His eyes were ivory, his cheekbones level and wide. While his head and ears were small and neat, his other features were big. His nose stretched across more than the middle third of the face. His jaws thrust forward, both upper and lower lip thicker than any two of Arnold's fingers. His chin was small and not prominent. At every point where something beautiful might lodge in a man's face, in his sat something startlingly brutal. Yet the totality of his mild expression—its firm relaxation—made him the most extraordinary-looking man Arnold had ever seen. The nick of a small scar prevented a wedge of hair from growing in the left eyebrow.

Arnold stared.

Perhaps in response to Arnold's gaze, the man smiled.

To the right, an upper tooth was gone.

The imperfections threw into relief, however, his tenebricose vitality, interrupted only on the side of his dead-black shoulder by the raised nickel of a smallpox vaccination.

Arnold looked up at the smile, which seemed to have swept here from the Universe's far end, herding before it all of night and masculinity, to resolve, a grand orchestral cadence, in Arnold's doorway.

Arnold stammered, "What . . . *uh* . . .um . . . *why* are . . .?"

Still smiling, the man—was he twenty-five? thirty-five?—said, "Ah bo' ya' chiggen an' yo' swee' 'taitahs." It was not a voice so much as a rumble that called up a sympathetic buzz in the base of Arnold's throat, even as Arnold was oblivious to all meanings in it.

Standing and staring and trying to say five different things, Arnold moved his mouth—while honestly forgetting, one after the other, what each was, till he fell back on: "Who *are* you . . .?"

"Ah' Bo'muh."

"What?" The elided "m" or "n" would have made it comprehensible; but, there in east Boston, Arnold spoke the standard New England English Dr. W. E. B. Du Bois himself had been raised with, a hundred miles to the west.

"Ah' Bo'muh—mah name Bo'muh. Who you?"

"Oh . . . *Uh* . . . Arnold Hawley! Won't you come in? *Please*, come in!"

Still smiling, the towering fellow said, "Okay, if ya' wan'," and stepped inside.

Arnold stepped back, a heel catching on the rug's edge. Though he didn't stagger, for moments Arnold had an ecstatic image of himself sprawled on his back over the floor while this amazing fellow stepped over him.

"Please . . . *um!*" Arnold spoke from the depths of bewilderment. "*Please*, sit down . . .!"

Again the man smiled. "Sho' . . . Okay." He turned and dropped to the red, black, and white check blanket covering Arnold's daybed. Leaning down, he put the white paper bag beside his scuffed work shoe on the rug.

For moments, Arnold had intimations that something in the bag concerned him. But . . . for his life, he couldn't think of what.

The man—Bo'muh?—let his knees fall wide, while, with hands larger than Rachmaninoff's legendary foot-long reach, he patted the blanket, ran them out over it, either side, then back to his hips, and looked around.

Perhaps because he was looking at only *one* of the hands, it never occurred to Arnold that the man meant other than *Come sit here*. He stepped to the bed, turned, and dropped on the spot. For a moment, Arnold felt he was falling. The black smile rushed up to hang above the spherical shoulder, already higher than Arnold's eyes. He (Arnold thought for the first time) was at least six-seven, even six-eight, though muscular as a bull or boar.

Something moved beneath Arnold's buttock—and tugged free. "Oh, I'm *so* . . .!" Arnold had *sat* on the hand—but was too astonished to leap up.

With their deeply-ridged dead-black knuckles, the long fingers that had been under Arnold's rump hung before him, then dropped on Arnold's knee—and *rubbed!*

Arnold stopped breathing and looked down at the hand moving forward and back, the brown material of his slacks folding and unfolding.

The man said, "Ya' wan' yo' chiggen an' yo' swee' 'taitahs?"

Arnold pictured himself turning and leaping from the bed, from the room! But, bending, and, with the blue-black field of Bo'muh's biceps before his eyes, what Arnold did (instead) was grasp Bo'muh's arm with both his hands. "Oh . . . *Oh* . . . Uh . . ." he started, leaning forward, three times. It took bodily will for Arnold not to press his face against the arm—thick as a thigh!— that he clutched, that he pulled closer, while the pressure moving along his own thigh grew greater.

Below bass, the voice asked, "I bet ya' wan' I should do sumpin' wit' ya', huh?" Though, on the simplest level, Arnold had finally understood each word, for all he took in, the man might have been speaking Venusian.

Bo'muh's hand moved forward to Arnold's knee.

Bo'muh's hand slid back to Arnold's hip.

When, again, it moved forward, the fingers spilled his thigh enough to graze Arnold's genitals beneath the cloth.

Arnold's hands tore from the arm. Arnold's thigh pulled from the fingers. Like flesh seared to steel, Arnold's leg ripped free of Bo'muh's, as if it burned and bled. Things Arnold had occasionally imagined Junior Johns or Doogie Mallone doing with him did *not* return. But the maelstrom of shame and pleasure that always followed those imaginings swirled through Arnold's body.

Now Arnold leapt forward, and while he managed to remain upright, both his hands and his legs pulsed, below pain. Before the door, he turned, repeating, "But you've got to *go*—now! Please, *please*, you've got to go! Go on! Go!"

"You don't wan' me t'do nut'in' wiff' ya'? Huh?" Bo'muh sat waiting, a long time (while Arnold realized he, himself, was panting—that, dizzily, he might fall). Finally, when Arnold began to think he had not been understood, and his eyes began to water in frustration, Bo'muh said, "Oh. Okay—maybe nudda time." Slowly, even sadly, Bo'muh returned his hands to his own knees, leaned forward, and stood.

From the ceiling hung a light in a shade of yellow-and-orange glass. Bo'muh stepped in front of it, his irregularly tufty hair brushing the bottom, so that his right shoulder and ear were edged by a flare, red-gold. The hand that had rubbed Arnold's leg swung randomly at hip and thigh, to stop between Bo'muh's legs, where, absently— at least it seemed to Arnold—he began to rub his own white cloth work pants. "Ah stay an' do sumpin' wiff ya' if ya wan'. Da'd be good. You go'n like it." In rubbing, his hand rose to bunch the cloth at his waist, lifting one pants cuff six inches and the other, four.

Looking down, Arnold saw that, with the oversized black work shoes, Bo'muh wore no socks.

The cuffs dropped, rose, dropped, rose, dropped, rose *again*—

"*No!*" Arnold blurted, looking up. "No . . . Please, you have to *go!*"

"Okay . . . maybe sum udda time," and, still rubbing, still smiling—at Arnold—he ambled forward, passed him, and went out the door.

From the hall, Arnold heard rug-dampened footsteps thump further and further off, till, changed to the clops of soles on wooden steps, they descended into silence.

Arnold moved back and sat—almost missing his desk chair, so that its far legs lifted from the floor, then clacked down, scraping! With one hand, Arnold slapped the desk top, then worked himself awkwardly back in the seat. His right leg was quivering; a muscle in his shoulder twitched. Sitting on the chair by his desk, Arnold took long, gasping breaths, while what had happened slowly cleared. Since Arnold knew he was the only male who'd *ever* had such feelings for another man—and never before at such intensity—it made no sense.

As he looked around the room, Arnold saw, a foot from the bed, the white bag that Bo'muh had left. For the first time he recognized it as Miss Merelda's.

Yes, it *had* been a new delivery boy!

That's my chicken, Arnold thought suddenly. *And my sweet potatoes!*

He'd phoned the order into Miss Merelda's place half an hour ago!

Arnold stood up . . . shivering. In the April warmth he was shivering. Bending unsteadily, he grasped the desk's edge, because, for a moment, he thought, again, he might fall—and lifted the bag. Standing once more, taking a breath, he stared into the mouth at the napkins folded over the containers inside.

I didn't pay him!

• ◆ •

Once a week—sometimes twice—Arnold ordered his dinner from Miss Merelda's. (Actually, Bo'muh had brought his *second* dinner from Merelda's that week, as Chinese Sam had brought his first.) After a mostly sleepless night, next evening Arnold counted his quarters, nickels, fifty-cent pieces, and dimes, then went to the payphone in the hall, pushed a dime into the back of the middle vertical slot, where it dropped from under his thumb and rang, then dialed.

"Hello? Merelda's Home Cookin'. Wha'chu want?"

Arnold placed an order for just five pieces of chicken. Twenty-six minutes later, he was as astonished as he had been the previous night when, knocking on Arnold's carefully half-opened door with Miss Merelda's white bag, Old Chinese Sam came in, in his knitted cap, with wispy Mandarin beard and moustache.

"But what happened to the *new* boy?" Arnold demanded. "The one who was here before . . .?"

In his drab watch cap, Sam shook his head, as, in wild frustration, Arnold counted out eighty-six cents in change into Sam's rough, lightly lined palm. "That boy crazy." Sam chuckled, blinking up at Arnold with bright, dark eyes. "He real *crazy*." Leaving Arnold with the bag, on which chicken grease made a translucent map, Sam turned, hobbling out into Arnold's second-floor hallway. "He not good. No. He *crazy!*" And Old Sam was gone.

For a second night, with the smell of fried chicken in his room, Arnold lay in sleepless confusion, which lasted beyond three. Because he was three years older than most of the other students and had only been there half a term—by temperament Arnold had always been isolated—he had no one at school he wanted to talk to: certainly not the other two students on the first floor who shared Mr. Hitchinson's Negro rooming house. Besides, they'd never struck Arnold as serious.

What, the previous day, had occasionally invaded his mind as absurd possibility now fixed itself as absolute necessity. He *must* talk to Aunt Bea, though for all its imperative thrust, it seemed no more possible than it had last night. Suppose she figured out about his . . . disease? He could imagine her dying on the spot, from misery and shame. Finally, after endless imaginary dialogues, he reached a conclusion: I'll *say* it's a woman! Indeed, at three-eighteen that second morning, twenty-three-year-old Arnold Hawley was convinced he was the only human being who had ever fixed on this particular solution to his problem.

This was a long time ago.

The next morning Arnold overslept Dr. Cohen's eight-o'clock Renaissance History course, got up, and wandered around Boston most of the morning. At ten, he walked by Miss Merelda's and, through the screening on the gray-framed door, read on the oak-tag sign behind the sagging metal mesh: *Open at 11:00 A.M.* Because he knew his people, Arnold didn't come back till five past noon.

Inside, sweat drops along the edge of her rough hair, Miss Merelda stood behind the register, the open drawer pressed into the belly of her flowered print, while she shuffled a handful of produce bills, holding them far down to the side, below the counter's back edge, to read them with glasses she had not had changed in twenty years.

"Miss Merelda." Arnold walked up to the counter and leaned a forearm there.

Behind her, the deep fryer was a chattering Charybdis.

"Your new delivery boy is very nice. Really, he's awfully pleasant—"

Miss Merelda put one bill behind another. "That boy's *nuts*"—she reiterated Sam's pronouncement from last evening—"is what he is. I had to let him go 'fore the night was over. See"—through her wire-framed hexagonal lenses she looked up at Arnold—"he was messin' up the money. I can't have nobody messin' up my money."

"Well, actually"—Arnold rubbed at an ear—"that's one reason I came in. We got to talking, him and me, and when he went I realized I'd . . . well, I never paid him. I just forgot. It wasn't his fault. But I must owe you . . . a dollar-five for the chicken and sweet potatoes I got that night. And a ginger ale. I don't know why I didn't give it to Sam yesterday. But I think it's a dollar-five—that's what it is, isn't it?"

"That's right responsible of you—but it's all right." Miss Merelda went on shuffling pink and yellow receipts. "If it had only been you, now, that'd be one thing. But he didn't get my money from half his customers." Again she looked at Arnold. "I know you young people at the colleges don't got a lot of cash—not like some of these white boys. But collectin' his money, makin' his change, that's his *job!* You see, the boy's retarded. I just took him on as a favor to Joey. You remember Joey—? Or maybe Joey'd

already left by the time you started coming in here—the one takin'
pictures all the time? Now Joey was a *real* responsible boy—I
mean, I never had no problems with Joey. Everybody told me I
was crazy, hirin' a white boy to deliver to coloreds. But I never
had no problems with him. He was on time. He didn't make mistakes. Everybody liked him—me, too. And he took some nice pictures. Though, yes, I'm a little mad at him this morning, for
bringin' in a boy to work here he should'a known couldn't'a done
the job. But, you see, Joey was polite. And he worked his butt
off—excuse my French. So when he come back here last week,
askin' about a job for his friend, I wanted to oblige him. Such a
big, strong, good-lookin' boy, too. Joey felt sorry for him and, I
guess, so did I." Miss Merelda shook her head. "So I said he could
come in the next evening and work. Was *that* ever a mistake!"

"Miss Merelda, do you know where he lives? Bo'muh—that
was his name . . . ?"

"Bowman," she said. "Slake Bowman—that's what Joey said
his name was."

"I mean, I feel I'd like to . . . well, at least apologize. To tell
him I'm sorry. I mean, *part* of it was my fault."

"It weren't yo' fault, sweetheart." Miss Merelda looked up
sharply. "The boy's crazy-retarded. That's all. He should be in a
hospital, somewhere. It ain't like he's just slow or somethin'—he's
retarded. He can't take care of hisself. If he can't take care of hisself, you got to put him in a hospital. The boy ain't competent."

"Do you know where he lives?" Arnold insisted. "*Please* . . ."

"I think Joey's got him stayin' with him—'cause Joey's a
good, kind boy. He cares about people."

"Where does Joey live, then?"

"Paradise Hill, over where it crosses Eighteenth. Least, that's where he used to live. Joey was away a while, but he ain't moved. Seventeen Paradise Hill. But you don't have to go over there—"

Arnold was already out the screen door.

Arnold didn't go to Paradise Hill that day. He walked around some more. And when it started to rain, he rushed home, toweled himself off, and sat moodily at his desk, or sat on the edge of his bed, or walked out into the hall, or wandered up into the attic and looked at the old mattresses and left-behind trunks. About nine o'clock that night, when the lines would be clear, Arnold went into the hall and, at the black pay phone, put in a nickel to get the long-distance operator to put in the call to Aunt Bea in Cleveland, where she'd been living permanently a year now. Then, with the earpiece to his ear and one hand around the mouthpiece, he stood listening to it ring, till Bea answered: "Hello . . .?"

"I have a collect call, person to person, for Beatrice C. Hawley, in Cleveland, from Arnold Hawley, in Boston. Will you accept the charges?"

"Yes, ma'am. Thank you so much."

"You're welcome," the operator said, and his nickel tinkled back into the cup.

Then Bea repeated: "Hello?"

"Aunt Bea—hi, there!" He forefingered out the nickel to put it back in his pocket. "It's Arnold."

"Hi, sweetheart. How's everything at school?"

Which is to say, their conversation took off on the reassuring trajectory it had assumed once every two weeks, first from

Pittsfield, then from Ohio, since Arnold had gone away to school. Only a bit more jerkily than usual, at least on Arnold's side, it continued on that trajectory, till, at once, Arnold asked:

"Aunt Bea, do you know anything about sex?"

"Arnold—what a question to ask *me!* Do I know about *sex?* I know it makes a whole lot of otherwise intelligent men and woman act like perfect fools!"

"I called you 'cause I had to talk to *somebody*, Bea!"

"Now, if you're about to tell me, there at college, that you got some little girl in the family way, though I'll always love you, honey, you gotta know that as soon I put this phone down, I'm gonna cry my eyes out, to see you throwin' away your whole life and education like this, after you've worked so hard to—"

"No, Aunt Bea. No! It isn't *that*—"

"You sure? Well, at least that's somethin'!" Then, tentatively, Bea asked, "What is it, then?"

"It's just, Bea—but . . . well, what does it mean when you feel this funny way about something—some*one*—someone you don't even know." Arnold was both surprised and relieved that as far as the sex of his obsession, Bea was doing the work for him. "And you can't get them out of your mind. And you're all upset about everything, and you can't do anything you're supposed to be doing right. That's gotta be bad. I mean, unless you're doing it with the right . . . *person*—the right woman, when you're married, to make children, that's *gotta* be bad, isn't it?"

"Well, I don't know if I'd go *that* far, honey. 'Cause then there'd be an awful lot of bad people in the world—probably most of 'em."

"You never did it with anyone, did you, Bea?"

"Arnold, what are you talkin' about—'*course* I never did it! I'm not a married woman! How could *I* do somethin' with somebody? I don't have a husband. Besides, between my teaching work at the high school and raisin' you, sweetheart, I had plenty to do without getting myself involved with no fella and all *that* craziness."

"And you never *wanted* to do it, either . . .?"

At the other end of the phone, there was a long pause. "Well, now, that's a little different. There might have been a couple of times, when I was younger, when one or another crazy idea got in my head. Still, an idea is just that—an idea. Everything you think about, though, you don't necessarily have to *do*."

"You never were just . . . *curious*, maybe? What it would be like? How'd you keep from wondering?"

"Like I said, wondering—thinking—isn't the same as doing." Then, on the other end of the phone, Bea chuckled. "Me, to be perfectly honest, I always figured it was like peach ice cream."

Arnold said, "*Huh* . . .?"

"Yes. Peach ice cream." Bea chuckled again. "You've had peach ice cream."

"Sure."

"Where'd you have it?"

"You know, Bea. At Anita's. You can't get it from Breyers or Sealtest. That's the kind somebody has to make at home."

"Right. And peach ice cream is pretty good, isn't it? You know how Anita makes it in her freezer, there—how you used to always want to turn the crank and put the rock salt in the wooden holder with the ice around the metal freezer barrel, and then you could only turn it nine or ten times 'cause you'd get tired—so I'd have to crank it for you."

"Oh, yeah! I remember—"

"That was when you were five or six. And it was some *good* ice cream, too. I could see somebody, in the right mood, get on a bus and travel halfway across the country for a taste of that ice cream."

"I think that's why I came out to Appleton for Easter—"

"That's what you told me. And it *was* real good, with that pound cake Anita makes. Probably it's one of the best things in the world. But you know, a whole lot of people never *had* peach ice cream, honey. I mean, not the way Anita makes it, with Grandma Logan's own recipe for her jarred peaches. But, then, see, if you *never* had it, you wouldn't miss it. I always figured it was more or less the same way with . . . well, that kind of love. Since I never tried it, I don't figure I'm really lacking anything. Me, I always thought the Catholics had the right idea—at least about that. Now, your aunt has always been a good, chaste woman. Don't let anybody ever tell you different about me. I never understood why men couldn't be the same way. Perhaps some of the very good ones can. But I think you're more likely to keep a clear head about all that stuff if you—well, maintain some objectivity. You have to think of it as a wonderful flavor ice cream you never had and so you don't really want it—at least you don't have to want it if you know it's not good for you. But you get all messed up in it yourself, and, believe me, you won't know which end is up."

"That's sounds awfully intelligent, Bea. You're a smart person. . . ."

They talked for another fifteen minutes. On the tarpaper roof over the board ceiling covering the front half of the two-story rooming house, the rain chattered like Miss Merelda's deep-fat fryer. While they talked, Arnold wondered sometimes if what his aunt was saying *did* relate to what he felt. At other times—when the comfort of her words quieted his feelings—Arnold wondered if his own behavior weren't the essence of sexual and poetic madness, the beginning of the insanity that must claim him. But by the time they'd finished, he could say, sincerely: "Hey, Bea—thanks *so* much! I feel a lot better—a *whole* lot better! Good-night."

"Well, that's what I'm here for, honey. I *hope* you're feelin' a little better. When I first heard you on the phone, there, I knew you were hurtin' about somethin'. I don't know if I said anything useful, but you *sound* a little better. And that makes me feel better *for* you. Oh—and by the way: you know now, there *is* such a thing as birth control. I said I thought the Catholics were right about *some* things? But I *sure* don't think they're right about *that* one! And I don't see how anybody who lived among colored folks and seen what happens to all those babies can help but agree with me—"

"Oh, *Bea*—!"

"Don't 'Oh, Bea!' me, honey! I'm talkin' sense to you! So if there's a little girl *you* got to talk some sense to, you *do* it, hear me? Don't let yourself get all shy, so you end up in a nasty pickle. If you got to say something to her, you *say* it! But I know you'll do the right thing, 'cause that's how you were raised."

They said good-bye again, good-night again, and—as they

had done twice a month, all-but-forever—hung up. (At his three different colleges so far—Boston University, Brown, and now BU again—Arnold had taken four years to reach his first term as a junior.) He chuckled at the preposterous thought of himself and a girl; though just *how* preposterous that was was something he could never let Bea know.

The next morning, Saturday, it rained—and thundered, as Arnold woke. The door to the closet in the corner of Arnold's room was thick oak, with carved paneling, notably more solid than the gray plywood walls on either side.

Mr. Hitchinson had painted the oak door green.

It broke Arnold's heart, and in his first week at the place he had talked about it with Bea. Would there be any way to take the paint off and restore it to its original grained splendor? But Mr. Hitchinson, who wore a beret like a Frenchman (though he was a tobacco-colored man from the Caribbean), said that years ago some children had drawn pictures all over it with ink that had seeped into the wood and *wasn't* going to come out, though he'd tried sanding it down—which is why he'd given up and painted it. Some things were ruined, and you had to let them go, which was how, actually, Arnold had always thought about his own sexuality.

When the two students from down on the first floor finished closing medicine cabinet doors and sliding metal rings along the shower curtain rod in the communal bathroom at the hall's end on the second, and the slap of their slippers moved off down the stairs, at eleven Arnold got his toothbrush from the desk drawer where it was wrapped in a paper napkin and went in to brush his teeth, shower, towel off, and put on his underwear. Then he came back to his room, put his toothbrush back in the drawer (the other students left theirs in glasses on the bathroom shelf, which Arnold was not yet brave enough for), and opened his closet. Behind the door his upright army-surplus steamer held half his clothes, still folded on the trunk's cross-shelves. Beside the trunk was his umbrella—Aunt Bea's umbrella, which he'd begged to be allowed to take with him to school.

"That's a *woman's*, honey," Bea had explained. "Why don't you let me get you a nice, dark-colored *man's* umbrella."

"Oh, come on, Bea," he'd said. "I've *always* used this one. Maroon's a dark color. You don't ever use it. Let me have it."

So the deep maroon umbrella, ringed with immense scarlet blossoms, had gone with him, first to Boston, then to Providence, and—now—back to Boston. From a distance, Arnold knew, it looked like a big, brown, family thing, with *something* around its edge. Only when you got closer did the bright flowers bloom into recognizability.

They *were* beautiful.

•◆•

Standing under it, Arnold looked up between the metal spokes holding the cloth wide, to see through its fabric a frizzy blot of light.

From the scalloped rim, rain curtained off the edge onto the broken pavement, as Arnold walked the tree-lined Roxbury streets. When wind jogged the umbrella in his hand, the droplet curtain in front of him shook before the rainy porches and velvety tree trunks, while, now and again, water-weighted leaves brushed the cloth, which, under their glittering spillage, was the color of old blood.

In the Saturday-morning torrent, Arnold had been walking for forty minutes, mostly moving toward Paradise Hill. Could someone like Slake Bowman, Arnold wondered—perhaps because he *was* retarded—glimpse that overturned bowl of stretched cloth with its rim of scarlet azaleas, and see how beautiful it was, how rich, how fecund, how productive of dreams, when you walked under it in the rain?

On the sloped sidewalk, great pavement pieces were gone. Mud and grass spread the gaps. Water rushed by and around Arnold's shoes.

When the rain stopped, Arnold swung his umbrella down, to see he was walking on a street of small houses. Two women hurrying and clutching shopping bags, and a father gripping his son's hand, announced what the rain had kept largely invisible, despite what the houses' condition and the window boxes of tatty geraniums and broken begonias suggested and Arnold had basically surmised: Paradise Hill was a colored street. With the tug of a breeze, a few drops blew against Arnold's wrist. He turned with the umbrella, and—as he slid the catch down the handle's ivory-inlaid stick to close it—up on a lamppost he saw the metal holder, and, beneath the white glass bulb, the blue sign within its frame with white letters:

PARADISE HILL

On the door of its screened-in porch, the next house said 33. 17 could be no more than a block or two off.

Tapping the umbrella's ferule on the wet cement beside him, Arnold walked up the slope, while down beside brown porch newels metal drainpipes poured water onto the leafy ground.

The last numbered house was 21.

Then, beyond a cross-street, only a suggestion of a sidewalk ran on.

A quarter of the next block was vacant. (If it *was* a city block.) Within it, as in a swamp, he saw, behind long weedy growths, wide pools.

Two other houses sat askew from where his sense of the street told him houses should stand. The larger was four floors, ornate, parapetted and bay-windowed. Thirty yards away, the smaller could have been a two-story carriage house, or some other outbuilding for the larger, though a graveled driveway ran between them.

Was that the street?

Along its pebbly length, here and there, it became dim steel, under recent water.

Arnold did not follow the gravel because on the other side of the smaller house was a front porch—this one large—with columns holding up its slanted roof over the verandah-wide plat-form. Several tree trunks rose beside it, to leafy branches full of spring green.

Down the other way ran the pavement bits, through tall grass and taller saplings. A rustling roar filled the leaves, and droplets hit Arnold's face and hands. Deciding it had started to rain again, once more Arnold lifted Bea's umbrella. Before he could open it, the leaves above the house dipped, rose, dipped again, and rained water upon its half-opened furls, as if some titanic sponge had been rung out above him.

As Arnold realized that it was only the water already collected in the leaves, water cascaded down on all sides of the porch, two, three, four seconds, hiding rails and newels in silver.

At the same time someone stepped—beyond the falling drops—up on the porch by side stairs Arnold couldn't see, who, as the water ran away and became only drippings here and there, was . . . yes, gigantic Slake!

Umbrella half open over his head, Arnold felt as if something had struck him in the chest. He swayed above the leaves and stones he stood on. Because he could not have moved backward, with banging heart Arnold staggered three steps forward, closer to the porch's broad stairs.

Up on the boards, Bowman was barefoot. His plaid shirt hung completely open down his chest and practically off one shoulder. Looking at Arnold, he smiled.

Arnold—who'd thought he'd remembered every pore in Slake's flesh—had forgotten the missing tooth. Arnold said, "*Uh* . . ."

Slake Bowman said, "'Lo, deah. You come see me? Hey, now." Then, with a gesture of his mallet of a fist, a nod of his head, and basso seriousness, he added, "Da's purdy." The hand dropped to the raveled jeans and, between his legs, began to rub, again. "You come t'do sum'pin' wiff me?"

If Arnold could have turned and run, he would have. But what he felt, he would decide later, was a species of joy as immobilizing as death.

Someone opened the door at the back of the porch and called

out. "Hey, Slake—come on in. You don't got no *shoes* on, now! You're gonna catch your death." The *a*'s had the flat elongation of the Boston Irish. The man who stepped out onto the porch boards—a white man—in a white T-shirt with a gold cross at the neck was a thick-legged Italian. In his late twenties or early thirties, he had a belly, though his arms were nearly as massive as Slake's. (Were they weight lifters . . .?) His jeans were shoved into the top of his engineer's boots. The boots had buckles on their sides. "What you standin' out there for?" he asked, jocularly. (His "What" was more like a "Whaaaht." The "th" at the head of his "there" could have been written with a *d* as easily as Slake's.) "Come on, stop playin' with yourself, and get in here!" He looked over and, now, saw Arnold. "Hey, don't mind Samson, here." He stood up a little straighter. "He's kinda slow and don't know what he's doin' a lot of times." He turned back to Slake, taller than Arnold by a head and a half. "Come *on*, now, Slake! Cut it out!"

With his astonishing smile, the Negro said in a rumble as low as wind in leaves, "He mah fr'en'. He come to see me do sumpin'."

The white man, whose black hair clutched down over his ears and the back of his neck (men just didn't *wear* their hair that long; it looked a little crazy) glanced again at Arnold. "You're a friend of Slake's?"

"*Um* . . ." Arnold said, "Uh," and then, "*Yes* . . ." A sound, practically a sob, propelled the syllable.

"Hey, I'm sorry! Well, come on in, then! Come on. Get out of the wet!"

Arnold took another staggering step over the rocks and

leaves toward the stairs. As he climbed, the white man said, "That's quite an umbrella!"

"Thank you," Arnold said, and coughed, coming under the porch roof.

Barefooted Slake drawled again, " 'S purdy."

Waiting at the door, the man had his hand out to shake, thick, callused, the knuckles rough, the fingers soiled. When Arnold hesitated half a second, he seized Arnold's hand and pumped it. "Hey. I'm Joey Salieri. I look out for Samson, here. He's stayin' with me—we're *real* good friends, Slake and me. I brought him up from Alabama, when I was down there this summer—'cause his damned folks didn't want 'im. I don't mind takin' care of 'im, 'cause he's a really good boy. He helps me out a lot. But a lot of times, he goes out and meets people all on his own and brings 'em back. That's fine with me—I don't care. We mess around, but we're not exclusive or nothin'. There's a room in the back you two can fuck around in, if you want. I won't be in your way." He stood there, still pumping, not releasing Arnold's hand but gripping it tighter.

"Um," Arnold said, "should I put this"—he gestured with the half-closed umbrella—"out here on the porch?"

"Naw," Joey said, "bring it on in. Slake likes it."

"Oh!" Arnold looked up, to see that Slake himself was standing beside him, inches away. Then Slake leaned forward so that his entire body was against Arnold's side, thigh to shoulder.

"Come on," Joey said. "Back off, Samson. You're gonna scare your friend to death, here!" Still holding Arnold's fingers, Joey pulled Arnold through the door.

Inside smelled funny—like paint and gasoline and something else. On the mantle over the fireplace stood three large extinguished candles. One whitish one was at least six inches thick and ten inches tall. In the three-quarter dark, all around the floor, rectangles leaned against the walls, many overlapping. From the glistening here or there among them, many seemed to be glass covered—paintings or pictures, Arnold realized, though it was too dim to make them out.

Near one heavily draped window stood a high bench with some kind of headrest on it, and, on a rack beside it, half a dozen bar bells. On the wooden floor beside it, a dozen circular weights overlapped. (So they *were* bodybuilders.) Across the room stood two dilapidated armchairs. A large crucifix hung on the wall, palm fronds folded behind it.

The walls were paneled. No lights were on.

Because Joey had still not released him, Arnold only now realized that Slake's hand had also dropped to his shoulder. As the three of them walked across the room, Bowman was rhythmically squeezing.

—which was suddenly frightening.

Joey was saying, "You gotta give your friend a chance to relax and settle down, now, Slake." In the dim room, he smiled at Arnold. "You wanna sit? We don't got no electricity. But we have a coal stove goin' in the kitchen. I can make you some boiled java, if you want." (His *java* had flattened into a term unique to Boston.)

"Oh, no," Arnold said, looking around for a place to leave a wet umbrella. There was no stand or rug, even by the door. He bent a little, to lay it on the hardwood. Only then did Salieri's hand come loose. "Is it okay to put it here . . .?" Arnold's palm tingled. "Maybe I should take it back outside on the porch—"

"Da's real nice," Slake said.

"You can drop it anywhere. Hey, I'm sorry we don't got no electric right through here. But they turned it off last week."

As they walked across the room, Slake said, "I jus' seen the 'lectric man—out back."

"You did? The fuckin' scumbag *bastard!*" (As was *java*, so was *bastard*.)

Arnold flinched. He had met college students (white) who used such promiscuous profanity, but not with a complete stranger, just entering your home.

Slake said, "Ah did sumpin' wiff 'im."

"What—?" Joey stopped and looked across at Slake with total incredulousness. "You did? Well, where the *fuck* did you do it?"

Slake's black face settled into a mocking grin. "Out back."

"Jesus, Slake! I *told* you about that! You can't *do* that shit out in the middle of the goddam backyard! Somebody might see you, and you're gonna get in trouble! This is the big city. This ain't the Alabama woods. We got our bedroom for fuckin' around. That's why you bring 'em back in here."

Through the smile, Slake said, "Ain't nobody seed us. 'Sides, he cum but I din't—see," and again Slake reached over and squeezed Arnold's shoulder, "I save' dat fo' you."

"I guess you figured it out," Joey said, in only somewhat frustrated explanation. "Slake likes 'em big, soft, and brown—like you, there." He winked at Arnold. "Me, I like 'em big, black, and hard—like ol' Samson, here. At least I used to. . . . But since Slake and me been roommates together, I'm slippin' to the brown and soft side, myself. That's some funny shit, how what you like can move around that way and get you all influenced. But I guess that's what they call love. Hey"—he pointed toward a door—"in there's the house fuckroom—you know, the bedroom, I mean. You guys can go in there, whenever you want. And I got my dark-room in *there*—" he pointed to another door. "Hey, lemme show you this—" Bewildered, Arnold followed him across the floor to enter an even darker space, Slake behind them both.

Through some drapes at a tall window, the black shade had been raised to show a splattered pane. (*Had* it started raining again?) A circular ring handle hung from the cord's bottom. Out-side, trickling droplets distorted leaves and branches.

That chemical odor was stronger in here, resolving into the slightly rotten and vinegary smell of photographic hypo. Arnold recognized it from the two weeks he'd spent in his high school photography club.

In the room's middle was a large table. Something dark and mechanical towered in its center.

"Got this baby just after we came up from Alabama—Slake and me. It's rebuilt—but it's a beaut. Cost me twelve goddam dollars."

Arnold said, "What is . . .?"

Joey said, "An enlarger. An Eastman—not the best. But it does the job." Both from the top and halfway up its four-foot height, as Arnold's eyes began to adjust, he made out rods thrusting from the sides, four and six inches. The bottom half looked like a square bellows.

Again squeezing Arnold's shoulder, Slake said, "Joey makes some *nice* pitchurs."

On a table under the window stood three white enamel trays. Before the rain-streaked pane, he could see their rolled red rims. Across the middle of the room hung what looked like four clotheslines, with a dozen or more clothespins along them. Absently, Joey was saying, "Samson brings a lot of college kids back here—is that where you're from? One of the schools?"

As he nodded, Arnold saw that from one line hung a curled sheet of paper. Another line across the room just above head height, Arnold realized, was an electrical cord. Slightly irregular, it lacked the others' smooth curves.

Joey said, "Slake likes the pictures of hisself, best—the nastier, the better. In fact I think those are the *only* ones the big fellow's really interested in. I love to take 'em, too. I could take some of you, if you wanted. Just regular portrait work, I mean."

"Oh," Arnold said. "Thank you. That would be . . ." and realized he wasn't sure if the offer were gratis.

Then the lights came on.

In a ceiling fixture missing two bulbs, a single one, unfrosted, flared, its filament a white hole twisted into the day. Sitting on the table, a lamp without a shade but with a red bulb did *not* go on—though at least Arnold could see it.

He hadn't, before.

The enlarger itself had also gone on, shining a beam of light up from the top onto the ceiling and another down from the bottom, onto an enameled plate banded with metal.

Joey said, "Oh, Jesus . . ." Leaning over the table, he flipped a switch on the black faceplate of the box near its base. "I forgot that was still on." The enlarger's lights went out.

At the same time, in another room, a refrigerator turned over, halted, turned over again, then hummed.

Stepping back, Joey rubbed the back of his head.

Now that Joey had moved away, Slake moved closer to Arnold and slid his immense arm around Arnold's wet sports jacket shoulder. "He say he wa' go'n' come back and turn 'em on."

"Put the *lights* back on?" Joey exclaimed. "Even though we hadn't paid the bill?" Grinning, he shook his head. (Joey was missing both front incisors, Arnold saw now, which added an air of derangement. Suddenly his oversized muscles and over-long hair looked weird.) "Come on, Slake! What the fuck *did* you do to him?"

Slake's free hand was, Arnold realized, again rubbing at the fork between his own legs. "Ah stood back there, doin' wiff myself like Ah do an' I tol' 'im I thought sumpin' was wrong wiff' mah dick, an' would he look at it t'see if he could figure out wha' it was."

Joey broke out laughing. "Slake! You are the *only* person I know what could get away with that!"

Slake drawled, "Da's 'cause they think Ah'm stupid. He went and played wiff it and then he sucked on it—and I held his head and kinda pump' in 'im a li'l, and then he said he' put the lights back on for me, but I shou'n't tell nobody."

Arnold looked over at the black angular face. He'd started to feel dizzy.

Slake shook Arnold's shoulder. "But don' worry. I din' cum

none. I tol' 'im I was savin' that for my frien' what was comin' to see me." Again he smiled at Arnold.

"Slake," Joey exclaimed, "you are a lyin' sack of shit!" He laughed again. "If he put the lights back on, you know damned well you gave that man a load! But don't you worry," which was to Arnold. "Slake's got enough for you and the electric man and the milkman and the iceman and me and the grocery boy and probably two or three more besides!"

Arnold listened in a haze of mortal fascination and horror.

"Well," Slake said, "yeah—I cum a *little* bit wiff 'im. But jus' a li'l. An' I can do it a lotta time'. An' when Ah do, I squirt a whole lot, too." He leaned toward Arnold. "Ya wanna see?"

"Like half a damn milk can." Joey rubbed one hand on his jeans hip. "Well, now you seen where I do my work. Hey, thanks, Samson—for gettin' the lights workin' again. Maybe while you guys are fuckin' around, I can get some work done, now we got some juice. Come on." Joey led them back to the door into the living room.

A tingling in Arnold's face blurred his vision. Was this what criminals in the electric chair experienced the instant between the thrown switch and death . . .?

The awkward step through the doorway, with Slake's arm still around his shoulder, revealed the living room was also lighted. Arnold's insides felt like clear water.

"Why don't you guys go into the fuckroom—excuse me." Joey grinned. "I mean the bedroom, there"—In both a floor lamp by the armchairs and in a ceiling fixture, lights were on— "and have yourself some fun. I'll look in after a while. The sheets aren't the freshest, but basically nobody sleeps on 'em but Slake and me. Well, somehow he manages to drag *someone* home here with him about every third night. I'm glad we both like threesomes. Like I said, I guess that's love. And you probably figured it out, I really *do* love this black bastard." Joey cast a grin over at Slake. "That's why I stole him away from his fuckin' crazy Alabama family—you know his father lives with two wives and has children by both of them *and* one by one of Slake's sisters—"

"An' Ah got one, too," Slake declared.

"Yeah, yeah," Joey said. "We know all about *that* crazy woman. She's eight years older than Samson and tried to poison him three times—and stabbed him, so that he ended up in the hospital, when she caught him with some boys." He looked at Slake. "It ain't that you like her or was married to her." Again he looked at Arnold. "That's why I brought him up here with me—before somebody killed him down there. See, he don't understand the ordinary boundaries, like you and me. Anyway, if we could just find some work Slake could do, we'd have it hunky-dory."

"Down home when I was hitchhikin', guys used to gimme money for fuckin' 'em up deh behinds—white guys, too."

"Yeah." Joey shook his head. "But I don't like you doin' that stuff. You said you didn't like it, either. Besides, down there, you knew 'em all already. They was all friends of yours. It ain't the same as up here, Slake." He took in a breath that was all frustration and looked at Arnold. "So if you get any ideas—for jobs, I mean—I hope you come back and tell us. Hey—who knows? Maybe I'll come in after an hour or so and take some pictures of *you* guys—that always tickles Samson. I mean, if you don't mind. I never take any picture if you don't want me to."

As he stood beside Arnold, holding him around the shoulder and rubbing at his own crotch, Slake Bowman said, "Ya' wanna look at my dick? And maybe play wiff it some, like d'electric man—an' see if there's somethin' wrong wiff it? Ah' let ya' suck on it. An' Ah'll do stuff wiff ya', too. 'Cause I really like—"

Which is when—in the light—Arnold looked at the sixty or seventy framed photographs, some prints as big as seventeen or twenty-four inches, leaning along the room's baseboard.

Slake Bowman was in more than half—in all but two, he was naked. In one, he wore only a sleeveless undershirt. In them all were other men, also naked. All were flagrantly entwined in las-civious and—for the moment Arnold looked—incomprehensible acts: white men, colored men, and one who, just to the right of the fireplace, at once and with a surge of terror, Arnold saw was Old Chinese Sam!

Though otherwise naked, Sam wore his knitted cap.

Some were younger, some—like Sam—were older. Two photographs—Arnold only saw now—showed Slake embracing women, their breasts clearly visible. One was young, white, blonde, and curly haired. The other was older and colored. On the black-and-white print, her heavy mouth glistened darkly with lipstick. Across them all, bedsheets and pillows and blankets rip-pled and folded and coiled, here hiding a foot, there an elbow, in one a shoulder, in another an entire arm.

All that had occurred around Arnold had happened with preternatural clarity. But he retained only a third of what the

two men had said. It lay outside any conversation he'd encoun-
tered before, a kind of rhetorical confusion, overturned, splattered
about. Arnold felt colder and colder, tenser and tenser. His
mind moved faster and faster, leaping to understand what was
going on in this terrible house at the side of its half-existent
street. Arnold's mind vaulted further and further to find something among his own experiences, learned or lived, that would
make sense of what was happening in this building whose very
foundations were diseased images, most of which Arnold could
not even identify, however much things near them had trou-
bled his dreams or musings, even as he kept returning to what
was before him—

"You . . .!" Swallowing, Arnold jerked from Slake's encircling
arm. "You're . . . blackmailers!"

Joey Salieri frowned. "Huh?"

"You . . . you're a vice ring! You get . . . women and—people.
And lure men in here, and—and you take photographs of them!"
That, Arnold was sure, must be how, *basically*, it worked. "And
you *blackmail* them!"

"Me?" Salieri returned a bewildered grin. "You mean *me* . . . ?"
He pulled back. "Aw, come *on*—!"

That Arnold's own condition had allowed him to recognize
those images, however secondary a part they played in the danger
here, meant Bowman and Salieri were somehow even low enough
to take advantage of *that*. . . .

"No!" Arnold declared, backing away. "I have to get out of
here! This place is *dangerous!*" Somehow the whole of the living
room had gotten between them.

"Oh, hey," Salieri called across the floor, "that's *crazy!* Why would I have everything out here if—"

"You're *blackmailers!*" At the door, Arnold turned and, staring at the small drape hanging across the little window at the top, managed to open it. "Yes. You're a . . . a *vice* ring—aren't you!" Arnold ran out on the porch.

Rain poured as Arnold went crab-wise down the warped boards. He had started to shake again—the way he had the first night Slake Bowman had come into his room. In the downpour, his teeth chattered. And sometimes, as he walked, he cried from fear. Three blocks away he realized he'd left Aunt Bea's umbrella in that terrible place.

Still, returning for it, Arnold knew as he trudged through the water rushing the sloped sidewalk around him and the water cascading from the trees above, would be insane!

•—•

The psychological dismantling and rendering inactive of a passion such as Arnold's is one of the most painful things the self can undergo. Only poets and a few saints can accomplish it with any ease, because it entails a revision in one's conception of paradise as well as any entitlement the self may have to it. That Arnold was able to finish the fundamental business over the next week (three more days of missed classes spent largely in his room, followed by the weekend) is, therefore, astonishing. In that period, he returned to stand across from the corner and look at the house on Paradise Hill only three times—the first at five-thirty the following morning, as the sun bubbled like molten copper at the horizon to make the April waters ice bright between the saplings and the long growth beyond the porch; the second at all-but-pitch black two in the morning, four days on, while one window, in what was certainly the living room, leaked yellow light around and between the drapes, till, after he'd stood there, watching in the dark for forty minutes, it went out.

Neither time did he see anyone enter or leave.

The third and last time, Arnold came to stand there a mere three minutes on Sunday afternoon, when, under the full branches, the gray-green siding was drying. It had rained once more, earlier. Patches on both walls and pavement were still wet, crossed by dry ribbons under the silver sky.

Arnold was still too frightened to walk up the porch steps, knock, and ask for Bea's umbrella—which was what he had come for.

For a while, though, he considered going to the authorities. ("They stole my umbrella—! My *aunt's* umbrella . . .") But Arnold had no idea of the ring's extent, or what vengeance its other members might inflict—for all he knew, their tentacles spread across *all* the New England states—not to mention how he might explain the way he himself had come to know so much about their operations.

Besides, he would sound like a fool.

Because his firsthand experience of sex had convinced him of Aunt Bea's rightness—that what you had never partaken of, you could not really miss (an ethical conviction that, even when, a decade later, for the company, Arnold began to go to gay bars with a few witty black male friends, he never really revised)—

twenty-three-year-old Arnold Hawley returned to school and threw himself far more seriously into both his studies and his poetry.

•—•

Arnold Hawley had considered himself a poet since, at thirteen and fourteen, he'd read the translations of Villon, Radiguet, and Rimbaud that Aunt Bea had on her shelves between the Edna Ferber and the James Michener; and shortly tried to do his own.

(Arnold's Pittsfield elementary school was one of many at the time experimenting with the early teaching of languages—in Arnold's case, Latin and French. The displacement of this onto Russian in college was just perversity: the cold war was raging.)

A year and a half after the Bowman/Salieri affair, that renewed energy yielded Arnold his own first single-author pub-lication—the chapbook, *Waters*, from the Back Bay student collective. It held those first fifteen deeply felt—and actually *published!*—poems. (By now he was twenty-six.) Yes, they were all Boston and Appleton—and precious little Pittsfield, where, with Aunt Bea, he'd actually been raised.

On the night of publication—it had been the day of Presi-dent Kennedy's funeral, and riders on the Boston busses were still muttering about the televised murder of that poor untried man in the Texas jail, though Arnold couldn't have cared less— singularly drunk he had staggered about on Commonwealth Avenue, shouting, "Keats is dead! Long live Arnold Hawley!" throwing his first copy high into the air . . . and usually missing it, when it came down.

A year to the day after *Waters* appeared, Arnold moved to New York City.

For two weeks he slept on a friend's couch in Brooklyn's Bed-Stuy, then finally managed to snag—it had come through Lamar, actually—his own apartment in New York's East Village: '68 was really the height of his friendship with Noel Crichet and Lamar Alford and Bobby . . . what *was* Bobby's last name? It was astonishing he couldn't remember it since he had gone on to write an entire book with the man! But '68 was an astonishing year, when everything in the country, including Arnold, had changed—and changed so much. That summer a small press called Old Stone accepted *Air Tangle*, his second book—well, his first *real* book—and put it out, at eighty-four pages, with three (glaring!) proof-reading errors, one in the first poem's second line.

The seventy-five dollars they'd paid him—expanded by ten borrowed from Bobby . . . *Horner*, of course! (How could he forget *that?* At the kitchen table, Arnold found a piece of paper and, with a ballpoint, wrote it down six times: Bobby Horner, Bobby Horner, Bobby Horner . . . Now, he knew, he'd remember it.) Yes, from Bobby Horner—had gone, despite the ravings of Edmund Wilson, for the Bollingen edition of Nabokov's translation of *Eugene Onegin* with notes, put out by Princeton University Press. Arnold had wanted it above all things since it had come out in '64. It was eighty dollars for the four volumes—twenty dollars per book! Certainly they were the most expensive books Arnold had ever owned. (He had his own Russian edition of the anomalously complete ten-chapter novel-in-sonnets, purchased secondhand, for thirty-six cents, up in Rhode Island.)

Nabokov's monograph on Pushkin's African grandfather, Abram Gannibal, was the first thing in it he read (and then reread; and reread once more) with open-mouthed delight at its precision and beauty. For a decade they were the most expensive things in his apartment. But how could you be a lover of both Russian and English and *not* have them?

In New York, the majority of Arnold's reading was not poetry—much less black poetry. Still, black poetry was an important minority current. Within easy walking distance, both the Tompkins Square branch of the public library and the Otten-dorfer branch, on Second Avenue just up from Saint Marks Place, had several books on Hart Crane, which Arnold read straight through, going from volume to volume, as they were listed on the frayed index cards in the card catalogue's dull wood drawers. Right after that, however, in the catalogue at the Otten-dorfer, three cards were devoted to a poet named Martell Crane, whose work Arnold read in the week immediately afterward. Sandwiched up on the balcony shelves, one was a pamphlet—a chapbook like Arnold's own *Waters*. In its maroon cardstock cover, it looked as if it came from the '30s, the '40s, or before—but lacked all date. Another Martell Crane book was a slim yellow hardcover, published by Turner Press in Raleigh, also sans date. (By now Arnold knew that usually meant pre-World War II.) The third was an even slimmer volume published by Congdon & Sons, of Arlington, Virginia, that bore an introductory paragraph by one Jessie B. Rittenhouse, dated 1922, which confirmed what Arnold had already suspected from some of the poems: ". . . one of the most accomplished and moving elder singers of his race . . ." wrote Rittenhouse. (Jessie Rittenhouse had an impressive bibliography. But though, up at the main reading room at Forty-second Street, he had looked at a dozen of *her* books, Arnold could find no other mention of Crane.) Martell Crane was black.

At least five of the Crane (Martell) poems had a clarity and hardness Arnold liked—but apparently he had never come to the attention of Locke, Cullen, Watkins, Bontemps, or any other broadly known black anthologist. Two more afternoons at the Forty-second Street Public Library and six hours uptown in Harlem on Columbus and 136th Street, at the dusty Schomburg Collection in the room off the Children's floor, upstairs at the Countee Cullen branch, had found no further mention of Martell. At Tompkins Square and Saint Marks, Arnold moved on in their catalogues to Stephen Crane, and was soon buried in the Beer, Stallman, Gilkes, Berryman, and Linsen biographies and memoirs.

•◆•

Arnold had read *Kalaidoscope*, Hayden's anthology of black poets, backward and forward, as, years before, he'd read *Caroling Dusk* and *The Negro Caravan*—because Aunt Bea had had copies on her shelves—and everything else there: *The Saracen Blade* and *Auto da Fé*, *Mandingo*, *The Recognitions*, *Raintree County*, *Forever Amber* and *The Ponder Heart*.

Hughes?

Generally Arnold found him a bore—though, now and

again, something would happen in Arnold's life, and a month or a year later he would be thumbing through some collected volume and realize Hughes had written about it. Even if he didn't have much of interest to say, Hughes had covered it—and that was interesting.

As a sixteen-year-old, he'd loved *Maud Martha*. Though he didn't read it till he was twenty, he adored *Annie Allan*. (By now he'd heard the story from Bobby Horner: "Who let the coon . . ." It still made him set his back teeth.) As a thirty-year-old, he had studied *In the Mecca*, trying to unravel the fine stitching in the all-but-invisible seam between the politics and the poetry—far finer, he felt, than in the poets who had inspired Brooks's conversion.

Well, poets in old age often needed younger poets to inspire them onward. The young Pound had galvanized the elder Yeats to his greatest work. Would some young poet eventually come along and, in the unimaginable future, do the same for Arnold Hawley? Now that was an interesting thought, but not one to ponder at any length since, if only because of his condition, he probably would not live that long.

•◆•

The third time Arnold went with Bobby and Lamar to the Stonewall over on Waverly Place, an incongruous black and Hispanic gay bar in the middle of the West Village, Arnold sat on a barstool between them. Two down from a tall black man with a shaved head and a red ostrich boa looped around his neck, who only smiled when anyone said hello, over his second beer in the bar's dim orange, Arnold mused: "When you consider that only one in five thousand men is queer, then you come to a place like this, the only thing you can assume is that every single one of them must have come to New York City and every single one of them must show up here on Wednesday night."

Bobby, who was looking away at the crowd, glanced back at Arnold. "One out of five *thousand?*"

Heavy Lamar leaned forward over the counter in his black turtleneck. "Who in the world told you *that*, darlin'?"

"Actually, dear heart," Arnold returned, "it was a *doctor*— so there!"

"One who never read Kinsey *or* Freud," Bobby said.

Just then the jukebox came on with the Four Season's "Walk Like a Man"—already half a dozen years old. In response five youngsters strutted onto the dance floor, the metal taps on their heels clacking, each diminutive backside sashaying ten inches to right, then left, with each staccato step. Half a dozen people squealed. Others laughed. Still others joined them, while the Seasons wailed in falsetto:

> *Walk like a man, talk like a man,*
> *Walk like a man, my so-o-on-oo!*

The fellows, mostly Hispanic, pranced about, one fist at the waist, the other, forefinger extended, like chastising Mrs. Palmer herself (Arnold thought, suddenly and surprisingly), shaken in denial toward anyone who smiled.

"Really," Arnold said. "It was a doctor. I'm not kidding—

when I was twelve. I asked him, in the hospital, when I was having my tonsils out—and I *do* think a doctor ought to know. Of course," Arnold allowed, "he also said Negroes couldn't be faggots."

"*Ha!*" Lamar declared. "Do you see a white face anywhere *in* here—other than Dago Joe, over there?"

"You mean that cute, *cute* butch number?" Bobby nodded toward the incongruous black-haired Italian, standing by the wall, in a white T-shirt, his denim jacket unbuttoned over it, and jeans, thumbs under his belt, one set of grease-soiled fingers clutching the neck of a Rheingold. "I just thought he was an Italian truck driver who'd delivered something, and was hanging around to laugh at the queens and have a beer."

"He *is* an Italian truck driver," Lamar said. "But he's here every night. His name is Joe Soley. He's from Fishtown, in north Philadelphia. He has the nicest uncut cock you *ever* saw—which he keeps very clean, by the bye. And while, yes, he *does* have a faint smell of gasoline about him—he does most of his own repair work—his ten-wheeler is parked on Greenwich Street. And he is the easiest pussy in the place!"

"Oh, he's *so* cute!" Arnold exclaimed, from within the music and laughter, which meant no one—certainly not Soley—could hear.

"He's so *butch*," Bobby added.

Arnold said, "You really know him?"

Bobby demanded, "You've actually *had* him?"

"Sho' 'nuff, honey-chile." Standing, Lamar leered along the bar. "And if you want him, *all* you've got to do is walk up to him, put your arms around him, and whisper in one or another of his cute little guinea ears, *I wanna fuck you* soooo *bad, white boy!* I promise you, in ten minutes, you're gonna be over by the river in the sleeper of that Dodge, the two of you, and he'll have his jeans around his ankles—the man wears *no* underpants at *all* (I'm speaking from experience, here)—and as long as you still got some spit to grease yourself, you can bang that dago butt till the *sun* comes up!"

But Bobby and Arnold had collapsed against one another, with their own squeals.

(The jukebox began the next song: "*From a Jack . . . to a Queen! From a Queen . . . to a wedding ring!*" which elicited more shrieks from that night's sixty or seventy patrons.) "But, you see," Bobby said, finally sitting back, "that's what I want *him* to do to *me!*"

"Well," Lamar said. "I wouldn't have minded trading places for a while, myself. But that's not Joe's thing. Maybe that one out of five thousand—what your doctor *meant* was that there're only one out of five thousand full-fledged, legitimate, and unrepentant tops. Now *that* I'll go along with. Still, playin' the man for the night has its rewards. But if you want him, that's *all* you gotta do."

"You make it sound so easy," Bobby said, his voice hovering on complaint. "But just suppose I did do what you said—and *he* said, 'Sorry! Get lost, faggot!' I would die"—Bobby's voice soared into its own falsetto—"*die* of embarrassment!"

Lamar spread his hands along the bar. "And that, my dear, is why it is *not* easy—and why it never *will* be easy. But remember: 'not easy' is *not* the same as 'impossible'!"

Arnold listened, feeling that all this, from the verbal exaggerations to the assumption of sisterly affection, was a vast pretense, which he was sure he would probably pull away from soon. It was fun, yes—but it lacked . . . something.

"Seriously," Arnold said. "What do you think it is? I mean, how many of us are there?"

Bobby drew a long breath and sat back up on his stool. Then, squarely, he looked at Arnold. "Would you believe one out of five?"

"Oh, come *on!*" Arnold dropped his shoulders and looked back with mock outrage. "That's impossible. Be *serious*, now!"

Bobby arched a brow on his teak forehead. (Arnold had always felt that Bobby was the best-looking of the three of them. Yet Lamar—even more overweight than Arnold—always seemed to have the most scandalous successes.) "You stop off at my place on your way home," Bobby retorted, with equally mock superiority, "and I'll show it to you in black and white, in my copy of *Sexual Behavior in the Human Male.*"

"You actually *own* that?" Arnold demanded. "Aren't you afraid somebody might find out?"

"I keep it right next to my copy of *Psychopathia Sexualis*," Bobby said. "It's a good way to scare them off from borrowing it."

"He's translated all the Latin parts into English in pencil in the margins," Lamar said, nodding. Then, in a voice he clearly wanted to sound as if he were quoting, he intoned: "'In the United States, one out of five men has had significant sexual relations with a member of the same sex.'"

"Oh, for God's sake!" Arnold said. "*I* haven't had significant sexual relations with a member of my own sex—yet!"

"You haven't come out," Lamar said. "When you do, darlin', we'll throw you a coming-out shindig that will knock people's socks off. The two of us like to keep a virgin around for luck."

"*I'm* not doing all that much better myself," Bobby said, ruefully.

"And *I'm* just this old whore who thinks you're both sweet." Again Lamar leered. "Hey, we'll rent this place here on some Tuesday night—put up balloons and streamers! Arnold Hawley Has at Last Done the Dirty Deed. Seriously, I'm not kidding about Dago Joe, there. If you want him, just take yourself over there and volunteer to pork him—you're just his type, Arnold. He told me, he likes 'em on the heavy side. He wants to feel some weight on him, he said, when he's sleepin'. Actually he's a sweetie—afterward, he took me back to his place on the East Side, over on B, and introduced me to his lover—"

"He's got a *lover?*" Bobby demanded.

"Yeah, another kid from Philadelphia. I forgot how many years he said they'd been together—seven, eight."

"Please," Bobby said. "*Don't* tell me that about him! I just want to go on imagining him returning home to Connie or Maria or Annette and their five snot-nosed brats on the far side of Queens—only maybe after the tenth beer or so, he'll let me do something . . . *nasty* to him, in the alley out back, when he's on the way to his truck."

"Actually," Lamar said, "he *was* married—when he was seventeen, back in Philly. There was even a kid. But that's what he left Fishtown to get away from. He's been living with a man since he was twenty-three. He's *thirty*-three now."

"He's adorable," Bobby said.

Arnold asked Lamar, "What—did you get his *entire* life story?"

"Pretty much," Lamar said. "He's just a *little* too much work for me. But other than that, he's rather sweet. So's his boyfriend. Really, if you want him, all you have to do is—"

"I'm sorry," Bobby said. "It all sounds *much* too complicated!"

Arnold asked, "It couldn't *really* be one out of five . . . could it?"

"Are we still on that? Well—you *know* it's got to be more than one out of five *thousand*, Arnold," Bobby said. "How many were there in your class?"

"Where I grew up, in Pittsfield," Arnold said, as the music stopped again, "our class was thirty-six—boys *and* girls . . . eighteen boys. And . . ." The specifics were something he had not thought about for a long, long while, if, indeed, he ever had. "I guess four of them were . . . well, *interested* enough to fool around together."

"Is that counting you?" Lamar wanted to know.

"Okay. Five—*if* you count me. But I just watched."

"So five out of eighteen, which is *more* than one out of four and *almost* one out of three!"

Arnold found himself terribly confused. "Is that . . . is that really supposed to count?" But the music had come on again. And, over by the wall, Joe had hooked the arm with which, in his hand, he held his beer bottle, around the shoulder of a very cute, very dark, very young-looking black kid.

The man two down stood up from his stool, turned, and dragged his boa and its reflection, both flamingo pink, from the polyurethaned counter.

Though not that night, eventually Arnold read a good deal of *Sexual Behavior in the Human Male.* He found it worrisome. Starting in 1948, the book had been a bestseller for more than a year—and, five years later, so had its companion, *Sexual Behavior in the Human Female.* Yet for all it contained, how little of that information had reached Pittsfield, where Arnold had spent those years!

One night, when he leaned the book against the lamp's bronze base and turned off the light on his bedside table, Arnold lay awake thinking: How . . . cruel! Even if it *is* the most debilitating of conditions (which, were it anywhere *near* as common as Dr. Kinsey said, made it seem unlikely): how cruel, to take us as children and impose such isolating loneliness. Tonight, Arnold thought, in Pittsfield and in Queens and in Appleton and in Fishtown and God-knows-where-else, children are awake, in bed, as I am now, pondering their approaching deaths from this . . . disease, in the midst of a loneliness sharp enough to clog their ears and scatter their eyes and cloy their throat with grave dust. And, as he had not in a while, Arnold began to cry. Why, why, why lie to them as I was lied to?

●◆●

Arnold was thirty-two when he received his first copy of *Air Tangle* from Old Stone Press on October 7, 1968. The botched second line in the first poem drained all his enjoyment from it. You saw it on the first page—"dimself" for "himself"—as soon as you opened the cover. The Great God Muddle was determined to transform Arnold into a Mr. Bones. *Could* a black poet have a worse typo? Such a wondrous thing: to make a poet black and scatter typos . . . Arnold was sure anyone who looked at it, white or black, must snicker.

Three reviews were good, however. A fourth was grumpy. Whoever wrote it was clearly (one) young and (two) not into poetry: "Most of these poems are silly. They don't rhyme. They don't tell stories. I have no idea what the poet thought he was doing—and I don't think he did either. The paragraph on the back says he's black."

(Not even six months after the conversation between the library schemers in his living room, and people like *this* had switched from "Negro" to "black"!) "But one of the poems, to the extent it's about anything at all, has something to do, as far as I can tell, with not being able to go to the opera. That's just dumb." Well, wasn't being misunderstood *part* of being a poet? (He hoped the negative reviewer was white—but had a niggling suspicion it was a spiritual relation of Cousin Harold's.) None of the four had mentioned the typos, which only made Arnold distrust them all.

◆

At thirty-four Arnold made his final visit to Aunt Bea's Pittsfield house, in western Massachusetts. The tenants who had lived there for the last fifteen years had moved, and Bea was selling it—though she hadn't been able to come back from Cleveland to see about it. So Arnold went in her stead. He stayed with Mrs. Winterson, in her musty, sloped-ceiling guestroom. The following afternoon, he wandered about the old place, saying good-bye to familiar cracks in the walls, squeaks in the stairs, stains on the upstairs wallpaper, there since he'd been a child—ignoring the gross changes the people who'd lived there had made.

(In what had been Grandma Logan's bedroom on the second floor, the peach-and-yellow flowered paper had been stripped from the walls and the room painted the harshest blue. They'd left a television in it, for God's sake—obviously because it didn't work.)

The child in the house, Arnold thought. Like Pater's Florian Deleal. But Florian gone all mocha . . .

He stood in front of the pantry's heavy swinging door, its brown coloring lightened just a little high on the left, from how many trips, shouldering into the dining room, carrying tureens of split-pea soup with ham, serving dishes of sweet potatoes and butter, rhubarb pies, and turnips, platters of roast pork, legs of lamb. He remembered Dr. Josephson, his elementary school science teacher, in his brown suit, perched on his desk corner, explaining how the swinging door had started as the navy's response to contagious diseases, especially syphilis, which, back then, they'd believed might be spread by contact with doorknobs. Eventually the knobless doors made their way into hotels, restaurants, and other public places, especially where food was prepared, and finally into homes. Dr. Josephson held up the jar in which a lemon had been all but enveloped in soft green mold, with irregular white around the edges. He pointed out the gold droplets. That had been in '49, a year after Moyer had taken out his patent on the mass production of penicillin.

No, they hadn't had sex education classes. But they'd learned *something* back then—even if it wasn't what kids learned in school today.

In one of Bea's old photo albums, in a trunk in the upstairs hall, just brought down from the attic, so that it could finally be shipped to Ohio, Arnold found a picture taken of him on the night after his high school commencement. He'd just turned eighteen—sixteen years ago and how much younger!

On the album page, the color photograph showed a stocky young man, wearing blue jeans and a sports jacket, with a ball of frizzy hair (an Afro years before anyone had called them that;

Arnold smiled) and an equally frizzy beard. His hair was nearly the same rust brown as his skin. His eyes had that coppery-yellow tint, which made him, Arnold had always felt, look slightly exotic. "Dark they were and golden eyed . . ."

And, yes, even then, tending to fat.

Arnold brought the album down, and on the blue-flowered cushions of the sofa the tenants had also left behind, in the same place where, on the gold couch (now in his New York apartment), as a child, he had read so many, many books, Arnold sat back, the album open over his thighs. Outside the sitting room window in the leaves (the white lace curtains had already been removed, making the tan shades, raised now to let in air and light, look stark), balmy Pittsfield July nudged its breezes into and out of the house. (Like Arnold, the poet Adelaide Crapsie had been born in Pittsfield, three hundred miles from Rochester, where, at age thirty-six, she had had coughed out her dying days, with her feeble, bleeding lungs, sitting on her bed's edge, clutching Jean Webster's hands. While at Smith, Crapsie had invented the Cinquain. Almost twenty of them were scattered throughout Arnold's first four books. One reviewer, only three months ago, recognizing them in *Pewter Pan*, had called Arnold the form's contemporary master. And what might they say of him tomorrow?) With slender fingers and their overlong nails, Arnold tried to pick the photo loose, planning to write on its back:

The poet Arnold Hawley,
Spring, 1954, BU, age 18.

But the photo started to tear—what sort of mucilage *had* Aunt Bea used on these things? Finally, Arnold let it alone—and put the album back.

❖

What was Arnold's relation to the *black* poetic tradition? On his East Village apartment shelves, treasured first editions of Hayden, Braithwaite, Bontomp, and Tolson leaned against the camp volumes of Countee Cullen and Angelina Weld Grimké, secretly enjoyed. He read and reread a nineteenth-century edition of *The Life of Oludah Equiano* ("Written by Himself") till the board backs were falling off—as he'd reread *Beetlecreek* and *The Catacombs*. The Black Arts Poets? Larry Neal and Sonya Sanchez were both heroes to Arnold, but he found a stridency—or perhaps, better, a lyric self-involvement—in Jones/Baraka that not so much repelled as bored him. He liked Baraka's freewheeling prose, though: *The System of Dante's Hell* (he'd had read the first part of it in *Trembling Lamb*, which he'd purchased in a very small Cambridge bookstore years before when he'd gone with Aunt Bea to hear a Boston Pops concert. There was a close-up of Jean Harlow on its black matte cover) and *Tales*. Soon, though, he decided he didn't like the people who expressed the same opinion, so he stopped mentioning even those.

Several years after he'd moved to New York, in his folding metal chair in the St. Mark's Church basement, Arnold had sat waiting ("They're coming in from Newark," someone said. "The traffic's heavy. . . ."), when, in dashikis and brocaded fezzes, Baraka (since Brooks liked him, Arnold felt he had to give him a chance) and his entourage strode into the room, waving real guns, firing blanks at the ceiling.

At the first ear-deadening and echo-laden retort, one woman screamed. A second and third shot crashed out. Several people laughed uncomfortably. Another uptilted muzzle flashed silver in the fluorescent lights, spitting sparks and its shattering crack— and Arnold bit the inside of his cheek hard enough to make his eyes water. Walking home later, across the Tompkins Square, still shaken, still tonguing torn flesh inside his mouth and sometimes tasting blood, he wondered: after that, how were you supposed to remember, or even pay attention to, any of the damned poems the poet happened to read?

• ◆ •

A year and a half after that marriage—and three months after *Dark Reflections* had gone to press, but several weeks before he actually saw a copy—Arnold was walking back up his apartment steps, looking at the sunlight falling from the colored panes of the airshaft window over the bowed marble, when he remembered the bright details from the evening he'd gone to the clinic for his Wasserman. Actually, none of *them* had made it into *Dark Reflections*. He remembered moments after the publication of both *Waters* and *Air Tangle* when he'd realized things he'd hoped to put in this or that poem had eluded him completely. He stopped. He looked. "Peach ice cream . . ." Arnold muttered, not thinking about any flavor of ice cream at all. He started walking up the stairs again. But weren't those the revelations, Arnold thought, that always made writers lose interest in past work, that consigned it to inadequacy, to mediocrity, at least on one's personal scale?

That night, Arnold went up to Twenty-third Street, and, just
on the sidewalk, started talking to a black kid named Eddy, in his
midtwenties, who, standing outside one of the bars, had smiled at
him—Eddy didn't want to go in because someone might be inside
Eddy didn't want to see. Otherwise, he seemed nice enough,
though he was all skin and bones and shook your hand like a girl.
(Whatever *had* happened to Dago Joe? That night it came back to
Arnold: another evening at the bar, when, on a dare from Bobby,
he had gone up to Joe and said, "You seem like a very interesting
. . . person." Joe had turned, smiled, and answered: "Yeah? Well,
so do you." And then put his hand out to shake. Joe's grip had
been firm, thick-skinned, and as manly as you could want—nor
had he released Arnold's hand. At all. "Perhaps some evening
we'll actually get a chance to talk." "I hope," Joe said, "we do. I
hope we get a chance to do more than talk." "Really?" "'Cause
you look a like a real nice person, too. I like meetin' nice people.
Talkin' with 'em. Gettin' to know 'em." Which is when Arnold
realized Joe was *still* gripping his hand—and that he, Arnold, was
getting an erection. He'd pulled loose, turned, and fled back to
Bobby. They'd laughed together, clutching at one another and
giggling for ten minutes—though that grip had trouble him for
weeks, for months actually.) Arnold brought Eddy home. They
even had coffee. Then they went to bed. Afterwards, Arnold gave
him the twenty dollars he asked for. At least Eddy had gotten
hard, though neither one of them came, and—after Eddy left—
Arnold was astonished at how depressed that made him. (The
firmness, the friendliness, the straight black hair over the neck of
his T-shirt, the faint embarrassment that clearly Joe had felt, too,

but just a clearly he was not going to let master him—everything with Eddy, so many years later, had been the exact opposite.) "You do what you want with me" were Eddy's only instructions to Arnold. "I don't care." But that was just not the first thing you hoped to hear on your first sexual encounter. It couldn't have been because Eddy was black and Joe was white. Or that Eddy was hustling and Joe was not. Or that . . .

It was, Arnold decided, at any rate, not an experiment to repeat. Although, over the next couple years, he did—with Tony, with Big Ukrainian Mike—twice.

• ◆ •

Visiting the city that summer, her hands steady even at seventy-eight, Aunt Bea took the picture with her aged Rolleiflex, while Arnold stood, looking thoughtful, next to the brick newel at Tompkins Square's east entrance. Arnold's hair was all but marine short. He'd given up on the contact lenses years ago and gone back to glasses—so that, in pictures, the coppery-gold of his irises was simply no longer so striking. Since the photo only showed the top of his crewneck sweater, one might not realize that Arnold's belly was, as it had been in the vanished picture of him at eleven, again broader than his shoulders. When it had come in the mail with Aunt Bea's familiarly florid script on the envelope (she still wrote letters with a fountain pen and refused to use ballpoints), Arnold took it out and, before he got up to the apartment, sat down on the stairs and wrote on the back:

The poet Arnold Hawley
Autumn '79, New York City
The East Village, Tompkins Square
Age 43

That had been the visit when she'd brought Arnold the black cashmere: the night before she was leaving, he'd waited up for her to get back from the Metropolitan. In her purple dress, her hat still on, Bea sat primly on the edge of the couch, across the green glass from him, sipping a small bit of sherry—she'd brought the glasses in her suitcase and purchased the bottle the day she'd arrived. But instead of talking about the opera, she'd told him: "When I went over to Appleton for the funeral, of course he'd left it in the office closet at the garage, if you can imagine—an eighteen-hundred-dollar *coat!* Somebody was just going to walk off with it. That is *so* Harold. Anita was four years older than that man and just as proud as a peacock that she'd caught him. And there he went and dropped dead of a heart attack—at fifty-nine. It's not as if they had any children, and Harold was just your size. Anita said she didn't even want to *see* anything again from that garage. So I went over with my shopping bag—and since it was hanging up in the office closet, I took it for you. I had it cleaned, to get the cigar smell out. Those three white boys he had working for him can argue about which one ran off with it—if they even knew it was in there. You remember the youngest one, with the awful teeth? At the funeral, even though he was wearing a suit and tie—the poor redheaded one with the ears?—he *actually* smelled, Arnold! Really! I felt so bad for him. Sitting there in the church, with all those black people around them, those three poor white fellows looked . . . well, the only word to describe them is 'forlorn.' They all looked . . . just forlorn! I think all they had was Harold. Especially the redhead. Not even thirty and only six teeth left in his mouth. Really, they loved that man. *Where* did Harold find them? There were some beautiful silk ties hanging up in there, too. But you were never a suit-and-tie person—so I left those."

·—◆—·

Days, Arnold worked in a cubicle with green shoulder-high walls at the City Employment Administration.

Nights, he . . . well, sat in his East Ninth Street apartment and read. Or, sometimes, in warm weather, he sat in Tompkins Square. And read. He wrote a lot in his notebook. He wrote book reviews and covered neighborhood events for a couple of local throwaway sheets. Arnold owned not one jazz album. But, by the end of the '70s, he'd become fascinated by country and western—George Jones, Ferlin Husky, Jessi Colter, Ray Stevens, Waylon Jennings, Merle Haggard, Tammy, Tanya Denise Tucker, Loretta, Crystal, Dottie, Reba, Bonnie Raitt, and Bonnie Tyler. With its barely suppressed fascist worldview, *this* was the music all other American arts either accepted or reacted against—*including* black jazz!

This music was ubiquitous over working-class radios—in the cabs of all-night truckers, in the crowded white-enameled kitchens of Pullman dining cars, on transistor sets at the backs of garage workbenches. (Uncle Harry had played it in *his* garage, once he'd finished with the morning services on Appleton's black religious station.) It played over the public address systems in prisons and in supermarket cellar stockrooms, in every state, New York, California, Florida, and Kentucky. Arnold's own obsession, as he explained to any number of slightly nonplussed friends, black, white, or whatever, was finally no different, and *certainly* no less American, than that of how many white folks who got twisted up over Robert Johnson, Bessie Smith, Thelonius Monk, Gillespie, Davis, or Coltrane. Wasn't this the art, the music, the American voice you *must* know and love (or hate—although, despite its dismal brutality, Arnold loved it) to be an American artist?

Two years later Arnold wrote an article to that effect, which was accepted at a journal that had started in the mid-'70s, *Spectacle*, published by Nathan Corner, reputed to have some actual money. Arnold saw the first copy on the journal shelf at St. Mark's Bookshop on the fourteenth of September, 1979, and the next day the postman squashed the fat mailer with his contributor's copy into the lobby mailbox.

When a black poet friend whom he ran into at a St. Mark's Church reading by Michael Harper mentioned he'd read the piece and Arnold asked him what he'd thought, in his brocaded dashiki in the church cellar lobby his friend said: "Arnold, it left me totally . . . bewildered! Man, I thought it was *insane*—in fact, I thought it was *so* insane, it turned around and started to be interesting. I just assumed it was a joke or maybe a parody—that began to take itself seriously . . . like, you know, 'The Portrait of Mr. W. H.'"

Now Arnold was nonplussed—and though he still loved those wails over flights from crime in Indiana, the despair of blue-eyed Oklahoma boys at ever finding love, the glories of male friendship in Nebraska roadside honky-tonks, and the agonies of men and women cheated on and cheating, he phoned Bea that night. "I don't see why it's any different from McPherson's championing the stories of that poor white West Virginia kid who killed himself—what was his name? Pancake?" James McPherson was the black writer at the University of Virginia, who'd won the Drew-Phalen for fiction last year ('78).

Somewhere in Cleveland, Bea said, "I think McPherson wrote a story saying *he* liked it, too."

"He did?" Deflated, Arnold turned his thumb on the green glass table. "Oh, *dear* . . ." Not only was it a silly notion, it wasn't even Arnold's!

Bea said, as he had been sure she would, "Arnold—if you like that stuff, you like it. You can like or not like *whatever* music you want, honey. That's your right as a black American." (He remembered her saying "colored American" in his childhood.) Still, his liking it would have been more dramatic if he'd been blacker and not so nondescriptly brown. To the extent that such predilections *were* social gestures, they registered with more force if you made them in clear, bold hues—like Bea's, or . . . indeed, Harold's. He felt better, as he always did, talking to Bea. Still, with his New York friends he discussed his country-music obsession rather less.

The next day he went back and worked at his cubicle at the City Employment Administration.

How, how, how to give it a higher tone, make his appreciation of it not only his own but more than a homily? Arnold sat surrounded by those half walls like gunwales in an already sunken lifeboat—his office comprised some forty cubicles, forty lifeboats, all already foundered. . . .

Talking of it less, he listened to it less.

But he was working on another book, the prose poem this time, listening through evenings of Giovanni Pierluigi da Palestrina, through nights of Bonnie Tyler. . . .

Then, somehow (". . . lovin' till your arms break. Then he lets you down . . ."), the fifth book was done and even country music was something Arnold *used* to like.

• ◆ •

At forty-five Arnold had never been associated with any particular group of poets, black or white. Several times he had rather radically changed his emotional life in order to withdraw from one artistic community or the other that he felt was taking too great a purchase on him. His lonely and ascetic principle was: art is the one human enterprise in which, when you are doing what everyone else does, you are doing something wrong. But now he found himself fascinated, fixated, obsessed—it beat out his onetime fascination with country and western—with that self-consuming lyric eruption in the first years of the 1890s in London, the Rhymers' Club. What, if anything, besides a love of Verlaine and Pater, a fascination with Zola and Olive Shreiner's extraordinary transvestial *Story of an African Farm*, had held those young men together for the three or so years the club could be said to have existed in its upstairs room at the Cheshire Cheese, as one or another of its members stumbled drunkenly off, one to Paris, one to Istanbul, one to New York, another to Dublin? Richard Le Gallienne, Victor Plarr, and Ernest Rhys had left substantial memoirs; as had Greene, and Hillier, and Rolleston—and Yeats (of course). There was Longaker's reasonable biography of the young-dying Dowson and memoirs by the now-and-again deranged Symons; even Davidson had done one, not to mention frequent nonmember drop-ins, like Edgar Jepson. But what about Lionel Johnson, after Dowson (". . . Gone, gone with the wind, flung roses, roses riotously with the throng, dancing to put thy pale lost lilies out of mind . . .") the most important poet, save Yeats, in the group?

In the reading room of the 42nd Street New York Public Library, Arnold stood with one hand in his pocket, looking up at the flickering numbers on the call-board above the brass-barred reception window, as the clerk nodded to him. Arnold went over, to receive the photo-offset copy of a bulky typescript, bound between boards, yes, like an actual book—but without a photograph, end to end.

Subject of that extraordinary essay by Pound, Lionel Pigot Johnson had been a major influence on Hart Crane, a friend of Pater's, a subtle religious thinker (a physical stature like Pope's or Napoleon's—Johnson had been practically a midget): he had been the first person to read aloud *"Non Sum Qualis Eram Bonae Sub Regno Cynerae"* at the Cheese's monthly meeting, because Dowson had been too nervous or too drunk . . . and only a *typescript* biography?

Without a *photograph?*

That's when it occurred to Arnold that the black American poet Arnold Hawley could probably expect not even that. Though Aunt Bea had personally given Miss Polk copies for her library in

Cleveland, as far as Arnold knew no other library—certainly none in New York City—had any of his books.

Not even the Schomburg. Once, he made a trip up to 135th Street to check. My God! What had once been a cluttered room off the second floor of the Countee Cullen, under the management of that pleasant Mrs. Delany (she also managed the Russian Collection, housed on the other side of the same room), was now an entire new building! And still there was not a Hawley volume in their catalogue—though Arnold's *Pewter Pan* had just arrived downtown on the shelves of the St. Mark's Bookshop.

(He had still not found a publisher for *High-Toned Homilies with Their Gunwales All Submerged*, though someone had mentioned some people who were just starting a new press, called Croaton. . . .)

Six weeks later, in that way life has of confirming unpleasant truths in widely dispersed families, Aunt Bea phoned to say that the house in Appleton had burned down two nights ago. Cousin Anita was dead. "Died in her bed—of smoke inhalation. That's what the autopsy said—though, later, she was burned . . . badly." It was an unsettling replay of his own parents' death in the Maine fire, thirty-nine years before, which Arnold had been too young to remember. If he couldn't get out for the funeral, Bea said, people would understand.

Would the Diamond Harbor photograph of the poet Arnold Hawley (age eleven) have survived . . .? Almost certainly not.

So Arnold ceased pursuing Jepson and Symons and Dowson and Davidson—and stopped thinking about biographies at all. It was enough just trying to go on writing poems. And why *would* you put such a photograph in a biography of Arnold Hawley anyway? It's not as if Diamond Harbor were actually a place that had been meaningful to him. He'd visited it only the once and didn't remember it. Still, it had been a nice picture of a laughing, overweight, golden-eyed black boy.

Back in '72, the year it had came out, he'd read (two weeks before Bea) Bedini's *Life of Benjamin Banneker* and the same year devoured the black American travel writer George Washington Wilson's recently reprinted report on the Congo, as a supplementary text toward understanding *Heart of Darkness*. (He and Bea had talked about them an hour and forty minutes on the phone.) At a friend's suggestion he'd picked up Nella Larson's *Passing*, read it, and walked around chuckling for days over its macabre end.

These weren't the only black texts he read. (He'd read his Baldwin, his June Jordan, his Ralph Ellison, his Marilyn Nelson, David Bradley, Lucile Clifton, and *more* wonderful Brooks. . . .) But those were the ones that were most important to him.

·—·

When, at Lark & Dove, Vikki asked him for an author's photo for the back of *Beleaguered Fields*, Aunt Bea's was the picture Arnold sent her.

For some reason they didn't use it.

And by the time the book won its prize, the photo had disappeared from the office.

Whatever had happened to that fantasy of Arnold's (Arnold

wondered): someday someone would be writing his biography, and, somehow, all *those* three snapshots would magically turn up and join the photographs of his aunt Bea—who finally died in '97, another missed funeral that almost destroyed Arnold—and the pictures of his elegant, handsome parents. Bea's last postcard had said she was taking a class in Persian. The three pictures of Arnold, at eleven, twenty-six, and forty-nine, would all fall in a shiny sheaf between pages 324 and 325—the same pages that the photographs occupied in the Moldenhauers' 800-page biography of Anton Webern.

Only he didn't think about it now—much. (As to the photographs, Arnold was probably the only person who had *seen* all three.) Since he'd been eighteen, Webern had been Arnold's favorite composer; another enthusiasm picked up from Bea; though Bea herself preferred Berg. That had been one reason for her last visit to New York: the Met had finally mounted *Lulu* with the Friedrich Cerha orchestration for the third act. Bea had gone to hear it twice, once, with Arnold, on her second night in the city, and once by herself, a week later, the night before she left . . . when she'd given him Harold's coat.

•-◆-•

In '88, a year after he'd won the Alfred Proctor Prize in Poetry, three days beyond June's Gay Pride Day, Arnold was walking through the West Village. Somehow, Arnold reflected, the closet had just . . . dissolved around him. Nearly twenty years before, in the summer of '69, Arnold, yes, had read about the riots that had begun in his onetime stomping grounds, the Stonewall Inn. They occurred over on the other side of the Village, where no one Arnold knew actually lived. He had assumed they were as unimportant as any such city disturbance. But he kept finding more articles about them. Then more. His conviction was that this "Gay Liberation" business, which so clearly was just an imitation of "Women's Liberation," itself only a spin-off of civil rights, had to be a social aberration that would dissolve when people grew tired of it.

But it hadn't.

Arnold was always vaguely bewildered as to why. And though he knew that guns had been fired, windows and heads had been smashed to make it happen, the turmoil continuing day and night for most of week, he had hidden in his apartment, across town, to escape the flames and smoke and shouting that had filled the very streets he walked through, on this bright afternoon.

It was June of '88, the second year of his Proctor stipend. (When, a few years later, he'd finally gotten his courage back and stepped out for his three twenty-dollar experiments, he'd found only that Bea had been right. It *wasn't* as good as peach ice cream— and, indeed, since Anita's and Harold's deaths, peach ice cream, too, had gone from the world. Not Baskin-Robbins nor Häagen-Dazs nor Ben and Jerry could make anything near it.) Because he was a poet, all bookstores held a fascination for Arnold. Along with A Different Light, he'd always found the Oscar Wilde Bookstore oddly and unsettlingly interesting.

Whole bookstores devoted to forbidden books . . .

However bright and sunny they were, Arnold could think of them in no other way—and had stopped trying.

Still, somehow the terror at the prospect of sex with men had changed, changed with the DMZ III and Gay Liberation itself, the Lesbian, Gay, Bisexual & Transgender Community Center— the "Gay Firehouse"—on West Thirteenth Street, the Gay Community, the Gay Vote, the thousand lavender balloons released into the air, only last week, rising in protest before St. Patrick's as the cheers of thousands swelled, making a roar like the wind through wet leaves in a public park. The cheerers quieted . . . and, across Fifth Avenue, facing the cathedral's white-and-gray stone, in that brilliant June, on the platform erected for them, the Gay Men's Chorus began *Ave Maria* (standing among the thousands, watching, listening, Arnold thought: Now *that's* a protest with style. We can do *some* things right. . . .), all to mellow into a sort of gentle joke to which his three attempts at actually *doing* it had added their own anticlimactic irony.

For the last six years there'd been this awful AIDS business. . . .

Still, it even extended to characters on television shows (there'd been Beverly on the Archie Bunker show, *All In the Family*, an episode of which Arnold had actually gone to a friend's house to watch—he still had no TV), and now there were stores and sometimes you saw men walking hand in hand; which was simply and endlessly uncomfortable for Arnold, even as he smiled at them, because he never wanted them to feel the terror he once had.

Still, the annual citywide demonstration—Gay Pride Day— was not only reported on the TV news but made the front page of all the city newspapers, not just the alternative press; and had been, more than a decade now. Given the fears he had grown up with, Arnold understood the politics of "coming out" and its obviation of blackmail as well as anyone. But he was still unsure of what there was to be proud, in gay life. It was like celebrating the loosest and most lascivious behavior among black folk as the core of civil rights. It seemed some wholly and absurd internal contradiction that, if anyone really exposed it, would reveal all progress to be a sham and topple the entire liberatory project.

Passing by the wrought-iron steps that led up to the bookstore, Arnold saw, in the Oscar Wilde's window, a display of three oversized photography books—all featuring male nudes.

One caught Arnold's eye, however. On the cover, across an extreme close-up of the black-and-white reproduction of a muscular black chest, white letters proclaimed:

SALIERI

Arnold frowned, totally unsure why the name should stop him. The only thing it brought back was a recollection of Mozart's musical rival. Pushkin had done a playlet about him, inspiring the poet Mandelstam to a meditation on the two composers and what such rivalry had to say about art. Shaffer had made a full-length play from the same encounter. (Arnold had missed the movie.) Why, Arnold wondered, after looking up at the oversized book in the store window almost a minute, should he turn and climb the stairs? Or (he was within the store now), why should he look here and there until he found the oversized hardcover, on a table, propped on a white wire book rack?

The answer only came when he opened the cover to read the book's inside front flap:

This selection of ninety-seven beautiful and historic photographic prints from the more than seven hundred pictures that remain from the work of Boston photographer Joseph Salieri (1929-1975) is long overdue. Salieri died from pancreatic cancer at the age of forty-six in a Delaware hospital twelve years ago. He is one of a number of mid-century photographers who pioneered the serious homoerotic photograph. At the time he took them many of his pictures were considered pornography—and were even sold as such—but in more recent years people have begun to appreciate their extraordinary composition, as well as the astonishingly fresh vision of an all-but-utopian joy, even a revolutionary sense of *agape* and *philos*, along with their blatant celebration of *eros*—certainly the first thing we see among them. Raised in a New England orphanage, Joseph Salieri came under the tutelage of a wealthy Boston Brahmin, Frank Fines, who eventually gave the young man the use of a house in Roxbury's Paradise Hill, where much of his early work was done, a neighborhood where Salieri did many odd jobs to make ends meet. He worked as an auto mechanic's helper, a carpenter's assistant, and delivered food for a black soul-food restaurant, while putting every spare penny and free hour into his photographic work. . . .

It was continued on the back flap, where Arnold read on:

After two years as a newspaper photographer, in

1968 Salieri was convicted of contempt of court when the sexual nature of his project occasioned a police raid and he refused to reveal the names of his models or customers. He spent two and a half years in the Massachusetts State Correctional Facility, making him one of the many political martyrs in the movement for gay civil rights. A tragedy of this period is that the mentally deficient young black man featured in many of of Salieri's photographs, 'Samson' Bowman, to whose care Salieri had committed himself on a trip to Alabama, four years before, disappeared some two months after Salieri began his jail term and was never seen again.

Arnold looked up from the book.

Slake . . . he thought. His throat tightened and, quite surprisingly, his eyes began to fill.

When the keystone of a life structure that you have erected turns out to be a falsity falsely fixed, the *whole* does not necessarily collapse to the concrete in a cloud of steel, masonry, and glass. Too many microstructures have been set in place to support things, so that the initial keystone bears no present condition for any reality it might once have sustained.

On the bottom of the back flyleaf, a small square photograph—according to the caption beneath it—showed Joseph Salieri, dark haired, in suit and tie, smiling . . . with a full set of teeth.

A memory flashed up before Arnold: the thickset Italian, smiling at him, in his newly illuminated darkroom, with his missing incisors. But the unimpaired smile on the photograph, apparently—from the date—taken after his release from jail, could of course have involved a later dental bridge.

The tiny image returned nothing to Arnold of the T-shirted fellow with the gold chain he remembered from that rainy Roxbury April.

Turning back to the front of the book, Arnold began to page through the photographs; and immediately found two of Slake Bowman—Lord, Arnold thought, looking at the ripped Goliath. I hadn't realized, at the time, he was *so* young! Four pictures on, another stopped him—again, of Slake, naked and lying on a rumpled sheet with a naked Asian. The two men, Slake (Samson?), massive, the Asian, slender and notably older, already had their legs entwined. One of the Asian's legs was bent in an unnatural way. The only thing he wore, which for some reason did *not* look the least incongruous—was a knitted watch cap.

Well, Arnold thought dryly, so much for the myth that Asians are necessarily not as well hung as blacks. As impressive as Slake's equipment was, the Asian's was extraordinary! But perhaps that was just because Old (Old? In the picture, he couldn't have been forty-five!) Sam was erect and Slake's gunmetal dark equipment, at least in that photo, was soft . . . Was that *really* Old Sam, beneath Salieri's lens and paired with Samson, how many years ago? (My God, Arnold thought. How many times did he bring me fried chicken? I had no notion he was carrying *that* around!) Yes, the Asian's wispy moustaches hung perhaps three quarters of an inch down at the edges of his smiling mouth. He wore an inch-length goatee—what, today, the kids called a fly. In Arnold's memory, Sam's facial hair had been of Fu Manchu length—probably because Arnold had never seen one before outside the movies. Neither man in the picture was anywhere near as old as Arnold. (Arnold had not actively thought of Sam in more than twenty-five years!) In conjunction with the rumpled lines of the bedding, the framing made their two bodies suggest the entirety of a world. The contrast in tones, and their two expressions, as their faces neared one another's, moments before a kiss—which you could read as joy a moment before it became mutual and torrential laughter (as it quickened both bodies; at least here the flap copy seemed accurate)—was, yes, a lovely picture!

More than lovely—the pleasure in looking at them was actually thrilling (the backs of Arnold's hands had begun to tingle), even delicious.

Because they were beautiful—and because he *was* a poet—Arnold pondered: Though I have never lain like that with anyone, nor do I particularly fancy going through what it would take to make it happen, nevertheless Joey Salieri (Miss Merelda had always called him Joey) has made them into heroes for me . . . even if they'd fooled around no more than an hour in the fuckroom. It was a bit unnerving that he could remember so clearly when, unhung, leaning, and overlapping among so many along the baseboards, what must have been the same picture (or one in the same series) had so terrified him. (What was it Rilke had said? Beauty is only the beginning of the terrible. . . . But could it work the other way around?) Wasn't the classical job of art to provide heroes for the people—as Lamar and Noel and Bobby Horner had become for Arnold, as the resisting black and Hispanic queens at Stonewall had become for so many others?

With Horner's name came a remembered smidge of conversation with Bobby, from before Stonewall, from before AIDS:

Had he and Bobby been walking in the park? Had they been coming from St. Mark's when the bookshop was actually *on* St. Mark's Place? They'd been talking about the porn novel. Horner was protesting: "But the whole idea is that they stay together. Happily. One of them *doesn't* crash his car into a tree and die—"

"In the reign of the Emperor Hadrian?" Arnold had commented, in his driest tone. "I wouldn't think so."

"But this is *really* going to be revolutionary. It's—"

"—a porn novel," Arnold said. "Look, *I'm* not together with anyone. And I'm not planning to be. Neither are you. And we *all* die, eventually—even happily married heterosexual couples; and usually one a number of years before the other."

"But that's exactly what I . . ." Horner had stopped, looking at Arnold unhappily.

Arnold had decided to rescue him. "Look, Bobby. I said I'll write it for you—and I will. I'll follow your outline, and I'll make it as lush and lovely and lyric as I possibly can, no matter what nastiness you have your hero indulging in—or how mindlessly happy he is afterward. But as to what's revolutionary about it, I'm sorry. I don't get it."

As he looked at the photo of the two men from years ago— Salieri was dead; were either of them, Sam *or* Slake, alive?— Arnold thought: What's revolutionary is that they're happy—and someone put out effort to show it, beautifully. Not how long it lasted, hours, seconds, years . . .

But, at least for moments, Arnold wondered if perhaps, now, he did . . . get it. This is what Freud had meant when he'd written, *Wo es war, soll ich werden*—Where there was *id*, there shall by *ego*—another of those things it took an entire village to bring about. Arnold looked up and around at the colorful face-out displays on the bookstore shelves, at the men—and two young women, over there, together, shoulder to shoulder, one black, one white—in the store with him. And what an extraordinary village I am lucky enough to live in!

He looked down at the photograph.

Why should anyone even *want* to photograph Arnold Hawley? Clearly Slake's glorious physicality is what photography was for. It's what should have been—and *had* been—memorialized in silver salts. And the engorged genitals of the Asian were an extraordinary bit of news, retrieved from the unknown by the camera, a surprise evaluation of a piece of jewelry you'd thought paste for years, now presented him by time and Salieri.

Arnold turned another oversized page: God, whenever did they take *this* one?

On the wide Roxbury steps, Slake sat, again nude, with his extraordinary smile—in this one you could see the missing tooth. (Did they come out at five or six in the morning to snap it? Perhaps the electric man stood guard, just outside the frame, to warn if someone came by.) Imagine the Thinker—not Rodin's, but a primeval black man from the Olduvai Gorge—his problem untangled and his back straight, his lungs open with intellectual triumph, Heidegger's fundamental question—*Why are there somethings rather than nothing?* or, as a more recent North Carolina wit had put it, *Why, in an infinite universe, is there an infinite universe . . . ?*—definitively and forever solved!

The muffled bell had finally sounded, unmuffled!

The brief breeze had become a welcoming wind!

The confirmation of it was the expression on the face of a naked black man, who'd once sat on a Boston porch, with his neat, high, joyful, arrogant, and knowing head.

(Good phrases, Arnold thought. Were there any qualifications to get rid of? Wonder if I should try to review this book.)

What had stopped him, however, was that, on the porch behind Bowman, all opened out, leaned four, five, *six* . . . umbrellas!

With a surge of memory and a suddenly beating heart, Arnold examined one and another of the background forms aslant the porch behind the seated man. Slake's deeply marked muscles, in this portrait, looked oiled.

Two of the umbrellas *were* clearly women's—covered with sweeping floral patterns. But, caught in black and white, no, none was Aunt Bea's. On Aunt Bea's umbrella, the bright flowers had gone only around the edge, leaving the middle solid maroon.

Arnold went over them again—and again. And once again.

Could it be that, like Sam's moustache and beard, Arnold remembered it inaccurately?

But, no, they weren't Bea's—none of them.

(How many people *had* Slake brought over who'd run off without their umbrellas . . .? Arnold began to laugh. How many umbrellas had they stolen . . .?)

Then, checking the notes at the back, Arnold learned the picture was dated July, 1959, two months before the September he'd *started* at Boston.

Arnold mumbled, "Blackmailers . . ."

When a keystone is dynamited free, while it may not crumble the world, it makes things shift.

On returning home, Arnold went to his brag shelf and slid free one of the six copies he still had of *Waters*—the one which, on the inside flap, he had marked "setting copy" in case it was ever reprinted. Under the dedication to Beatrice Carmentha Hawley, Arnold wrote in:

And in memory of Joseph Salieri and

and, after another ten seconds, wrote:

Slake Bowman

Then he crossed them out and reversed them, putting "Samson Bowman" first. Then he crossed out "Samson" and wrote in "Slake" again. "Slake" *was* his name, after all. Samson was a nickname. And this was a mark of respect.

This was the copy from which the poems would be reset were there ever another edition. That was Arnold's plan. (It was Bobby Horner who had told him the old Jewish joke: "Do you want to hear God's laughter? Tell him your plans. . . .")

In his apartment, save two in the living room and three in the kitchen, every wall was covered with bookshelves, the books themselves—mostly paperbacks—dim and spine out. Really, it was like living in the storage cellar of a bookstore. Yet he'd have it no other way. For isn't this where, finally, the village had its heart? As Novalis (poet by night, young tubercular salt-mine inspector by day) had noted two hundred years ago (and Guy Debord had kept current, quoting it in *Society of the Spectacle* at the end of section V. 131): "Writings are the thoughts of the state. The archives are its memory."

(That's right. It was Bobby Horner who had given him his first copy of *Society of the Spectacle*—as well as *Laws of Form*. And his two-volume copy of *Decline of the West* . . . along with *Plato and Platonism*, one of Hart Crane's favorites. Books kept connecting with books. That's what made them live. . . .)

Standing in the hallway, by his shelf, Arnold turned to the sixth poem in his chapbook and reread it. "Blackmailers" . . . But though it had nothing to do with either Boston vice or the blackmail ring whose existence he had carried in the cellars of his memory till this day, and on whose existence so much of his life and work had been grounded, it was still the strongest poem in his earliest collection.

—November 2006,
New York City

HISTORICAL NOTE

Neither the Drew-Phalen Award nor the Alfred Proctor Prize in Poetry exists. But the barbaric comment poet Wallace Stevens is here reported to have made at the "1950 Drew-Phalen Banquet," a refrain not only throughout this tale but in the mind of any black writer contemplating his or her possibility for reward or recognition in America, Stevens did make at the 1950 Pulitzer Prize banquet, when that year's recipient, Gwendolyn Brooks, entered the hall. Today the NBA requires a nomination fee from the publisher. Among the minor characters here, names of the real and recent dead mix with the wholly fictional. Do not search for Martell Crane. I have invented him, though Jessie B. Rittenhouse was solidly actual. So was Lamar Alford. (Though his death was not commemorated in the *Boys Like Us* roster.) As did Arnold, I sat with him a number of evenings at the Stonewall, a summer before the historic riots of late June in '69. You can hear his voice on the CD of the Broadway cast recording of *Godspell*. Joe Soley was just as real, as was his younger Philadelphia lover of more than a decade, Paul Caruso. The "vandalism" in the New York public branch libraries, which, in record time, switched the country from (capital-N) "Negro" to (small-b) "black," perpetrated by, among others, Lamar and two of his friends, happened as I have described it, although as "African American" and (capital-B) "Black" now and again move to displace it, it may soon be forgotten.

—SRD